P9-CFK-232

RAVES FOR **THE SUMMER OF EVERYTHING**

"There's so much to love in Julian Winters' *The Summer of Everything*: A delightfully heartwarming, super-supportive, diverse group of friends, a beloved indie bookstore, and, of course, Wesley Hudson. Wes' struggles to figure out life and love were so incredibly relatable, and I cheered for him every step of the way. A must-have for every YA bookshelf!"

—SANDHYA MENON, *New York Times* bestselling author

"Absolutely packed with Julian Winters's trademark blend of heart and humor, *The Summer of Everything* is, without a doubt, the teen romcom of the summer. I can't wait for readers to fall in love with the epically nerdy Wes and his group of charming (and hilarious!) friends."

—PHIL STAMPER, bestselling author of *The Gravity of Us*

"Wes's problems are lifelike, and he's surrounded by eccentric, supportive, and inspiring friends who challenge and encourage him… his coming of age is endearing."

—*Foreword Reviews*

"Julian Winters always writes with tenderness and care and respect for teen readers. *The Summer of Everything* is a big-hearted romance that gives queer boys of color the happily ever after they deserve."

—KACEN CALLENDER, bestselling author of *Felix Ever After*

"*The Summer of Everything* is an ice cream cone by the pool on a sunny day. I felt like part of the Once Upon a Page family and didn't want to leave. An utter gem!"

—GLORIA CHAO, author of *American Panda, Our Wayward Fate,* and *Rent a Boyfriend*

"Winters does it again: a book about friendship, love, community, and the sometimes meandering path to adulthood, all in a great bear hug of a book that will keep your summer going."

—L.C. ROSEN, author of *Camp*

RAVES FOR **HOW TO BE REMY CAMERON**

Junior Library Guild Gold Standard Seal of Approval
American Library Association 2020 Rainbow Book List
YALSA's 2020 Best Fiction for Young Adults List

"The author pays homage to past and present LGBTQ wordsmiths Tennessee Williams and Benjamin Alire Sáenz, and has created an array of diverse characters without presenting them as preachy stereotypes and boxed-in caricatures... VERDICT Winters deserves a place in the YA literary canon."

—*School Library Journal*, Starred Review

"I always smile my way through a Julian Winters book. Remy's story of self-discovery is empowering and lovely."

—ADAM SILVERA, *NYT*-bestselling author of *What If It's Us*

"You've been warned: Remy Cameron is coming for your heart. I adored this tender, heartfelt love song of a book."

—BECKY ALBERTALLI, author of *Simon vs. the Homo Sapiens Agenda*

"An endearing novel that gives hope to those who know what it's like being different."

—*Kirkus Reviews*

"I don't often swoon, but I swooned HARD for this incandescent book. Julian Winters has crafted a deeply moving story of love, family, and identity that will stay with me forever."

—ADIB KHORRAM, award-winning author of *Darius the Great Is Not Okay*

RAVES FOR **RUNNING WITH LIONS**

Gold Winner, 2018 IBPA Benjamin Franklin Awards | Teen Fiction
Finalist, 55th Georgia Author of the Year Award (GAYA)
#1 Amazon Bestseller | Teen & Young Adult LGBT Fiction

"Funny, wise, and ridiculously romantic. It hit me right in the heart."

—BECKY ALBERTALLI, author of *Simon vs. the Homo Sapiens Agenda*

"A heartwarming freshman novel from an author poised to be a modern Matt Christopher for an older audience."

—*Kirkus Reviews*

"Full of heart and full of hope... I loved being reminded what it's like to be a teenager during a long, hot, messy summer, when everything is new and exciting, anything seems possible, and the world is opening out in front of you."

—SIMON JAMES GREEN, author of *Noah Can't Even*

WITHDRAWN

THE SUMMER OF EVERYTHING

a novel

JULIAN WINTERS

BOOKS

Fitchburg Public Library
5530 Lacy Road
Fitchburg, WI 53711

interlude ✿ press · new york

Copyright © 2020 Julian Winters
All Rights Reserved
ISBN 13: 978-1-945053-91-7 (trade)
ISBN 13: 978-1-945053-92-4 (ebook)
Library of Congress Control Number: 2020939803
Published by Duet, an imprint of Interlude Press
www.duetbooks.com
This is a work of fiction. Names, characters, and places are either a product of the
author's imagination or are used fictitiously. Any resemblance to real persons,
either living or dead, is entirely coincidental.
All trademarks and registered trademarks are the property of
their respective owners.
Cover and Book Design by CB Messer
Background & Emoji Vectors © depositphotos.com/ckybe/in8finity
Palm Tree Vectors Designed by Freepik
10 9 8 7 6 5 4 3 2 1

interlude 🧩 press ∙ new york

For everyone who hasn't figured it all out yet: You're okay.
You'll get there. Never stop dreaming. Enjoy the moment.

"No matter where this life takes you, there will always be someone in this world who loves you more than your imagination will allow you to understand. You're never quite alone."

—Savannah Kirk, *The Heart of the Lone Wolf*

CHAPTER ONE

IN EVERY KNOWN DEFINITION OF the word, Wesley Hudson is officially *offended* by what he's just read. He closes the paperback and stuffs it into his backpack. He wants to scream, "Where does she get this stuff?" But what's the point? It's only him on a bench outside of LAX's Tom Bradley International Terminal.

Savannah Kirk—better known as Mom—may be a *New York Times*-bestselling Young Adult author and adored by her millions of social media followers, but to Wes she's an anomaly. Not in a bad way. Wes loves that his mom is quirky, overly optimistic, totally liberal about *everything*, and funny as hell too.

But her books are… weird.

First of all, she writes Horrmance, which is a mixture of horror and romance. How is that a thing? How does one mix the styles of Stephen King and Rainbow Rowell and produce a bestseller? Well, besides a good marketing campaign. Wes hadn't known there were that many people who wanted to read books about werewolves fighting a blood feud while trying to find a date to the prom.

Obviously, Wes knows nothing about being trendy or the least bit cool. But Savannah Kirk's latest hit, *The Heart of the Lone Wolf*, is just so cliché. In the book, the antagonist has just given the conflicted main character an ultimatum: List the five things she cares about most, and the villain will consider sparing those things from the destruction that will come from creating his perfect new world— because, of course, the villain always gives you a choice.

Wes pulls out his phone and checks for new notifications. No texts. No voicemails. Nothing. His flight landed an hour ago. Ella's forty-five minutes late picking him up.

Actually, this is all Ella's fault. Wes rarely reads his mom's books. Had Ella been on time, something he doesn't think she's been once in her life, then he'd be halfway home by now instead of considering his own list of the top five things he cares about most in life.

What or whom would he save from mass destruction?

A line of honking cars wages war for curbside parking in front of him. People come and go in rushes, wheeling luggage or backpacks and sometimes fussing children. There's a lot of swearing, and middle fingers being tossed around from cars and SUVs.

One thing's certain: Wes definitely wouldn't spare LAX from Armageddon. But he's a born-and-raised Santa Monica kid, so California can't go down in a heap of flames.

He swipes to the notes app on his phone. Since he's stuck waiting for Ella, he might as well kill time with a list. If there's one area of impending adulthood Wes excels at, it's list-making. He only wishes his ability to break down life's most meaningless aspects into finely tuned bullet points impressed Calvin Hudson, his dad, in the slightest.

"Don't waste away this summer," Calvin warned before Wes boarded his flight out of Siena, Italy. "This is your chance to figure out what you're going to major in before college starts. Who do you want to be in five years?"

Frankly, Wes doesn't know who he wants to be in five minutes. An influencer? A teacher? Alive after suffering through that last chapter of his mom's book?

Whatever. Wes has no intention to "waste away this summer." He has plans. Huge plans. Life-changing-like-in-Netflix-movies plans.

Yes, he's eighteen and should probably be considering what he's going to do with the next four years when he attends UCLA in the fall. He assumed the whole "this is adulting" thing would happen post-high-school-graduation, but nope. A month in Italy with his parents didn't help either. He thought the trip was a graduation gift, not a "figure your shit out" ultimatum.

His parents are still in Italy, though. Calvin, a chef and a major fixture on the California restaurant scene, is extending his culinary base to Europe. They're spending the summer starting Calvin's new restaurant while Savannah works on her next book. So, Wes has space to solve this whole adulthood issue.

For now, he can continue to be—by far—the coolest comic book geek to exist. He can return to epic, boss-level living. That basically consists of chilling with his friends and working at Once Upon a Page. He loves that place. It's so laidback, Wes practically gets paid to kick his feet up all day.

But this summer isn't just about a strict diet of pepperoni pizza and reading Green Lantern comics, and maybe deciding what he'll study at UCLA—a hard maybe. This is the summer Wes finally wins the heart of the guy he's been crushing on since sophomore year of high school. He doesn't have an actual *plan* for that either, but it's going to happen.

Life owes Wes so hard for giving him nerdy genes, a pain-in-the-ass older brother, uncooperative curly hair, and the inability to skateboard.

"HAVE I TOLD YOU HOW much I hate coming to L.A.?"

Wes is mostly through with his list when he looks up. Ella emerges from the driver's side of a familiar crimson compact car parked curbside. She's wearing a long *Like a Virgin* T-shirt over black tights and has scuffed Vans on her feet.

"You don't hate L.A.," Wes says.

"Well, I hate LAX. Passionately. It's a traffic abomination."

"Big facts," agrees Wes. He drags his luggage to the passenger rear door. Ella pops it open, and he heaves his stuff inside. He turns back to her. "Is that how you plan to explain away your lateness?"

"Fuck off," Ella replies with zero heat. She tucks locks of her long, dark brown hair behind one ear. "Have you met the 405 at seven p.m. on a Sunday? Actually, have you met the 405 at any hour? It's vehicular suicide."

"You're still late."

"And you're still a virgin. We can't all win at life."

Wes frowns and pretends to be wounded by Ella's words, but he can't be. It's one of the many things he loves about Ella—her dry sense of humor. And how freaking brilliant she is. Plus, her kill-your-enemies-for-you loyalty.

She's the kind of friend Wes will never quit.

He thinks about Ella's place on his list…

The Five Things I Love the Most:
Number Three—Ella

Ella's the closest thing I have to a sister. She's got serious runner-up best friend vibes.

It all started two summers ago at the bookstore. My first "official" year as an employee. Ella was a new hire too. She had this badass energy, so I introduced myself. Then she said the eight most horrifying words ever:

"Do you give HJs on the first date?"

Full disclosure: I pretended I didn't know what an HJ was. I mean, I did—the internet does exist! But I wanted to make sure we were on the same page.

Turns out, she'd caught me staring at a semi-cute dude who'd been browsing the fantasy section five minutes before— the same dude SHE was checking out. On the Kinsey scale, I'm a hard seven, even though that rating doesn't exist. That's how confident I am in my gayness.

Ella was cool with it. To her, I was competition.

"And I definitely give HJs on the first date." She was so chill. I loved it.

After that, we were bonded for life.

Wes folds Ella into a hug. He's half a foot taller than her, something he never teases her about and, though an anti-hugger, she never complains when he does things like this. Wes likes to think he's the exception to all of Ella's rules.

He buries his nose in her hair and inhales. She smells like her favorite brand of grape bubble gum, the Pacific Ocean, and home.

"I can't believe you abandoned me for a month," Ella says into his chest.

"Did you miss me?"

"The only thing I miss in life is the ability to go to a coffee shop without the douchebag male barista mansplaining to me the superiority of an Americano." Ella pulls back, smirking. "You're very replaceable."

"I don't need your snark."

"Too bad. It's a built-in luxury."

Ellen Louise Graham—the last guy who called her that is quite possibly missing a finger—is a punk rock dream: forest-brown eyes, pale rose-white skin, and unreachable levels of confidence in her body.

"I'm fat and damn hot, okay?" she once told him before shamelessly hitting on some college dude loitering in the aisles of the bookstore.

Ella sizes him up. "You look good."

"Uh. Thanks?"

She slugs his bicep. "Take a compliment. I'm not handing them out like lollipops at the dentist's office."

"Fine. Thank you. You look good too."

"I mean, as if that wasn't obvious." Ella winks. "But also, I don't need your praises to validate my appearance. I reject your masculinist views on beauty and worthiness. My value surpasses physical attractiveness."

"I, uh…"

He's isn't sure how to reply to Ella, mainly because Ella loves a good argument. Wes? Not so much, which sucked growing up with an older brother like Leo.

Wes's parents were college sweethearts. The seriously nerdy— Calvin named Wes after Wesley Crusher, as in the kid from *Star Trek: The Next Generation*—accounting major who landed a hipster, creative-writing wallflower. After their first year of marriage, Leo was born. Four years later, Wes popped up. No one's said it, but Wes classifies himself as an "unexpected visitor."

A blaring horn startles Wes.

A very impatient woman with frizzy blue hair and a death stare honks from her Buick. She wants their curb space, and Wes's mini reunion is holding up the process.

"We're coming, Granny!" Ella shouts, dispatching an equally evil glare. She turns back to Wes. "I really hate LAX."

Wes jogs to the passenger side. Usually he'd be up for a verbal throwdown between Ella and Grandma Blue Hair, but he's just graduated high school and been an out-of-work-almost-adult for less than a month. He doesn't have bail money.

Ella pulls into traffic, slowly giving Grandma Blue Hair the finger in her rearview mirror.

Wes exhales happily. "Damn, it's good to be back."

"CAR, CAR... ANOTHER CAR!"

It's a shame that Wes is going to die young.

He's got one hand on the passenger door, another braced on the dashboard, and his small intestine is currently lodged in his throat: Ella whips her car around the 405 as if she's a Formula One driver. Above his head, a forest of tree-shaped car fresheners swings joyfully from the rearview mirror. A Taylor Swift Funko Pop figure, scribbled over with a black Sharpie to look dark and menacing, mocks him from the dashboard.

This is why Ella's runner-up in the best friend category: because Wes, who hasn't left his mark on the world or met his favorite comic book writer, Geoff Johns, and has only been to one Weezer concert in eighteen years of existence, will die an underachiever.

From the driver's seat, Ella cackles. "Chill, Wesley."

"Do not call me that," he says through his teeth. "Also, eyes on the freaking road!"

The car weaves between two SUVs, dodges a Corvette, and barely misses making out with the grill of a semitruck.

How is she able to drive at these speeds? It might be eight o'clock on a Sunday evening, but there's no lack of traffic in Southern California. In fact, there's never a shortage of traffic in the entire state of California.

"Did you piss your Spider-Man briefs yet?"

"I hate you," grumbles Wes, but his words are drowned out when Ella cranks the volume on her cheap stereo system.

The real travesty is that Wes is going to die while listening to "High Hopes" by Panic! At the Disco.

Ella is aggressively in love with her emo-pop-punk music. Wes, on the other hand, is a '90s alt-rock singer stuck in a geek's body. He's hardcore about garage bands and summer punk anthems—without the tattoos and flannel overload, of course.

As they merge onto the I-10, the traffic smooths. Ella decelerates to NASCAR-levels of road debauchery. She lowers the volume on the stereo and cracks the windows just enough for Wes to breathe in a lungful of sweet, sticky California air. There's this flavor to it, as if the ocean is so close, as if the sunset tastes like heat and oranges. It's still early July, but summer is alive and kicking this close to Santa Monica.

"Now that you're done being all Euro-hot," Ella says with a sly grin.

"That's not a thing."

"It is."

"It's very much not a thing," Wes argues. "Besides, I've always been way hot."

"Like, anyone can edit the definition, Wikipedia hot?"

Wes's body betrays him with a snort, then a chuckle. Ella isn't *that* funny. He kicks his russet-orange Pumas up on the dash, nearly knocking over Evil Taylor Swift, then slouches in his seat. "Listen, El, I'm not some cynical, self-deprecating Netflix teen who complains about how boring he looks, when in actuality I'm super-attractive after you peel back my 'nerdy layers.' Geek is the new hot."

"So, you're like Michael Cera in *Superbad*?"

"Like Michael Cera in *anything*."

"It's the curls, right?" Ella teases.

Wes can't disagree. His distinguishable hair genes—along with his severe jaw line—are from his mom's side of the family. But he mostly favors Calvin Hudson—tall with a long nose, full lips, more-brown-than-green hazel eyes and a need to shave *everything* since he was fifteen. But Wes didn't inherit his father's rich brown skin; neither did Leo. Wes's complexion is more like a pale tan.

"So, now that you're sexy-as-fuck," Ella says, still driving as if Wes doesn't want to see his nineteenth birthday, "we can start finding you some prospects? Or are we waiting until classes start in September?"

Another great thing about Ella: She's going to UCLA in the fall too. Wes won't be alone as he experiences his first post-high-school existential crisis.

"I don't need any prospects," Wes replies with as much nonchalance as a lying politician.

"You don't?"

"Nope. I'm good. Happy and single."

"Single, yes," Ella agrees, then raises her eyebrows. "Happy? Depends on how you classify it."

"I classify it as Wes Hudson, a guy on the verge of getting his shit together."

"So, the utter opposite of happy."

"Ella, I'm not going to spend my summer chasing after boys to fill some emptiness you think exists."

"Well, not boys," she replies, "but hopefully you won't be chasing the same boy."

Wes's hands curl into fists in his lap. He knows where this conversation is going. "You can stop implying."

"I will when you stop avoiding."

"I'm not avoiding anything," Wes hisses, but he is. He most definitely is. "I just want to spend this summer kicking back. Go to a party or two. Read comics. Avoid Leo. Hang out as much as possible at Once Upon a Page. That's it."

Ella sighs heavily. "Oh, here we go…"

Yup, here we go.

Wes is certain they've had at least ten different versions of this discussion over the short span of their friendship.

"All you do is spend time at the bookstore," says Ella. "As if all you want out of life is that damn place and Nico."

There, she's said it. Now it's all Wes will be thinking about for the next fifteen minutes.

Not as if Wes hasn't thought about this one thing since, well, tenth grade. But he's a realist. He knows discussing his massive crush on his best friend with anyone has never solved the problem. If *talking* about all life's problems solved anything, people might actually be a lot further along with their goals than just hashtags on social media.

"Listen," Wes says, angling his body in Ella's direction. "Life's good. We're done with high school. I smashed my college essay, and we're headed to my dream school…"

"Your parents' dream school," Ella corrects.

Wes's parents are UCLA alumni, not that that had a direct impact on why he chose to stay closer to home. Santa Monica is his life. So maybe he wanted to be somewhere all his memories with Nico exist, since Nico won't be at UCLA with him. He doesn't think that's a bad thing.

"What I'm trying to say is, the rest of this summer is going to be killer."

Ella rolls her eyes. "Whatever you say, pal."

The car pulls into the parking garage behind a pale pink building. Wes doesn't care if Ella agrees with him. He's home. He has two months left to execute his nonexistent plan. And he's damn sure going to make the most of what he's got.

CHAPTER TWO

**The Five Things I Love the Most:
Number Two—Once Upon a Page**

I don't know if I believe in magic. REAL magic. Not the stuff in Marvel movies. But I think everyone has that one place where they believe anything is possible.

For me, that's Once Upon a Page.

When I walk inside, I feel like I'm safe. I'm invincible. The Adult World can't touch me. I don't have to worry about leaving my mark in life. College? What's that? Career, who?

Maybe there really is a spell cast on the bookstore's doors. Once you enter, you're a kid again. You're free. Nothing—not even goblins like Leo—can take this away from you.

I guess I do believe in magic.

I believe Once Upon a Page is my gateway to being myself.

Paseo Del Mar is a pastel pink building that sits proudly on the corner of Colorado and Ocean Avenues. It's framed by gray sidewalks and palm trees. A series of twinkling fairy lights connects the property to the metal fence surrounding Tongva Park. A few paces down the sidewalk, a giant pedestrian intersection is mobbed with people, no matter the hour, all entering and exiting Santa Monica Pier.

But that's not why Wes is standing in front of this building as the dying sunset melts the peach from the skyline.

He's not here for the landmark of Paseo Del Mar, a mom-and-pop pizzeria named Little Tony's Big Slice that hogs a corner of the turf.

It's still open; the glass door swings ajar to exhale the scent of basil and flour and greasy pepperoni slices.

He doesn't want to slide into Brews and Views, the coffeehouse where Kyra works and where all the anti-corporate coffee people huddle instead of the three nearby Starbucks. Aerial, the surf shop, is already closed, though there's a light in the back indicating JoJo, the owner, is probably sleeking new boards before she hangs them in the display window tomorrow morning.

Wes is here for the place sandwiched between Little Tony's and Aerial: Once Upon a Page. He's here for the independent bookstore that he knows better than his own bedroom. Like Aerial, the bookstore is already closed, but Wes doesn't care. He just wants to look. He wants to absorb that last bit of charge—one he can never name or describe—from the parents who were dragged into the store today by their excited children or the quiet girl who camped in a corner, devouring every mystery book she could find. He wants to imagine himself behind that front counter, ringing up customers or introducing a new, wide-eyed teen to all his favorite comic series.

At the pier entrance, a young amateur rapper spits rapid-fire lyrics. From farther out come screams from Pacific Park, where patrons ride the solar-powered Ferris wheel or the rollercoaster. But all Wes can hear is the collection of '90s tunes he usually plays while he's at work.

Once Upon a Page is Wes's first job. It's his *only* job, so far.

He stares into the store's display window. Someone forgot to turn off the BOOKS sign. Its pink neon light illuminates the New Releases display, a tower of books whose covers show dragons and blood and flowers and breathtaking colors.

In the reflection, Wes swears he sees a small boy with out-of-control curly hair and large eyes bouncing in anticipation of getting his sticky fingers on the newest issue of *Green Lantern* with John Stewart on the cover. A boy who huddled in a corner of the bookstore for hours, reading. A boy who had to be escorted home more than a few times by Mrs. Rossi, the bookstore's owner, because he missed dinner or had homework to finish.

Wes isn't that boy anymore.

"Let's talk priorities," says Ella as she stands next to him. "Like hauling your luggage upstairs. Taking a shower because, while I love you, you're foul from being on an airplane for half a day."

"I don't stink," Wes replies with a curled lip.

He doesn't. After disembarking the plane, he very discreetly took a whiff under both armpits and, as a precaution, applied a thin layer of deodorant in a tiny restroom stall. Gym class and an awkward puberty had taught Wes many valuable lessons about hygiene.

"Fine, you don't." Ella sighs dramatically. "Are you gonna go inside?"

He could. Unlike the rest of the teen staff, Wes has a set of store keys. "No." He shakes his head. "Tomorrow."

"I'm going upstairs." Ella elbows his hip. "I have a date to get ready for. Don't hump the glass while you're down here."

"Gross. I'd never do that," Wes says, but Ella's already turning the corner, headed for the side entrance. He stands there for another second, smiling at his reflection. Then he remembers what she said. "Wait! You have a *date*?"

"Are you eating, Wes? You look frail."

Wes refrains from exhaling loudly through his nose when he looks at his mom on FaceTime. He flops backward onto his bed. "Mom, I just left you like twenty hours ago."

"You look like you're losing weight," his mom comments.

Wes shrugs lazily. Maybe sixteen hours on a plane snacking on salt and vinegar chips and pretzels have left him starved and gaunt. Or maybe his mom is a natural worrier.

Probably the latter.

"Why are you up so early?" he asks, glancing at the time in the top corner of his phone. 9:01 p.m. "What time's it there?"

"Just after six."

In the screen's background, Wes can spot the rising sun leaving the sky a bleeding pink. She must be outside the house his parents are renting for the summer. Savannah is wide-eyed, her graying brown hair is tied in a messy ponytail, her lips stretch into that smile he loves.

"I had to get an early start on this next book," she says, as though he should already know. As if Wes hasn't watched his mom wake up early, for as long as he remembers, to sip coffee and stare blankly at a laptop screen until words magically appear. "I couldn't disappoint my five-a.m. writers' club."

"That's just a social media hashtag, Mom. It's not really a thing."

"It is!" Her giggle crackles in his phone's speaker. "I'm already at ten thousand words."

Savannah doesn't call anything she writes an official book until she's pecked out at least ten thousand words on her ancient laptop.

"Hashtag 'amwriting' and killing it," Savannah adds.

Wes can't remember the last time he thought of her as Jordan Hudson, her real name. Since he was old enough to squeak out words, it's either been Mom or Savannah. She says it's for confidentiality, to protect their family from invasive social media predators or overzealous fans. But Wes thinks she simply loves to lead the life of someone else, like her book characters.

While his mom drones on and on about her next book's plot, he scans his bedroom. Wes loved the house in Italy—he loved *everything* about Italy, especially the boys and the ocean and, well, mainly the boys—but this room is a comfort he couldn't find in Siena.

His graduation cap and gown hang on the back of his computer chair. Hanging above his desk are a UCLA pennant and his dad's old basketball jersey. A standing lamp shines a beam on his shelf of Funko Pop superhero figures. The walls are covered in posters: Wonder Woman with her magic lasso; Nightwing in a battle stance; a Kim Possible he should probably take down.

Then again, he sleeps on Green Lantern bedsheets and has a pair of adult Spider-Man PJ's, so maybe that poster isn't the most embarrassing thing about his room.

"Has Ella settled in well?" Savannah asks, drawing Wes's attention back to his phone.

Judging by the mounds of clothes spread across his mom's favorite, ugly, green sofa in the living area and the tower of unwashed dishes, Wes would say Ella's settled in quite nicely.

"She's all good."

"Have you talked to her parents? Do I need to call them?"

"Nah. They're fine."

At least, Wes thinks they are.

Unlike Wes's relationship with his parents, Ella's communication with her own parents is best served minimal and lukewarm. Her dad's an investor who spends more time "investing" in young, surgically enhanced twenty-somethings around their Corona del Mar city limits. Her mom dines on red wine and prefers consuming Netflix documentaries to being actively involved in Ella's decisions. Their only interaction is her constant commentary on Ella's body. Neither of them seem to care that Ella has spent the summer living in the Hudsons' loft-studio apartment hybrid.

Wes can fully admit his family's pad is dope as hell. Located above the bookstore, it has the ultimate view of the pier and Santa Monica Beach. It's a floor of former office spaces, gutted and renovated into a one-floor living space. Though it wasn't always the ideal space for a family of four, they made it work: three bedrooms and two bathrooms, a gnarly kitchen that's fully equipped thanks to Calvin. Neither Wes nor Leo have any cooking talent. Unfortunately, the Hudson boys are known for three meals: cereal, Pop Tarts, and microwaveable burritos.

"You two stay out of trouble," Savannah warns, but she's never mastered that authoritative voice his dad has. It's stern-ish at best.

"No problem, Mom," Wes replies, saluting her.

"No parties."

As if Wes is that high on the cool people chain.

Also, per his agreement with his parents to crib-sit for the summer, Wes has to deal with Leo making unannounced visits to check on him. That's just what Wes needs—more time with Leo.

"No problem."

"Maybe just a small, intimate movie night with your friends," suggests Savannah.

His friends. Wes likes to limit that group: Ella and Nico; Zay, who's very chill with a great sense of humor; and Kyra, who makes Zay seem uptight. Wes supposes Anna is in that elite squad now. She's his "replacement" at the bookstore while he's been gone. She's also pretty much the anti-Ella, which Wes needs occasionally.

"Only movie nights, Mom. Promise."

She smiles sweetly at him. "Call me tomorrow."

"Deal."

Just as Wes hangs up and drops his phone on the bed, Ella twirls into his doorway. Backlit by the hallway lights, she's a stunner in a bowler hat, jeans, and leather jacket. All black, of course. The only exception is a white, flowy blouse under the jacket.

Wes sits up for a better view. "Wow, really channeling '80s Madonna, huh?"

"She only wishes she was me at our age," Ella says.

"True that."

"Though, even now, I'm positive she'd still try to hook up with this Long Beach State freshman volleyball player I'm going out with."

"LB State? Nice flex."

"I know," she says, winking.

"So, this is happening?" Wes rubs his jaw. "You're, like, going on a *date*-date?"

"Correct."

"But…" He pauses to choose his words carefully.

Thing is, Ella doesn't date. Well, occasionally, like on Leap Year Day. She doesn't conform to any heteronormative directives. She rejects the idea that anyone should seek out romance as an agency to existence. Monogamy might as well be a foreign language to her. All this, Wes totally respects. But it makes incidents like this, when *Ella is going on a date*, kind of weird.

"Why?" Wes finally asks.

"Because I'm bored, and you haven't been around for a month, and…"

"But I'm back."

"Obvi. But I already made plans. And maybe I like this guy."

"Okay." Wes wants to call bullshit.

"It's my prerogative, Wes. He's cute, I'm a hottie, so why not?"

"Huh." Wes nods approvingly. "That's fair."

"Great," Ella says through her teeth. "Now do the gay bestie thing and comment on how amazing my hair looks."

"Uh, that's stereotyping."

"You are a stereotype."

Fact, but he's not *that* stereotype.

"You look…" Again, Wes considers his words. "Like a material girl."

Ella flips him off with a snort-giggle. Wow, he's really missed that noise. "Whoever this dude is, he doesn't stand a chance," Wes adds, because it's true.

Ella hovers in his doorway. She never hovers.

"What?" Wes asks.

"Wes," Ella says, gently.

Wes's spine goes rigid. This is it. This is how every scene before someone announces, "They're dead!" starts. Wes can feel his heart crawl into his esophagus. He's already trembling.

"Is it Mr. Rossi? Is he dead?" he stammers. Mr. Rossi's at that age where "natural causes" is sure to be scribbled on his death certificate. "Wait… is it Zay?"

Wes still hasn't shaken the guilt about teaching Zay how to play Beirut with Fireball whiskey over winter break this year. What was he thinking? Zay just turned seventeen. But that was kind of Ella's fault, too, so if Wes is indicted for involuntary manslaughter, he's taking her with him.

"What? No," Ella says incredulously.

Wes inhales deeply. His forearm hairs stand tall, but he's prepared. He can handle this.

"They closed Book Attic," Ella eventually says.

"Book Attic?"

"Yes. The bookstore on Fourth Street."

"Yeah, I know," Wes says nonchalantly.

Book Attic has been around almost as along as Once Upon a Page. Their staff was very competitive. Wes believes the store had decent foot traffic, though not as great as his bookstore, which is located near the pier. People constantly stop in at Once Upon a Page for a good beach read.

"What's the big deal?"

"Book Attic is *closed*," she repeats. "They shut down that Barnes and Noble near Third Street Promenade months ago."

"I thought they relocated?"

"To where? Mars?" Ella's boot taps loudly on the hardwood floor. "Are you picking up the clues, Sherlock?"

Wes *pffts* at her. "That those stores had poor customer service and lowkey bad realty selections?"

"Maybe..."

"Not going there, Ella." Wes's neck is tight, but he still manages to shake his head. "Once Upon a Page is an institution. Nothing bad's happening here. Those two bookstores closing, out of the ten around us plus the twenty in downtown L.A., are just wild coincidences."

"Hella wild coincidences, don't you think?"

"No, I don't think," Wes says with a lightheartedness he hopes she accepts.

The corners of her mouth quirk. "Not very well, at least."

"That's what my SAT scores say."

Ella doesn't mention anything else about the bookstore. She tugs her phone out of her jacket. She has a My Chemical Romance phone case. Wes is aggressively disappointed by her choices. "I better go before this guy thinks he's unworthy of my time," she says.

"If he can't lift Mjölnir, then he's unworthy of your glory."

"That's some kind of nerd, DC joke, right?"

Correction: Wes is aggressively disappointed by Ella's comic book knowledge.

"Whatever." Ella waves. "Don't wait up for me!"

"Do I ever?"

"Good boy."

"Use protection!" he shouts, but the door's already slamming shut. Fine. Wes isn't Ella's guardian anyway.

Wes spends ten minutes on his phone, updating his social media accounts with photos and videos from Italy. He scrolls through a few hilarious Reddit posts and watches random YouTube videos of talking cats and epic fails. But he can't escape how quiet the loft is.

Why can't Wes be more like Ella when it comes to life and dating and, well, sex? Ella's ridiculously confident about that topic. She's all, "No biggie. Sex is just sex. It's not a defining moment in your life."

It's not that Wes is ashamed of his inexperience. He's always had this idea in his head: Wes wants his first time to be with someone he can imagine being with for more than a month or a week or *that moment*. He wants his first to be someone he can share his comics with, someone who's cool with his geekiness, someone who won't pressure him because, honestly, Wes isn't sure he's ready for sex. But when he is, he wants that person to be cool if he's nervous or if he can't figure all of it out.

High school was this epic buildup to a deadline. By the time he turned eighteen, Wes was supposed to know what college he was going to, see what his future would look like, and no longer be a virgin. And here he is, unable to figure out any of those things or even what to do on a Sunday night in the heart of summer, which, of course, is why someone knocks at the door.

Wes groans, rolling off his bed. Ella's undoubtedly forgot her keys or wallet or phone charger.

The knocking grows louder.

"Seriously, I'm not in the mood if you're about to tell me this Long Beach dude is bringing friends and you need a wingman," he shouts as he pads over the hardwood floor toward the door. "Ella, I'm not that guy. I have zero game."

When he pulls open the door, it's not Ella awaiting him.

It's Nico.

CHAPTER THREE

"DID YOU SAY YOU HAVE zero game?"

Nico leans in the loft's doorway. His dark hair is a swoopy, tall mess. It always draws attention from the way his ears stick out. His crooked smile is magnified by the laugh lines around his mouth. It's impossible for Wes to look anywhere else.

"You're wearing your glasses."

Okay, Wes is aware his comeback is weak, but it's just that…

Thirty days and an entire Atlantic Ocean separating them has made Wes's cottonmouth, racing-heart issues more pronounced. All the Instagram posts with the worst filters, and TikTok videos of Nico doing the most random things because he's *that person*, and poorly coordinated FaceTime calls can't compare to seeing him in person, in his doorway, standing two feet from Wes and wearing black-rimmed glasses.

Wes wishes he could come up with a better way than dark brown to describe Nico's eyes. His mom's a bestselling author, for fuck's sake. His grasp on adjectives shouldn't be this tragically limited.

"Yeah," Nico says, adjusting his glasses. A faint red hue blossoms on his cheeks. "Didn't feel like being bothered with my contacts."

Nico's passionately against wearing his contacts if he doesn't have to. "You shouldn't just go poking your eyes for the hell of it," he grumbled the day before their freshman year of high school started.

"Plus, I needed them to read the takeout menu." Nico holds up a big brown paper bag that Wes hadn't noticed before. A quick inhale coaxes a lazy smile across Wes's lips.

Chef Zhang's Kitchen, Wes's favorite Chinese cuisine restaurant on Wilshire.

"Unless," says Nico teasingly, shaking the bag in front of his face, "you're not hungry, Wesley."

Wes's stomach grouses like a cranky bear. Nico knows Wes loves that place, the asshole. As if he'd ever turn down beef and broccoli and quality time with his best friend. Wes wonders how anyone in this galaxy could survive without Chinese takeout and Nico Alvarez.

"Get in here," he finally says, almost reaching for Nico's shirt to drag him inside.

Nico strides in, automatically stepping out of his Adidas. He walks to the sofa as if he owns the place. He spent most of middle and high school occupying the same corner of the sofa or Wes's bed. They fought alien invasions on Wes's game system and did homework while sharing chicken tacos. They were two inseparable friends arguing over what movie to watch on Friday nights, which makes the fact that Wes is currently admiring Nico's ass as he unpacks the food inescapably awkward.

The first time Wes noticed Nico in a non-platonic way was a complete accident. Algebra worksheets were destroying Wes's life, the PSATs were looming, and his parents were hovering a lot, providing him with inadequate "private hand therapy" time. And there Nico was, in mid-November, playing a pickup game of beach volleyball with some rando teens they'd met an hour before on the pier. Nico, fresh out of the awkwardness of puberty and shirtless, was like zero hour of the apocalypse for Wes. His mind kept saying, *He's not hot, he's not hot*, but the rest of his body didn't comprehend.

It was a day of epiphanies—Wes was *really* into guys—and utter catastrophe—Wes was *really* into his best friend.

Nico props his feet on the coffee table, right next to Savannah's stack of research books on cryptids and mythological creatures. "Drinks?"

Wes chokes out, "Sure."

But he lingers. His eyes scan Nico: He's wearing a worn-soft, faded, reddish-maroon T-shirt and skinny jeans frayed at the knees. Nothing special. *Nico's nothing special*, Wes tells himself. *Just a friend. What's there to crush on?*

"Wesley?"

"Drinks!" Wes shouts, startling himself. Nico raises an eyebrow and, yep, that's Wes's cue to exit.

In the kitchen, Wes pulls out his phone. He considers texting Ella. Maybe she'd have some sage advice on how to reclaim his chill. Or she'd scream at him in all caps to GET IT TOGETHER WES, IT'S JUST NICO. Instead, he clicks on his notes app. He reviews his list. Most of the Top Five are interchangeable, depending on his mood—*sorry, Ella*—but one spot will never shift.

Number One—Nico

Nicolás Andrés Sebastián Alvarez. As in NASA. As in, Nico's out of this world.

The problem with Best Friend Crushes—besides the fact that one shouldn't pine after friends, period—is that I'm too chickenshit to even mention the topic of dating with Nico. Us dating, to be clear. My biggest fear is it might jeopardize the gold-standard friendship we established way back in our juice-box-drinking days. Hell no. I can't ruin that.

I don't even know what it is about Nico. I mean, I do. It's the way he's geeky but in that too-cool-to-be-a-nerd way. It's the glasses. The laugh. The ass. Did I just type that? But he's also a genuine friend. He looks out for me. He doesn't care if I'm extremely into comics or get super nauseated at the scent of seafood. That I'm gay. We haven't had The Talk about Nico's own sexuality, but I'm fifty-fifty he's this wicked-adorable bi legend.

He's like the accidentally charming sidekick in a Netflix movie that you're not supposed to fall in love with, but you do. You fall hard.

So, yeah, I'm that guy. You know, the kind that draws hearts around our names in Sharpie on my Five-Star notebook.

THIS IS JUST A CRUSH, OKAY?

Wes quickly locks his phone.

"I'm cool," he whispers. "I'm hella cool."

He raids the refrigerator. It's obvious Leo has stocked it recently: grapes, sliced carrots, water bottles, deli meats and cheeses, and microwaveable meals. Thankfully, he bought Coke, which Wes grabs for himself, and Nico's favorite, orange soda. While Wes is certain Leo's a certifiable dick three-hundred days a year, he finds it lowkey sweet that Leo thinks enough of Nico to buy a whole six-pack of glass-bottled orange sodas. Personally, Wes believes orange soda tastes like Tang-flavored piss.

It's telling that Wes would sacrifice prime refrigerator shelf space for Nico's favorite drink.

He's been whipped for a long, long time.

NICO IS HIP-TO-HIP, SHOULDER-TO-SHOULDER WITH Wes as they eat. He's built like Wes—lean but toned. It helps that Nico's always been active—skateboarding and beach stuff—while Wes can thank Calvin for his gene-lottery win.

"Oh. For you." Nico passes him a cup of teriyaki sauce, because Wes lives and dies for that stuff.

Cheeks flushed, Wes mumbles, "Thanks."

Nico's crooked grin reveals an overbite and the fact that his canines are slightly above average in length. Growing up, Nico was always self-conscious about that. He never flashed one of those toothy smiles in photos. A few of the jerk-faces they went to school with called him a vampire in the halls.

But when it's just Wes and Nico, he doesn't hide his teeth. Wes likes that.

"How'd you know I was home?" he asks between bites.

"Your mom," Nico replies with a shrug. "Also, don't pretend like I didn't stalk your flight path on Delta's app."

"You did?"

"Duh." Nico dusts his hands off on his jeans. He yanks out his phone, showing Wes his itinerary on the app. "I could've picked you up."

"You got no wheels," Wes teases, using an unopened pack of chopsticks to poke Nico in the ribs. They never got the hang of using chopsticks. Plus, Wes is a messy eater with basic tools like forks and spoons.

"I got wheels," Nico argues with a puckered mouth. "My skateboards."

"Yeah, no."

"Whatever." Nico resumes thumbing through his phone. "Check out this sick sunset." He holds up the screen for Wes to view. He swipes through a few shots on his camera roll. Crisp images of the sun skidding behind the horizon. Everything is unfiltered. Nature at its greatest. By the angles, Wes presumes Nico took the photos from his bedroom window.

"Put a few up on my Pinterest."

"Nice," Wes says with a mouthful of beef and rice. "I like that one." He points to the last shot: a smear of tangerine representing the sun. Palm tree silhouettes layer the bottom of the photo. It's this unbelievable composition that Wes can't look away from.

"Me too," Nico says softly.

"I've missed—" Wes pauses before "you" leaves his mouth. It wouldn't be weird if he said it, but it feels awkward on his tongue, as if he'd be saying it with a little too much emphasis.

You don't confess your lifelong crush on a friend with beef and broccoli bits on your shirt.

"The sunsets," Wes finally says after a gulp of Coke.

"Whatever. This place has nothing on Italy."

Well, it doesn't have you. Does Wes's mind have a reset button?

"True that. Santa Monica sucks balls compared to Siena."

Nico rolls his eyes, bumping their shoulders. "Keep telling yourself that, Wesley."

They laugh at each other. Wes knows nothing beats Santa Monica. And nothing's as great as their friendship, which is why Wes isn't going to say a damn thing tonight about how kissable Nico's mouth looks.

Nico slouches on the sofa, leaning into Wes. "Dude, today was brutal. A bunch of ravenous girls almost tore Anna's face off when she confused *Twilight* and *Vampire Academy*."

"So, by brutal, you mean hilarious?"

"Exactly." Nico fills Wes in on what he's missed. It's not much, but Nico talks as if he's breaking down the plot to every Marvel film ever made. Wes finds himself smiling at how *normal* this is. At how normal they are.

"Oh, man," Nico says between laughs, "and Cooper…"

Cooper's the new guy. Wes hasn't met him yet. He's also not sure if he's flattered Mrs. Rossi had to hire *two* employees to replace him while he was away or if he's been undervalued this whole time. He knows it's for the sanity of the bookstore, but maybe he'll *suggest* an increase in his hourly rate next time they're alone.

Wes kicks his feet up on the coffee table next to Nico's, nearly knocking over Savannah's books. At six-foot-one, Wes has a good four inches on Nico, something Nico's not fond of. But, thanks to fanfiction, Wes is absolutely obsessed with the height difference and the idea of leaning down to kiss Nico.

"…and he's cute, leaning toward hot—"

Wes snaps out of his daze. "Say what now?"

"I said he's kind of—"

"Yeah. Got that," Wes says, cutting Nico off. He hopes the stiffness in his voice isn't noticeable. The fact that Nico finds someone else attractive flusters him. But why? Of course Nico can check out another dude who isn't Wes.

Wes hasn't made any romcom-style declarations of his infatuation. Yet.

"So, is he, um, hotter than…" Wes is ashamed at how his voice trails off.

"Hotter than you?"

Wes's face scrunches. Slowly, he nods.

"Hold up. Do *you* think you're hot, Wesley?"

"I think." Wes pauses, tongue stuck to the roof of his mouth. "I think I'm acceptably attractive on a scale of one to that guy who's in all the teen Netflix movies." He's proud of that response. "I also think this city's—this state's—full of good-looking guys." A factual statement.

Nico stretches his arms above his head, then casually drops one around Wes's broader shoulders. "Well, then he's just any guy from the city, right?"

It's not the response Wes was hoping for.

They fall into an easy silence. The loft's windows are open. Downstairs, someone's car blares Tom Petty's "Free Fallin'," and Nico hums along. Wes does too. Another example of why Santa Monica's magic. They trade food cartons. Nico chugs soda while Wes picks at sesame chicken.

"This is good," he whispers.

"Always."

Heat radiates where their hips touch. The heady scent of ocean air sinks into the loft. Under that layer of iodine and salt, Wes can smell sweat and teriyaki sauce and Nico's deodorant.

It's a comfort. What is not a comfort for Wes is when he peeks down at Nico's rising chest and sees the emblem in the corner of his T-shirt. A white block S with a redwood tree in the middle.

Stanford.

While Wes has spent his life with UCLA as his endgame, Nico had another plan after sophomore year of high school. In September, he'll be attending Stanford. He wants to study premed. Nothing against UCLA and its rep, but they both know Stanford University School of Medicine is one of the premiere schools in California. Wes hoped Nico would at least complete his undergrad with him. But he knows why Nico's doing this. It's also more motivation to make this the Summer of Wes and Nico.

After they finish eating, Nico cleans up the trash. Wes acquires more drinks. He's deliberately not thinking about how cozily domestic this is. Who spends Sunday nights with their crush, crashed on the sofa, knees touching, tucked into each other's sides? Their faces are so close, Wes could lean forward and—

Do nothing.

Wes deserves an Academy Award for Best Actor in a Dramatic Friend-Zone Role.

"So, Wesley." Nico has a controller in one hand; the other fumbles with the remote. "Kill aliens or go Donkey Kong on your lame Yoshi ass."

Wes yawns, shrugging. "Whatever."

"I'll play, you watch?"

"Perfect."

"Hey." Nico unsettles Wes's very comfortable resting place against him to reach for something on the coffee table. "You forgot your fortune cookie."

Reluctantly, Wes holds an open palm for Nico to drop the cookie into. Wes can't lie—the fortune cookie is his favorite part of Chinese takeout. He cracks open the cookie and pulls out the slip of paper. He frowns at the message:

Change can hurt but it leads to a road paved with better things.

"Any good?" Nico asks, focused on the salivating aliens charging toward him on the TV.

Wes scowls. Even the fortune cookie companies like to mess with his mind. "Garbage." He crumples the shred of paper, then tosses it on the floor. He's jet-lagged and so freaking, ridiculously over this night.

He wiggles back against Nico's side. Nico kills more aliens. Wes thinks, *Stupid fortune, tomorrow's gonna be so much better,* and falls asleep.

CHAPTER FOUR 🛹

MORNING BLINDSIDES WES. IT HITS him like a fist, but mainly because he couldn't find a rhythm with his sleep cycle. *Thanks, jet lag.*

His phone's alarm assaults his eardrums. Outside his window, the sun pokes at the sky until it's pinkish orange. It's nearly eight a.m., and Wes hates everything.

He has two missed texts. One is from Nico, apologizing for ducking out last night after video games. He had to be up early to babysit his sisters. Wes barely remembers Nico leaving or crawling into his own bed.

The second text is from his dad.

From: Dad
Film and Television?
Received 11:38 p.m.

Attached to the text is a link to UCLA's School of Theater, Film, and Television. Calvin Hudson does this sometimes, sends Wes suggestions for possible college majors. It's supposed to be helpful, but it's really a reminder that Wes isn't anywhere near the stage of certainty about his future that his parents and brother were at his age.

After closing the text, Wes finally climbs out of bed. His eyes feel like sandpaper. He nearly walks into a wall stumbling to the kitchen for a Pop-Tart and leftover, room-temperature Coke. He's not functional enough to make tea, and coffee is a bitter, venomous sludge that Wes will have no part of.

He finishes off the Pop-Tart in three bites. He forgot to close the loft's windows last night. The air is blanketed by the scents of surf and seaweed and cool breeze.

Wes can smell it—today's going to be a good day.

He brushes his teeth, scrubbing the taste of sugar and flat Coke off his tongue. In the shower, he repeats, "You can do this; just tell him," while washing his hair. Anticipation buzzes in his system.

It's his first day back to work and, quite possibly, the day he wins Nico's heart.

In the bathroom mirror, while lazily fixing his hair, Wes assesses himself. He's wearing his very geektastic, lucky Green Lantern T-shirt. Last year at Comicpalooza, he won free passes to a new comic book movie wearing this shirt. So, today, Wes is going to get lucky, with his best friend. Maybe.

But he doesn't have time to think about that. The bookstore opens promptly at nine a.m. daily. He needs to haul ass downstairs, set up the till, dust the shelves, and check on his favorite corner of the store.

Wes skids down the hall's hardwood floors, passing Ella's room. Well, it's Leo's former room, now occupied by Ella for the summer. Quickly, he peeks inside. She's there, splayed out like an octopus and snoring at the ceiling.

He whispers to her, "Today's gonna kick ass."

Ella snores louder.

Wes shrugs, then runs for the door. He stops for his shoes, keys, and phone charger. On the way downstairs, he does a fist-pump that he's glad nobody witnesses.

WHEN WES ROUNDS THE CORNER, he's met by a grapefruit sky. It's a cool morning, but he knows the heat rises quickly in July. For now, he soaks in the quiet calm wrapped around the pier. The wind shakes the palm leaves hanging high over Tongva Park. He lifts his phone to catch a good shot of Santa Monica leisurely waking up, and text it to Nico before opening his notes app.

Number Five—The SoCal Vibe

There's a reason every movie and TV series doesn't have to try hard to make LA look so damn cool. It just is. But it helps that every city has a bomb-ass vibe that can't be replicated.

Downtown LA is obvi. That place is buzzing with so many people who want to make it big. But then there's La Jolla with its sick beaches and surf community that I love—even though I drown more than I surf. The views in Malibu are kickass. My selfie game is strong there. Venice isn't that far away and I 100% always live my best life down on Ocean Front Walk—all the music and faces and shops where you can get anything from clothes to art to weed.

Long Beach, Oceanside, San Diego... All great!

But Santa Monica is just so chill. I mean, it's fair to say, since I've been to ITALY now, I've never experienced anything like SM. It's more than the pier or the beach or the crazy-good restaurants everywhere. It's more than Nico. Or my family.

Santa Monica is this secret that I haven't fully unlocked yet. It's the kind of place that, once you're here, you never leave.

Wes pops his head into Brews and Views. He spots Kyra and waves.

"Welcome back, Crusher," she says, tucking a few of her big, loose curls behind her ear. Kyra is one of the rare people who gets his name's Star Trek reference.

Wes smiles apologetically, nodding his head in the direction of the bookstore.

"You're late." She wipes down a table. "You're never late."

"Jet lag," he says as an explanation.

Kyra puckers her mouth. "You're letting Ella influence you," she says with just enough accusation to make Wes yelp.

"How dare."

"Go open the store," she says, shooing him away with her rag. "They've missed you."

Wes sprints away without another word. It takes him a few turns of the key to jiggle the front door open. The lock has always been trouble. In his peripheral vision, the neon BOOKS sign shines like the North Star. Its pinkness makes him think of Mrs. Rossi and her vintage vibe, the one he fell in love with when he was eight years old.

Mrs. Rossi, like the bookstore, is some unrealistic version of perfect. She's a second mom to him. Some weekends, he finds a way to her house for home-cooked meals. Occasionally, he stays late at the bookstore just to listen to her recount stories from an era he knows nothing about.

"Home sweet home," he announces while flicking on the store's lights.

Rows and rows of deep, red oak shelves overflow with paperbacks and hardcovers. Bookcases line the walls and stretch into the store, connecting like Legos in the center. An endcap display of novels, every cover a different color of the rainbow, awaits customers near the front. It's a Pride presentation that Anna helped Wes with before he left for Italy. He grins at it as he passes.

He follows the thinning gray carpet toward the back. On the way is a showcase of all the latest teen apocalyptic-dystopian-fantasy sagas.

Each one has a title that starts with "Shadow" or "Queen" or "Dark." There's a generic theme Wes isn't commenting on.

In a back corner of the store is an office. The desk is a cluttered mess, one that only Mrs. Rossi can navigate. He unlocks the safe and grabs the till before exiting. Beside the office is a shoebox-sized bathroom and, thankfully, it doesn't reek. Wes would hate to spend his first day back scolding Ella over that.

He pauses at another section of the store. Wes's mecca, his Holy Grail, is the comics corner. It's common law amongst all employees at Once Upon a Page that this is Wes's territory. *Do not touch.* Wes has a system. He's got a sixth sense if anyone's messed with it. There might've been a mild tantrum—or five epic ones— in the past over people not respecting DC Comics domination.

His left eye twitches when he spots an Incredible Hulk comic overlapping a Green Lantern one. He almost drops the till. "Later, Wes," he whispers after a deep breath. "Fix it later."

He gave Nico one job while he was gone. One job.

Behind the front counter are a shelf stereo system and plastic bins filled with old compact discs, all the best stuff from the late '80s through the '90s. Outside the bookstore, Wes listens to everything on his phone or laptop, but the employees have a strict policy: If it's not on CD, it's not being played.

Wes has enough time to grab the *Blue Album* by Weezer and press play. At promptly nine a.m., he props the front door open to inhale the summer scents. "My Name Is Jonas," with its acoustic guitar intro, floats from the stereo into the street. Wes kicks his feet up on the front counter while checking his horoscope on his phone:

"There is a potential romantic interest in your life, Capricorn, and today is the day! Sparks are about to fly between you! This encounter could change your life."

Wes doesn't believe in horoscopes; he reads them for fun, but... *Sparks are about to fly between you!* Clearly, the universe is on his side. He smells clean, his hair is at least four-star-level Yelp-worthy, and he's wearing his lucky Green Lantern T-shirt.

He says to no one, "This is going to be the awesomest of awesome days."

BY NOON, WES'S PERCEPTION OF awesome has decidedly taken a giant belly flop off Reality Cliff.

"How do you not have a copy of that book?"

"Sir," Wes says through his teeth, "I'm sorry. We don't carry—"

"But it's the foremost research book on alien probing!"

Wes's mouth flattens into a thin line; his eyebrows droop into a frown. Mr. X-Files—it's what Wes is mentally calling this douchebag—is one of several customers who have royally ruined his morning. The universe, being the ultimate tease, gave Wes one very quiet customer during his first hour. Then the Hellmouth opened and in came the early lunch rush. Everyone needed his attention or a special order or, like Mr. X-Files, considered anyone in retail a personal punching bag.

"Oh, if you loved that series, let me introduce you to this one. Pirates, ships, and enemies-to-lovers-to-possible-enemies-again romance," gushes Mrs. Rossi as she leads a woman through the aisles.

Mrs. Rossi arrived an hour ago in a blast of lily-scented perfume and charm. She reminds Wes a lot of Frenchy from *Grease*—the movie version, since Wes has never seen a live musical. Mrs. Rossi is bubbly, a bit spacy, and not-so-accidentally dyes her hair cotton candy pink just like Frenchy. While she entertains customers with jokes and wide-eyed excitement, Wes is stuck dealing with Mr. X-Files, whose breath smells of raw onions and desperation.

"Sir, would you like me to order it—"

"I need it now," argues Mr. X-Files. "This research is vital."

"Really?" Wes raises a curious eyebrow at this guy's *'It's all good in the hood'* E.T. T-shirt. He's not judging; just observing.

Mr. X-Files relents with a grunt. "How long will delivery take?"

"For this book?" Wes clicks around on the store's semi-ancient desktop computer. "Ten business days."

"That's a millennium."

Wes peeks past Mr. X-Files to his comics corner. A young teen with honey-blond hair, green eyes, and a healthy distribution of freckles across their cheeks looks undecided between a Deadpool graphic novel and a Harley Quinn one. Every inch of Wes wants to scream. That's where he should be, instead of listening to this onion-breath monster's ranting.

"Would you like the book delivered to the store or a home address?" Wes finally asks, watching as Mr. X-Files turns an unhealthy shade of red.

After paying, Mr. X-Files stomps toward the door. Wes shouts, "And have a page-turning day!" because Mrs. Rossi loves to torture her employees by demanding they use the store's customary farewell for every customer.

He can't believe this is his life on a Monday afternoon.

"You're back!" Zay strides into the bookstore, greeting Wes with a fist-bump and a quick hug. Wes loves that about Zay—he has zero issues with showing affection with other guys, no matter their sexuality. In high school, Wes watched boys be casually demonstrative with each other, but if it ever got too physical, or there were too many eyes on them, they would always separate with a "that's gay" and a laugh.

He hated that.

But Zay isn't like those select assholes who ruined Wes's perception of PDA. Zay's still in high school. He's starting his senior year in September. He's got perfectly straight, white teeth, along with an awesomely soft, curly 'fro, the dreamiest sepia eyes, and a tawny complexion that Wes swears has never seen a pimple.

"Nice to have more melanin in this place," says Zay, jokingly.

This is another aspect of Zay that Wes loves. The one that doesn't walk around Wes's genealogy. Zay doesn't shame Wes's passing exterior because Savannah's white and Calvin's family is all very light-skinned. They both acknowledge Wes's privilege as much as they recognize they share the same community.

Zay's one fatal flaw is his poor choice in music, which he proves by cutting off Wes's epic air guitar session to Weezer's raucous "Holiday" and putting on Tracy Chapman.

"What the hell?"

"Wes, listen." Zay tilts his chin up. "I'm trying to educate you on great music the way my moms have informed me."

With Tracy Chapman? Wes is insulted on behalf of all the customers browsing the aisles. Zay's lucky Wes is too jet-lagged to chastise him about the differences between quality music, like Nada Surf and the Offspring, and whatever mellow nonsense is currently assaulting his eardrums. Plus, Zay's stupidly cute smile wins every argument.

In the teen fantasy section, a young girl stops to whisper-shout to her friend, "Fuck, he's bae-material."

On merit, Wes agrees. Zay's straight, and Wes really isn't into that whole turn-the-hetero-guy-homo thing he's read about online.

Also, there's that Nico thing he's currently navigating. Wes supposes it's a bit hypocritical to pinpoint his one reason for not dating Zay being the straight aspect, considering he's only about eighty-percent confident Nico's at least bisexual.

Thing is, Nico's been on dates with girls. He's kissed guys. Well, *a guy*. Wes doesn't vehemently hate Marco Carpenter for drawing Nico's name during a juvenile game of dirty dice—which was really the junior, home arts-and-crafts version Lula Fuentes made by taping dirty dares on the sides of Monopoly dice—at a party when they were sixteen. But he's not fond of the way Marco used his lizard tongue to attack Nico's mouth or the way Nico bit Marco's bottom lip. Their hands did a lot of moving too. It was kind of dark in Lula's basement, but Wes has read a lot of comic books; that's certainly given him partial X-ray vision by osmosis.

"Um, Wes?"

Wes blinks, then jerks out of his daydream—nightmare? —to stare at Zay.

"Wow," Zay says, nodding approvingly. "The power of Chapman."

"You should not be allowed near music."

"I dunno, homie." Zay points to the aisle between mystery and nonfiction. "Anna sure likes it."

Wes would like to remind Zay that they both believe Anna's part wood nymph. She has long, ash-blonde hair and large, rock-candy blue eyes. Freckles cover her fair skin. As she twirls, the hem of her peasant dress flutters. She's twenty, a supposed future assistant store manager, and so Bohemian-hippie.

"Anna's high," Wes comments.

"Maybe," Zay says, grabbing a stack of books that need to be reshelved. "But she digs it. The customers do too."

Throughout the store, people browse while swaying or bopping their heads. One guy mouths the words to "Fast Car." Traitors, all of them.

"Yikes. Scary."

Once again, Wes startles out of a daydream, this time to find Anna leaning over the counter. Popcorn flowers are braided into a crown around the top of her head. "Okay, help me out here," she says, tucking pieces of wavy hair behind her left ear to expose a sparkly line of piercings. "I have this customer looking for a funny book... but with aliens."

Wes's face pinches. *It better not be Mr. X-Files.*

"Uh."

Although Wes has spent more time in the bookstore than his own bed, he's not exactly the resident bibliophile here. That's Ella. But he knows enough about books to reply, "*The Hitchhiker's Guide to the Galaxy,*" without looking like a total novice. "Book's better than the movie."

"Aren't they all?"

Wes snorts. Truth.

"And that is...?"

Sometimes, Wes forgets how new Anna is. He only spent two weeks training her before he left. After that, she was in the very incapable hands of Ella.

"Sci-fi." Wes nods to a long wall opposite the front counter. "And if they really want a good book, tell them to get *We Are the Ants* also."

"Thanks," Anna says, skipping off with a smile too naïve for her to manage any portion of this store.

Wes settles onto the stool behind the counter. He's not jealous of Anna's situation. It's not as if he has time to go for a promotion. Not with college.

But if I didn't go to school…

No. Wes can't entertain that thought. But the problem is, it keeps creeping into his mind—not going to college but staying here, in Santa Monica, and helping Mrs. Rossi run the bookstore. Maybe it'll be easier to figure himself out in a place he knows than waste four years and end up in debt. And then what? A ridiculous amount of statistics show that most college graduates don't end up working in their field. So Wes is going to dedicate years to learning a subject, only to end up doing anything other than whatever he decides to study? It makes no sense to him.

But, all around Wes, everyone has their future figured out.

Ella Graham. UCLA. Communication.
Xavier "Zay" Jones. Plans to attend UCLA. Music Performance.
Anna Wooten. Santa Monica College. Business.
Nico Alvarez. Stanford. Biology.
Wes Hudson. UCLA. Undeclared. Most likely majoring in Loserology with a minor in Confusedonomics.

His chest is tight. Every time Wes's mind drifts like this, his vision goes mildly hazy. More than once, he's bitten his lip bloody. He should've figured all this out in Italy. It's as if Wes is the Chosen One, who's supposed to step into this destined role of well-adjusted, college-bound adult and conquer the world at eighteen. But now he's two months away from disappointing everyone in his life.

Wes stares pointedly at the chipped wooden surface of the counter until his heart slows down. It's fine. He's fine. This whole adulthood thing isn't going to ruin his summer.

CHAPTER FIVE

"It's so good to have you back." Mrs. Rossi rests a wrinkled hand over Wes's on the front counter, looking at him with tired, russet-brown eyes. Afternoon sunlight reflects off her bright pink hair. "These other kids are going to give a sweet old woman gray hair before her time."

Wes smirks. Mrs. Rossi is a certified fireball. Even in her late fifties, everything about her is still sparkly and captivating and lethal when handled the wrong way.

"Careful," he says in a half-warning, half-joking tone, "Mr. Rossi wouldn't appreciate that."

"Ah, that goofball. He keeps me dancing, you know."

Wes does. The Rossis remind him so much of his own parents. After decades together, they're still sickeningly in love. They have lunch together at least three times a week, go on strolls through Third Street Promenade while holding hands, enjoy the occasional dinner and a movie. They're *that couple*.

Mrs. Rossi sighs. "I don't know how I'd handle any of this without you."

Me neither. Wes's not exactly the model employee, but he's the only person under the age of twenty-one whom she trusts with a set of store keys. Well, besides Anna now. None of the others take this job seriously. Not the way Wes does.

"Well, the place didn't burn down while I was gone," Wes says, and the corners of his mouth tick upward. "That's a good sign. Maybe it won't be so bad when I…"

He struggles to finish that sentence. Wes has already told Mrs. Rossi he still wants to work weekends when classes start. But it still feels as though he's leaving her hanging. He doesn't know why. This is Mrs. Rossi's business. She ran it before him; she can do it without him constantly around too.

"It'll be fine," Mrs. Rossi whispers. Wes isn't sure if she's talking to him or herself. Another sigh deflates her shoulders. "Anyway, it's still nice to have you back. You're much better than…"

This time, it's Mrs. Rossi who doesn't finish. Instead, she stares out the front door with a deeply creased mouth and narrowed eyes. Without looking, Wes can guess why.

"Sorry, no selfies or autographs. I know you're all excited to see me, but please remain calm."

With a pair of big, dark sunglasses and an oversized, stretched-out sweatshirt hanging off one shoulder, Ella struts into the bookstore.

"You're late for your shift," Mrs. Rossi says in a clipped tone.

"I'm on Eastern time."

"Which, you know," Wes says, pinching the bridge of his nose, "makes you even later, right?"

"Thanks for the technicalities," Ella says dryly.

"This is unacceptable," Mrs. Rossi says. She's not typically a firm person, but in these instances, usually the ones involving Ella, she's fiercely strict. "If you're not going to be on time, at least communicate with me."

"Communication. Is that a mutual thing we're practicing?" Ella's smile is forced.

"Heaven help me," Mrs. Rossi mumbles, turning to walk toward her office.

Wes whips his head in Ella's direction. "What was that about?"

Ella lowers her sunglasses. "Not worth discussing right now."

"She's gonna fire you one day."

"She won't." Ella hops up on the front counter, crossing her legs. Every shift, the counter is Ella's throne, though she's been told repeatedly to sit on one of the stools like a normal human. She snaps her grape bubble gum. "I just got here and I'm already exhausted."

Without question, Ella's the biggest slacker around here. She helps when asked, which is never if Wes is available. But she also knows her stuff and has hand-sold more books than any employee who's ever worked at the store.

The digital clock near the register reads 2:07 p.m. Anticipation builds in Wes's stomach and bubbles to his chest. In less than an hour, Nico comes in for his shift. And then...

Wes hasn't had time to put together a detailed plan.

Just ask him out.

It seems simple, but Wes's execution skills have never been remotely flawless. He distracts himself by listening to Ella ramble about last night's date. She's shameless about the details, which Wes usually wouldn't mind except she doesn't refrain from any of the more explicit moments while Wes rings up customers.

"Afterward, I think he started, like, crying," she complains. "I know I'm amazing, but damn, Daniel."

"Oh my god," Wes mutters as he scans the stack of books in front of him. "Yes, ma'am. Would you be interested in one of our new bookmarks or buttons with your selections today?"

"It wasn't even my best effort." Ella snorts. "Usually I do that thing with my—"

"Di-did you find everything you were, um, looking for today?" Wes shouts nervously at the middle-aged man who is staring at Ella with wide eyes.

"He asked if I needed to cuddle, too. Like, dude, check your patriarchal ego at the door, please." Ella pops her gum. She doesn't budge from her spot on the counter so customers can lay their books down. "He's a soft five at best. There will be no follow-up."

Wes yells, "Have a page-turning day!" to his final customer before trying to brain himself on the counter. He's all for Ella destroying the patriarchy, crushing male ego, and having a little fun while she's at it. But he kind of wants to keep his job too.

"Oh, great," says Ella, exasperated. "Lucifer takes a human form."

Wearily, Wes lifts his head. Striding through the door is a white guy with gravity-defying sandy-blond hair and gleeful blue eyes. Wes recognizes him from Nico's Instagram feed—Cooper. He's shorter than Wes, thankfully, because otherwise he's quite attractive, one of those guys that needs to be in Urban Outfitters' social media ads. Wes swears California is nothing but beautiful people and tourists.

Slung across Cooper's chest is a messenger bag. His right hand plays with the strap while his left hand holds his phone out in front of him. He's talking to the camera, probably recording a video.

"Queen Ella," Cooper says, shuffling closer. "Say hello to my followers!"

Ella shoots him the stink eye, then turns to his phone. "Eat shit."

"Yup, that's my co-worker!" Cooper says as if Ella gave him a high-five instead of a verbal middle finger. "She's hella dope."

Wes mouths *What the hell* to Ella. She sighs, mumbling, "Social media minion."

Cooper wanders into the aisles, greeting customers and introducing them to his phone's camera.

"Is he always like that?" Wes says.

Cooper's cornered Mrs. Rossi and is half-hugging her while trying to take a selfie. She giggles and poses with two fingers up in the peace sign. A short line of customers waits to join the selfie movement.

"I don't like him," Ella says.

"Why?"

"Do I need a reason?"

If you're Ella Graham? Probably not. But Wes is too entertained by Cooper's attempts to angle his camera to catch the right lighting while standing with three young Black girls. Wes whispers, "He seems nice."

"Vampires seem nice until they find out you're a virgin who bleeds easily."

"You've read one too many Savannah Kirk books," Wes says, shaking his head.

"Yo, dude." Cooper slips behind the counter, holding out a fist. "Wes Hudson, correct?"

Wes warily bumps Cooper's fist. "Uh. Yeah."

Cooper pulls his hand back and makes this intense *ka-boom* noise with his mouth while wiggling his fingers in a weird, jazz hands way. Ella's right. This guy obviously can't be trusted.

"I'm your replacement," he says.

Wes's eyebrows shoot up his forehead.

"I mean, not like..." Cooper's cheeks flush. "I was your part-time fill-in while you were away. But Mrs. Rossi, the coolest of cool bosses, said she'd like to make my position at the store permanent, which would be sick, because this place is wicked. Books on books on books, you know?"

Wes nods, pasting on a smile.

Cooper smiles back, showing off a dimple in his left cheek. He slips off his bag and drops it amongst the other random clutter behind the counter. "It's a great gig. But don't touch the comics, right?"

"Correct."

Cooper leans uncomfortably close. His nose nearly touches Wes's. *Personal space much?* He whispers, eyes wide, "I heard you once stabbed a guy for dog-earing a Superman book."

Wes hadn't. It was a total accident involving a pen and minimal bloodshed. Also, it was two years ago.

"I feel you, bro." Cooper backs away, nodding. "I'm there."

Are you? Wes wants to ask. From the corner of his eye, he can spot Ella shooting them aggravated glares.

"So, like." Cooper's thumbs move rapidly over his phone screen. "Follow me back on Twitter. Add me on IG. And TikTok. Accept my Snapchat request. Oh, I'm still on Tumblr even though I'm not down with their censorship issues. I only Marco Polo with close fam and friends. But you fill those categories already."

Wes's own phone vibrates as if it's having a seizure. He has no less than five notifications from his various social media accounts. He's being followed on each one by Cooper "Coop" Shaw.

"FB's not really my thing anymore, but, you know, I make exceptions if that's your jam," Cooper continues.

"I'm sorry, what?"

"Feel free to subscribe to my YouTube channel too." Cooper briefly flashes his phone screen in Wes's face before returning to tapping away. "Do you Kik?"

"Um, sometimes?"

"It's all good, bro." Cooper pockets his phone, then rubs his hands together. "All right. Time to get to business. These books won't sell themselves."

Ella repeats, "I don't like him," as Cooper disappears into the aisles.

Wes isn't sure what the hell just happened, but Cooper's definitely likeable.

THIRTY MINUTES LATER, COOPER'S STARING at Wes with an absurdly creepy smile.

"What?" Wes grunts, too lazy to add any other words. The afternoon is melting perfectly with the weather, slowing time to a crawl. It's still fifteen minutes to three. It's been an eternity to Wes.

"Dude," Cooper says, dropping his voice to a whisper, leaning far too close again. Wes needs to have a serious discussion about personal boundaries. Soon. "Word on the street is…" Cooper looks around as if they're being watched. "Savannah Kirk is the beginning of your origin story?"

"She's what?"

"Your mom," Cooper hisses.

"Yeah," Wes says. "Something like that."

"Bro." Cooper smacks his hand on the counter, the noise like a crack of thunder. "Savannah Kirk is your mom."

Wide-eyed, Wes leans back. "Okay, first of all, *chill*," he says, holding up a hand.

"How is that possible?"

"Um. I believe my parents had intercourse?" Wes wants to take those words back immediately. It's cringeworthy. No, his parents did not have sex. That's gross. Wes was created from clay and magic like Wonder Woman.

Cooper repeats, "Savannah Kirk is your—"

Wes cuts him off. "Stop. I know." Thing is, Wes has met Cooper's kind before, the ones who worship authors as if they're superhuman. But they're not; his mom's not. She burns toast and overcooks spaghetti. But a small part of Wes can relate to Cooper's excitement. He went through a similar phase the first time he read *The Lightning Thief*. Not that Savannah Kirk has ever written a character as cool as Percy Jackson, but Wes understands the power an author has to unlock parts of yourself you'd never seen before.

"She's just a normal mom, you know." Wes's foot wiggles on the stool's bottom rung to whatever's playing overhead. "Her name's Jordan Hudson. She's just a writer."

"Just a writer—as if." There's so much wax and product in Cooper's hair, it barely moves when he shakes his head. "She's a goddess."

"Think so? You should try her meatloaf." Wes pushes fingers into his curls. "She's a mom. Nothing special."

"Uh, hate to break it to you, but moms are epic," Cooper tells him.

Wes is sure Ella would disagree, but when it comes to his own mom, she is pretty solid. She knows way too many hashtags, but she's also massively supportive of who he is. Plus, she gives great hugs. So, yeah, Wes's mom crushes epic.

"Sweet Brendon Urie, what is this?" Ella stomps up to the front counter, arms folded across her chest. Her annoyed expression, not to be confused with her burn-in-hell one, is in full effect: scrunched mouth and squinted eyes.

"What is what?" Cooper asks.

"This *noise*." Ella points toward the ceiling, indicating the music.

Admittedly, Wes has heard worse, courtesy of Zay. The song sounds vaguely '80s, though Wes's knowledge of that era is restricted to the music he's heard in movies.

"Uh. Don Henley," Cooper says.

"Don who?"

Cooper's jaw drops. "Don Henley, from the Eagles."

"You're sixteen. How do you even know what the Eagles are?" Ella replies.

"You have to know who Don Henley is."

"I do not," snaps Ella. "Don't threaten me with your bland music taste." Her eyebrow lifts sharply and... *there it is!* Burn-in-hell face activated.

Carefully, Wes turns his head and laughs into his shoulder.

"It's a classic," Cooper says, as if it'll matter. It's not punk and it's not loud and it's definitely not Ella.

She clears her throat. Back arched, hands cupped over her mouth, Ella shouts, "Canceled!"

"What? No." Cooper looks mortified.

Ella slides behind the front counter, reaching for the stereo system. "I'm cutting this shit off. I do not care about the heart of the matter."

From the aisles, Anna and Zay say, in unison, "Canceled."

Cooper crumples across the counter, head in his hands. "This is a mutiny. I've been betrayed."

"Sorry." Wes rests his chin on his knuckles. "It's a struggle in these streets."

There are three simple rules to Once Upon a Page:

1. Show up for every shift!
2. Participate in One of These Three Things—a game Wes and Nico invented their first year at the bookstore because they were bored out of their skulls and needed something to pass the time. It's now a must for all personnel.
3. Abide by the rules of Canceled!

As outlined by the handful of employees who have occupied Once Upon a Page before Wes began working at the bookstore: Every staff member gets two daily music vetoes during their shift. No more. If anyone hates the music selection being played, that employee can "cancel'" that band or artist for the remainder of the day. Usually, Wes saves his cancels for Ella or, on his aggressively annoyed days, Zay. There's no love lost at the bookstore for mediocre musical taste.

"Don whatever, you've been Canceled," Ella announces, unceremoniously dropping the CD into one of the storage bins without putting it back in its jewel case.

Delicately, Cooper fishes the CD out and re-cases it. "Did you guys steal the Canceled thing from *Empire Records*?"

Ella clutches her chest, feigning astonishment. "We don't steal around here, Lucifer," she says, indignant. "We borrow until asked to return."

"Damn right," Zay says.

Ella flips through a different bin of CDs. A minute later, she earns a microscopic amount of Wes's respect by putting on Blink-182. Humming "What's My Age Again?" under his breath, he shifts around to stare out the window. A neon orange flyer taped to the glass advertises a forgotten book club the bookstore used to host. Outside, the sun tickles gold beams across the sidewalk.

His heart beats fiercely when the alarm on his phone goes off.

It's one minute until three o'clock.

CHAPTER SIX

Unlike Ella, Nico's never late. At exactly three p.m., he whizzes past the bookstore on a skateboard, dodging pedestrians and tourists. He does a kickflip, then doubles back for an ollie. With his back to the store and head sloped, his shoulder blades are sharp angles under smooth tan skin. All his lines are perfect—narrow hips and straight arms.

Over his shoulder, Nico flashes a lazy smile. Wes's heart uppercuts his tonsils.

When Nico's out of sight again, Wes tries to fix his hair. The bookstore's air conditioner is inadequate. Pit stains are ruining his lucky shirt. And, unfortunately, he doesn't have any cologne or even a stick of deodorant stashed in the office.

Everything's falling apart.

Ella hops onto her throne, legs crossed, lips puckered. She's eagerly watching the door. Wes knows why.

He whispers, "I'm so dead."

"Yup," she says.

"This is going to end badly."

"I'm counting on it." She already has her phone out, recording.

Nico strolls inside, skateboard tucked under one arm. His other hand balances a cardboard cup with the Brews and Views logo on it. He's wearing a loose-fitting tank top, low-slung black skinnies, and Adidas. His hair's a little flat from the heat. A bead of sweat dribbles from temple to cheek to jaw.

Wes has never had a type. He's equal-opportunity when it comes to guys. But skateboarder Nico has always created extraordinary chemical reactions inside of him.

"Yo, Alvarez!" Zay marches from between the aisles for a high-five. "Saw your moves out there. A respectable eight out of ten."

Nico rolls his eyes, laughing. "¿Qué pasa, Jones?" He zigzags his way through the store to press a kiss to Mrs. Rossi's cheek. "Buenas tardes, Señora Rossi."

Ella says, "You're drooling."

"Shut up," Wes says, scowling.

"Just pointing it out," Ella comments with her phone directed at his face. Wes is certain this video evidence will haunt him for years to come, but he can't focus on Ella. Nico and Mrs. Rossi are almost finished talking. He needs to worry about what's going to come out of his mouth.

Which is... he's still undecided.

"Hey," Nico says, dumping his skateboard behind the counter.

"Hey," Wes says, forcing that one word through his tight throat. He looks down at Nico's board. "Sweet."

He can tell it's new—the wheels are still a fresh pink. On the underside are exotic florals and flamingos, a beautiful mash-up of greens and pinks.

"Picked it up last week," Nico says, way too pleased. "Breaking her in."

"Nice. How's she ride?"

"Wesley, are you thinking of taking up boarding again?" Nico's index finger rubs across the zigzag scar that splits his left eyebrow.

The last time Wes was on a skateboard, Nico was teaching him a basic trick when Wes promptly jacked it up, launching the board backward and airborne. The tail smacked into Nico's eyebrow. The result: a near-concussion for Nico, blood ruining his favorite *My Hero Academia* T-shirt, and stitches.

"I'm not very good at... uh, that. Boarding."

"Yeah, you're not," Nico says with an embarrassingly sympathetic grin.

Wes's face and neck are painfully hot. "How're your sisters?"

"Fussy and annoying as ever," Nico sighs. His mom works from home, but Nico usually babysits his younger sisters during the summer so she can focus on her job. His dad was a biochemist who worked long hours, so Nico's always had a role in watching over them.

"You love it," Wes teases.

Nico can pretend all he wants, but he enjoys being dragged away from video games to play dolls or hide-and-seek with his sisters. He doesn't mind helping with homework either.

"I do," he concedes. "Here."

Nico passes Wes the cardboard cup. Curling steam emanates from the hole in the plastic lid. It smells strong and earthy and delicious.

Though undocumented, Wes's relationship with tea dates back to when he was six years old. On weekends, he couldn't sleep at night until his dad limped through the front door like a zombie after working double shifts at the restaurant. He'd haul Wes into his arms and boil water for two mugs—one for each of them. Calvin would steep a sachet of fruity herbal tea for Wes. They'd camp out on the green sofa, Wes creased into Calvin's side, to watch reruns of cartoons until Wes finally succumbed to exhaustion.

The tradition continued into Wes's teens, though without Calvin, who shifted his schedule to be home at more reasonable times. But Nico replaced him on the sofa for homework and vicious battles on *Mario Kart*. And he'd always bring tea for Wes.

Wes pops the lid, inhaling. Darjeeling. He takes a careful sip, smiling around the lip of the cup. He whispers, "Thanks," but he knows what he should be saying: "I love you."

"No hay problema," says Nico.

"Okay," Ella grunts, hopping off the counter. "This is boring." Over her shoulder, she adds, "And I think I'm gonna hurl," with enough of a smirk that Wes knows she's been thoroughly entertained by his recurring inability to "man up."

He's glad someone's enjoying his failed romantic comedy.

NICO HAS AN OBSESSION—PINTEREST. LIKE a curator at a gallery, he collects artwork and quotes and scenic photography. He has mood boards for mood boards. It's a harmless hobby. But Wes would be lying if he didn't admit he loves the way Nico's eyes crinkle as he talks about each pin the way a wordsmith talks about their poetry.

Wedged between the wall behind the front counter and Nico's warm body, Wes drinks his tea. Every swipe to a new pin, Nico says, "This one's sick," while checking to ensure Wes approves. He always does.

"This is my new favorite," Nico whispers. Black and white text over a blurred photo of a bicycle clearly using the Gingham filter reads, *I'm not single, I'm not taken, I'm simply on reserve for the one who deserves my heart.*

Yeah. Mine too. Wes's future Instagram bio will read: "Whipped and pathetic since day one."

The words are right there, plain as day, in Wes's mind: *Do you want to go out sometime? As, like, more than friends?*

Nico swipes to another pin. Some sort of architecture. Nico's all over the place with his interests.

Just say it.

The next pin is Nightwing fanart.

Wes says, in a small voice, "I haven't seen you draw in a while." Nico used to love to doodle heroes and villains in the margins of

his notebook in class. He'd sketch on any surface that would hold
Sharpie ink. He'd use highlighters to outline capes and eyes and hair
on college-ruled paper.

The skin between Nico's eyebrows is pinched. "Kind of got away
from it, I guess."

He did. Right around... *Shit.* Wes is an idiot. Nico stopped
drawing after sophomore year. Just after Mr. Alvarez died.

Wes's shoulders pull tight. He glares at the dirty toe of his once-
white Converse All-Stars, studying the yellowed laces. He wipes his
sweaty palms along the thighs of his jeans.

How did he forget?

"Hey." Nico's bony fingers squeeze Wes's right knee. "The Smiths,
Pearl Jam, or Nada Surf?"

To other people, One of These Three Things is probably the
corniest, most childish, third-grader-bored-on-a-summer-road-trip
game. But to Wes and Nico, it's a keepsake, one they use to navigate
through slow days at the bookstore or times way too heavy for deep
discussions. It's a get-out-of-jail free card they've used frequently
when something awkward happens.

Admittedly, it's a knockoff of that old, stranded-on-a-desert-island
game. But instead of choosing three objects, players have to pick
the one thing they can't live without from three options chosen by
someone else.

Wes ponders his options.

"I think I know," Nico says.

"You do?"

"Duh." Nico's lips twist up smugly.

Wes loves that, though Nico's Spotify is crammed with current
hip-hop artists and a few guilty pleasure pop tunes, Wes can still scroll
through and find random songs by Foo Fighters or Gin Blossoms.

That he's influenced Nico enough to create an entire playlist called *Shit for Wesley*.

It's in this moment that Wes realizes he can't simply blurt out his feelings for Nico. Hell no. He can't half-ass this. Nico, who has playlists in his phone dedicated to Wes, who brings him tea, who doesn't call Wes out for being a forgetful friend and invoking memories of his dead father, deserves better than that.

Wes needs to conduct research; gather intel. If Wes is going to do this, he has to ensure there's no way Nico will reject him. This moment requires a bulletproof list of ways to ask Nico on a date.

"Dude." Cooper leans eagerly across the counter, interrupting Wes's thoughts. "You've got to go with the Smiths. It's *Morrissey*."

"No, no," Anna objects. "Pearl Jam. Relatable content."

"Are you stoned?" Cooper squeals.

Wes has no doubt that Anna is, but she continues to tie her hair into a loose braid, swaying as she says, "Oh. 10,000 Maniacs. Natalie Merchant is a goddess."

"Uh." Wes raises an index finger, remembering he still hasn't responded to Nico. "They weren't an option."

"10,000 *what*?" Zay's head pops up from between the aisles.

"Zay, my man, get over here. You're in desperate need of a full musical education," demands Cooper.

"I missed all of this?" Wes whispers to Nico.

They're close enough that Wes can smell Nico's citrus shampoo and the sugary orange soda on his breath when he says, "It's Nada Surf, isn't it?"

"Yeah," Wes exhales. He watches as Cooper and Zay argue over the definition of "quality music" while Anna draws Nico into a conversation about cows or aliens. Maybe both. He excuses himself. He needs some fresh air.

Outside, evening cups its hand around Santa Monica, leaving it warm under rose gold skies. Wes inhales the spicy scent of the meats being grilled at Taco Libre. Couples pass him, holding hands.

Wes unlocks his phone, then opens Google. He searches "how to ask out a crush." There are nearly two hundred million results.

"That's so rad," he whispers to his phone. After a deep breath, Wes bookmarks webpages.

SOMEONE'S WATCHING WES.

As he pulls on Once Upon a Page's front door for the fifth time, trying to get the lock to catch, he can sense the heavy stare.

It's twenty past nine p.m. The twinkle lights above Colorado dance overhead, moving with the breeze off the ocean. Wes would've been upstairs by now, devoting more time to his research, but in that last hour the bookstore was open, some Fratty McAsshats descended upon them, dicking around in the comics section. Wes spent twenty-five minutes restoring peace to his inner sanctum, which meant he was twenty-five minutes late counting the deposit, filling the till for the morning, and reciting the lock-up procedures with Anna.

He shouldn't have been the one training Anna, anyway. It's Mrs. Rossi's job. But she bailed three hours ago, looking haggard and pale. A month without him is starting to show in her eyes and the slow movements she made around the store. He hopes they both can survive his first semester at UCLA.

Now, he's tired as hell from working a double, starved—even though Nico brought him two greasy slices of pepperoni pizza before ditching to help wrangle his sisters for family dinner—and he has a stalker.

Anna sidles up to his left side and whispers, "Oh, my Zeus. Tall, dark, and extremely handsome watching you."

Wes pivots and groans. No, this guy is not tall and handsome. Dark? Definitely. In a side-by-side comparison, he's the guy that gets all the looks while Wes… is just there.

Leo Hudson, being firstborn and irritatingly dramatic in the most banal situations, is the Killmonger to Wes's Black Panther. Everyone's eyes automatically go to Leo's perfectly wavy, crow black hair, his pug nose that's on the right side of adorable, his gym physique, and the way he can pull off a suit.

"Ugh. He's nobody," Wes finally says. "Just my brother."

Number Four—Leo

I suppose I should include Leo somewhere on this list, right? We're blood. But I don't really know where to put him… besides in the trash.

That's not fair. I don't hate Leo. But I also didn't miss him much while I was in Italy. Maybe if we were like the younger Leo and me, the ones who only cared about collecting Pokémon or hanging at the beach, I would bump him higher. Seriously, where did those kids go?

I have genuine moments when I think I'm adopted. There's no way I could be related to Leo. We're like the distance from Earth to Neptune: 2,703,959,960 miles. I had to Google that. Right now. And that's the kind of thing I'd rather do than spend time with this alien version of my brother.

To be honest, I think the distance between us only grows the older we get. But he's my brother. And, sometimes, I miss… us.

Briefly, Wes glares at Leo before finally forfeiting the part of himself that refuses to be mature about this. "Hey," he says to Anna. "I'm good from here. See you tomorrow?"

"Are you sure?"

Nope. "Positive."

Anna pats his shoulder once, then disappears into the blur of people marching toward Ocean Avenue.

Tiny beads of sweat pop across Wes's hairline. He's more annoyed than nervous about talking to Leo. Hands jammed in his pockets, he crosses the street to where Leo stands outside Tongva Park.

"Sup?" Wes's playing this totally chill.

"You look thrilled."

Wes sizes him up. "And you look… the same."

Leo has most of their mom's features, with Calvin's mouth and the Hudson family's warm-fawn complexion. He's in typical Leo gear—crisp white shirt, sleeves rolled and bunched around his elbows, matching tie and socks, loafers. He's still studying for the LSAT, but he already dresses the part.

The only suit Wes owns is his prom tux buried in the back of the closet. It has a giant stain. Seriously, who drinks cranberry juice and White Claws? Santa Monica High students, clearly.

"Good trip?" Leo asks.

"Yup," Wes says, blandly.

"Glad to be back?"

"Yup."

"Is that all you got?"

Grinning, Wes replies, "Yup."

"Well." Leo pulls at his shirt collar, watching people shift around them. "Leeann's glad you're back."

Wes can't control the way his face reacts to her name. He loves Leeann. She laughs at all his accidental dad jokes, and, when he came out to her three years ago before a family dinner, she smiled, punched his shoulder, and warned him not to hoard all the local guys for himself just in case things didn't work out with Leo.

They've been together since sophomore year of college. Sweethearts, just like Wes's parents and the Rossis. Wes wonders if that's a running joke in his life. Is everyone destined to find their one great love in college?

He scuffs his shoe on the sidewalk. "How's wedding planning going?"

"I'm gonna pull my hair out before we even get down the aisle."

Wes doubts that. Not with their dad's genes.

"We almost picked a venue. Can't agree on flowers. I don't even want to think about a guest list." Leo brushes a hand over his low fade haircut. When they were kids, it was curly and dark like the ocean under a moonless sky. "She can't find a dress either."

"Mmhmm."

"Maybe you could help her with that?"

A prickling heat spreads in Wes's chest. He squints at Leo. "Why? Because I'm gay?"

He's so tired of this—the gay thing. The constant assumption that, because a guy is queer, he loves playing dress-up and lives for musicals and obsesses over *Drag Race*. He's sick of the morbid perceptions of the LGBTQIA community. He's sick of the stereotypes. There's no one kind of queer person. There isn't a right or a wrong version.

"What? No." Leo's eyebrows scrunch together. "It's not like that at all! Leeann loves you. She respects your opinion. You could tell her to wear a trash bag, and she'd do it. Not because you're gay. Because she freaking *trusts* you."

Wes blinks twice. No one thinks that much of his opinion. Well, Nico, probably. But no one else. "I'll, uh," he stammers. "I'll call her."

"Thanks." Leo fixes his wrinkled sleeves. "Have you started looking for a real job around campus yet?"

And there he is, the true Leo Hudson. Wes's been expecting this. "I have a job. I plan to keep it." He waves behind him at the darkened bookstore. "I get paid to—"

"Stack comic books?" Leo finishes. "That's real world-changing stuff."

Wes crosses his arms. Leo has always had a problem with him working at the bookstore, as if being a bookseller is a lesser job. He expects Wes to find something closer to his field of study. But Wes has no clue what that'll be.

"Dad says," Leo starts, but Wes tunes him out.

He hates this part too. Leo has the better connection with their dad. Yes, Calvin and Wes had their tea and cartoons on weekends. Yes, Calvin's the one who introduced Wes to the bookstore. But since Wes turned thirteen, it seems the gap between them keeps expanding. Leo and Calvin can talk on the phone for hours. They love the same sports teams and food. And all Wes shares with Calvin now is their inescapable geekiness.

It's not enough.

Leo exhales, as if he can tell Wes isn't paying attention. Wes rubs his forehead. He motions toward the pale pink building behind him. "Do you want to come up?"

"I've already stopped by."

Of course Leo has. He's probably washed the dishes, reorganized their mom's bookshelf, and inventoried their dad's cooking alcohol collection to see if Wes or Ella have snuck any.

"Tell Ella to clean up," demands Leo.

"I'll tell her you said hi," Wes replies smugly.

"And you'll call Leeann?"

"Sure."

"I mean it, Wes."

"Fine," Wes hisses. "I'll call."

Leo looks ready to say something sarcastic but doesn't. He whispers, "Thanks," in an almost sincere tone before nudging past Wes and disappearing into a fleet of tourists migrating toward the pier.

Wes finally drags himself to the loft. His first day back at the bookstore is officially a disaster.

"When it comes to matters of love, you're always dancing with devils." The music surrounding them was a din under Daemon's melodic voice. "Devils of temptation, constantly reminding you this love isn't enough. Devils of jealousy. Devils of uncertainty leading you to chaos and emptiness."

"You think love is confusing?" Elisabeth asked. A lock of her walnut-brown hair slipped from its neatly tailored bun.

"Love is the very definition of confusion."

Elisabeth smiled, though she wasn't sure if it was her or the itching noise around her pulling at her lips.

Beneath their feet, the ballroom's black and white pattern blurred. Dark, then light. Light, then dark. They danced in continuous circles—a waltz defined by helixes.

"Then there's the devil of heartbreak that drags you to hell. Always feeding your loneliness, your pain, with blackened memories. The 'what was' versus 'what was not.' Why would anyone want to live that way?" asked Daemon. Not a thread of his ice-blond hair had fallen out of place. Not a muscle in his pale face moved too earnestly, without a reason or a rhyme.

"And you?" Her control waned under the pools of black in his eyes. "How do you deal with such devils?"

The darkness shifted through her marrow like the chorus of a familiar song. The magic in that room, so thick and coated in blood, filled her lungs.

"I dance alone." Daemon smirked, exposing the barest hint of sharp canines. "I spin around until I don't recognize it's the devil leading me the entire time."

Elisabeth gasped, but could not escape.

They danced and danced.

—Savannah Kirk, *The Dark Prince*

CHAPTER SEVEN

IT TURNS OUT CONSTRUCTING AN exceptional list of ways to finally ask out your lifelong best friend doesn't happen overnight. It doesn't happen in two days. Wes's been home an entire week and still... nothing.

It's a Wednesday and Santa Monica breathes easy under a cloudless blue sky. People pass by Once Upon a Page in shorts and no shirt, tank tops and flip-flops. Everywhere, someone's wearing a shiny pair of sunglasses, reflecting all the good vitamin D.

Today's excellent weather promises one thing for the bookstore: sparse shoppers.

It means Wes can work on his plan of attack. He sits, cross-legged, in his favorite corner with one earbud in and his *Summer for Losers* playlist—a collection of mostly Lit and the Offspring and R.E.M.—cranked all the way up. Slouched over, elbows on his thighs, he scans through his phone. He's surrounded on three sides by wall-to-wall comic-book-cover murals. Each one has vibrant colors or large fonts and action sequences and characters he's imagined being too many times to count.

More than once, Wes's mind drifts to Metropolis or Gotham City. *Stop. Focus.*

Since opening the bookstore this morning, Wes has been doing what he excels at—perfecting a list. If Wes is being completely unbiased, it's one of his best yet. And though BuzzFeed, Reddit, Queerty, and a few other websites all highly recommend *not* crushing on a best friend, Wes has compiled a bunch of ideas from the personal stories he's read online. His tenacity knows very few limits.

Ways to Score a Date with Your Best Friend!!!

1. Take your crush to a lowkey coffee shop for heart-shaped latte art and sweet pastries and chill music! Avoid all Starbucks!
2. Go to an early showing of the latest romance movie so you have an excuse to invite your crush to dinner after!
3. Adopt a rescue puppy, pack a picnic, and get your crush out to a park for a swoon-worthy day of dog walking and sandwiches!
4. Cook your crush's favorite meal; you can always land a potential partner through their stomach!

Wes wrinkles his nose at the last two ideas. They're not the greatest. One, puppies are his kryptonite. He'd probably be too engrossed in those wide, hopeful eyes to remember Nico was around. Also, he lacks the fortitude to ditch the pup afterward. Two, Wes would most likely burn down the loft trying to recreate one of Mrs. Alvarez's awesome recipes before Nico arrived. That might not go down too well with his dad. Calvin would probably keep the puppy and put Wes in a kennel.

5. Use the beach to write a love note in the sand! Big, dramatic confessions always win!
6. Every geek's dream—dress up and go on a Cosplay Date!

Last Halloween, as a bookstore promotion, Wes and Nico dressed up as Kid Flash and Beast Boy. Wes, not thinking any of this through, agreed to be Beast Boy. Six showers later, he still couldn't get green paint from behind his ears and in places that didn't actually require him wearing the paint. His dedication to authenticity needs parental restrictions.

They strolled around in costume all day, handing out bite-sized candies to children and discount coupons to adults. He doesn't know if it helped sales at all, but it was fun. It also didn't hurt to admire Nico in a skintight red-and-yellow costume for eight hours.

Afterward, they walked Ocean Avenue together. Around them, masked heroes and monsters and one too many sexy animal costumes crowded the streets. Wes bought them frozen lemonades. They ate churros, leaning over the pier, watching the way neon lights reflected like stained glass windows against the ocean's dark surface.

It wasn't a date, but it was like one. Almost.

Wes wants to get rid of the "almost." He wants the full thing. He wants it to happen for a reason other than a holiday or a rare occasion.

"Dude!"

Wes nearly thumps his head into a shelf when Cooper flops down next to him on the carpet. A few feet away, someone squeaks like a mouse. Wes blinks at them. How didn't he notice anyone else in his comic book fortress? It's the teen from his first Monday back. Their blond bangs cut sharply over green eyes. When their mouth pops open for a "sorry" that's so soft Wes's not sure it's even vocalized, he notices a small gap between their front teeth.

"Have you read this?" Cooper asks, shaking a paperback in front of Wes's face.

Risking possible brain damage from being assaulted by the book, Wes leans closer for a better look. He's never read *The Dark Prince*, but he's a fan of the cover art. To be fair, Wes loves all his mom's book covers. They're done by the same person: a quiet, humble woman in Texas who never does anything in the same artistic style twice. She goes from almost anime-like drawings to real-life portraits.

"No," Wes finally says, dropping his eyes to his phone.

"Wesley of the Hudsons, future heir to the Savannah Kirk throne, protector of the—"

Wes has gradually been adapting to Cooper's randomness. He's funny, too. But two days ago, Wes spotted Cooper smoking up with Anna behind the bookstore, so maybe his humor is herbally influenced.

"How haven't you read this?"

"Uh." Wes still hasn't found the right way to break it to Cooper that Savannah Kirk's books aren't as mind-blowing as he thinks. "No time?"

Cooper leans back, eyes wide as if he's affronted. "But this section," Cooper opens the book and carefully turns the pages. He taps his index finger on a paragraph. "Elisabeth's connection with her friends is so real. They protect each other at all costs. It's the best."

Armed with his phone, Cooper snaps photos and records one of those time-loop videos before adding filters and captions and hashtags. "I'm bookstagramming this part. Hashtag bookworm homies. Hashtag SME…"

"SME?"

"Santa Monica Escapades," Cooper says proudly. "Gotta know the hashtags that bring the followers."

Oh. Right. Wes only knows the bare minimum ones in the comic book fandoms.

"Tagging you too," Cooper adds.

Wes face-palms. Up until junior year, Wes had managed to keep his name—and face—out of the Savannah Kirk fan communities. It's not that he cared; popularity for being the son of a bestselling author beats notoriety for being the guy who nearly blinded his best friend with a skateboard or who fell running *up* the bleachers at a pep rally. It was mostly his mom's concern. She wanted Wes and Leo to be free of the constant messages about her.

"What's her next book about?"

"Is she going to write a sequel to the last one?"

"Why didn't my two favorite characters hook up?"

"Why the hell won't she reply to my messages? Why won't she tell me her favorite perfume? WHEN'S HER NEXT BOOK COMING OUT?!"

People are strange. But then junior year hit like a high-speed train. A group of sophomores did a little research—nothing stays hidden on the internet forever—and started tagging him everywhere on social media.

Since then, Wes's little social media corner of geekery and Green Lantern fanart has been mobbed with the Kirklands, Savannah's hardcore legion. He ignores most of the messages, but it's still weird.

"Oh, this is adorable." Mrs. Rossi, hand over her heart, stands over them. "Take a selfie and send it to me. Then, Wes, sweetie, show me how to download it. Mr. Rossi bought me a new phone. I can't work it at all."

"He's just keeping you young."

"Well, I feel *old* with all these iOS updates or whatever," Mrs. Rossi complains.

"Never trust the Apple," Cooper insists, holding up his own phone. "Android for life."

Wes rolls his eyes. Under no circumstance would he trust an Android.

"Oh." Cooper stiffens next to him, cheeks flushed. "Sorry, Mrs. R. We should be working, right?" He closes the book and tucks away his phone before standing.

"No, no. It's fine." Mrs. Rossi surveys the store. She coughs, and then rubs at her eyes. "No one's here today." Then, looking down, she adds with a smile, "No offense, Lucas."

Lucas. The quiet blond in the hoodie.

Lucas shrugs, refocusing their attention on the graphic novel in their lap.

"Wes, sweetheart?" Mrs. Rossi turns to him. The shadows under her eyes are darker than usual. "Could you stay a little later today? Just until Anna gets in this afternoon."

Wes lowers his eyebrows. "No problem."

It's not as if Wes has some amazing, ask-your-best-friend-out plans to attend to today. He has to fine-tune this list first.

Before he can inquire about Mrs. Rossi's health, she says, "It's just a bug or something. Probably allergies."

Funny, Wes has known Mrs. Rossi for over a decade and she's never been allergic to anything except Ella's dramatics.

"I'm sure Anna can handle the store," Mrs. Rossi says, as if she almost means it.

Anna's improving, but even Wes wouldn't leave her in charge yet.

"I can stay longer to help if she needs it," he offers.

Mrs. Rossi's mouth stretches into a proper grin. "Thank you. But she'll have help if…" She studies the thin gold watch around her left wrist. "…*that one* ever gets here."

As if summoned through some demonic ritual involving a baby lamb's heart and Fall Out Boy's music collection, Ella pushes through the front door. She looks as if Hot Topic's summer collection vomited over her.

"El's Bells," Cooper calls, holding up his phone to record her reaction.

Ella squints at him. "I thought I compelled you not to call me that."

"Did you?"

"Yes." Ella snaps her grape gum. Neon green thunderbolt earrings swing from her ears when she tilts her head. "Put away the phone, Zuckerberg. I'm not in the mood."

Quickly, Cooper lowers his phone, but, from the corner of his eye, Wes can still see him typing away.

Mrs. Rossi *tsks* before folding her arms across her chest. "You know, Ella, it'd be wonderful if you were, I don't know, *on time* for your shifts. Especially in situations like this."

"Uh, my late is the new punctual around here," Ella says, hopping onto the front counter.

"You have no respect for this store or the customers."

Ella looks around. "Um, what customers? No offense, Lucas."

Lucas waves her off.

"Also," Ella says, smirking, "the customers *love* me."

Chuckling, Cooper hides his face behind both hands. Wes can't blame him. He wants to do the same.

"Be quiet, hellspawn," Ella snaps.

Wes turns his attention to Mrs. Rossi. She's gone from pale white to emergency-exit red. Ella leans back on the counter, unfazed. This isn't a new occurrence. Their arguments are part of what makes Mrs. Rossi and Ella's relationship functional. It usually involves shouting and storming off and doors slamming. And Wes, against his better judgment, is always the peacemaker.

"Just take your job seriously," Mrs. Rossi hisses.

"It's a bookstore," Ella deadpans.

"And it's my life!" Mrs. Rossi leans on a bookshelf, her hands shaking.

Ella, however, doesn't flinch. It's a testament to who she is. She's the type of person to stare a fire-breathing dragon in the eye and dare it to blow smoke her way.

"You're young," Mrs. Rossi says, the edge in her voice dulling. "You don't understand it yet, but the day you do, I hope you remember all of this. I hope you remember the person you *thought* you were. And I hope you don't regret missing what life has been trying to hand you, but you continue to act as if it's charity rather than an opportunity."

Ella's mouth is a thin, white line, but she doesn't crack.

Mrs. Rossi turns her sad eyes on Wes. Before she can speak, he says, "I'll make sure Anna's okay."

Finally, Mrs. Rossi exhales. The "thank you" is implied in her defeated smile.

The thick, eerie silence after Mrs. Rossi exits reminds Wes of being in the loft after his parents had an argument. He'd sit in the middle of his bedroom floor until Leo wandered in and sat next to him. They wouldn't speak. They'd barely make eye contact. But Leo would grab Wes's iPad and log into YouTube, and they'd watch funny animal videos together.

"Hey." Cooper lowers his voice. "She hasn't rejected my songs yet." He motions in Ella's direction.

She's still parked on the front counter, examining her nailbeds with a neutral expression. Wes expects that much. Ella never lets up on her poker face.

"I'm wearing her down," Cooper says, all teeth and dimples.

Wes highly doubts that. Cooper's playing Simple Minds. Unlike most of his peers, Wes liked *The Breakfast Club*. Don't get him wrong, it's problematic and cliché and John Hughes must've never met an actual person who wasn't white in the '80s, but he likes this band. He says, quietly, "Word of advice—stay away from Fleetwood Mac. Ella thinks Stevie Nicks is a fraud."

"Noted."

"This is bullshit," Ella huffs. She jumps down from the counter. "She can pretend all she wants, but I know the real deal."

"What're you talking about?" Wes asks.

Ella ignores him. She tugs out her phone and thumbs at the screen for a second, then stomps toward the door. Over her shoulder, she shouts, "And Coop? Canceled!" before disappearing.

UNQUESTIONABLY, KYRA IS ONE OF Wes's favorite human beings. If there was room for a sixth thing on his list of things he loves, Kyra would own that spot. She has huge, loose, dark-brown curls, an addiction to colorful sneakers, and a "California" tattoo running horizontally across the underside of her forearm. The black ink stands out so boldly against her golden brown skin tone.

But it's not Kyra wheeling into the store on the back of a skateboard that has most of Wes's attention. He adores her, a fact, but she'll never be number one on his list.

"Clear the way!" she shouts. One hand holds a cardboard cup above her head while the other grips a narrow hip that Wes only knows in a platonic sense.

Eyes scrunched, Nico kick-pushes them inside.

Cooper, the idiot, ducks and rolls from their path, though the bookstore's puckered gray carpet slows any momentum they built outside. Something thuds to the ground. Wes really hopes it's not the new "Fans of Becky Albertalli" section he and Anna spent forty minutes putting together an hour ago. He cares about Cooper's well-being, but not as much as the books.

Anna nods as Nico and Kyra dismount the skateboard. "Six out of ten."

"I give it a seven!" shouts Cooper from the floor.

"Seriously?" Kyra giggles breathlessly. "I thought it was an eight-point-five, easy."

"Hard eight," Wes offers. "Minus two for possible destruction to private property."

Kyra thrusts the cardboard cup at him. "But I bring tea," she insists. "And a Nico."

"Disqualification for bribing the judge," Anna declares. She walks away, smiling over her freckled shoulder.

"Ten for the tea," Wes says, eagerly grabbing the cup. After the showdown between Mrs. Rossi and Ella, he needs the caffeine. "Soft seven for the Nico."

"Oh, Crusher," Kyra says, leaning close with crinkled eyes. "Nico's an eleven, and you know it."

The implication in her voice sends a surge of heat from Wes's neck to his hairline. Is he really that obvious? Has his nonstop ogling—and he *hates* that word—translated to everyone in California except Nico being aware of his crush?

"Shut up," he mumbles into the cup's lid.

Kyra pats his shoulder and says, "You're my favorite romcom hero," in her least condescending tone.

"Sencha," Nico says, pointing at the tea Wes slowly sips. He drops his skateboard behind the counter. "Good?"

Wes hums contentedly. He loves that instant effect green tea has. It's calming, like watching the surf first thing in the morning. "Thanks," he says around a sip.

Again, Nico's eyes scrunch; the lines around his mouth deepen. His hair's flat today. He looks like he did when he was fourteen, hiding his teeth behind his hand whenever he laughed. Wes, in contrast, spent an hour at the mirror this morning with a palm full of product and a prayer as he tried to tame his curls.

"Why is fixing the nonfiction so daunting?" Anna asks, standing on her tiptoes to peek over a row of shelves near the back of the store.

"Hold up. That's my jam," Nico announces giddily. He edges around the counter, then stops to look at Wes. "Enjoy, Wesley."

Wes flops onto the stool, watching Nico disappear.

Cooper sits next to him, holding his left arm. "I think I broke my tibia."

"That's not your tibia," Zay says, strolling in with his backpack and a brown paper bag covered in dark grease spots.

"Are you sure?"

Even Wes knows that's not where the tibia is. But he's not sure how to let Cooper down gently.

Neither does Zay. "Not even close." He shrugs off his backpack. "Both my moms watch all those medical dramas. Rescue-hospital-anatomy-investigation. I know more about bones and diseases than I do about music."

"Wicked," Cooper whispers with raised eyebrows.

Zay peels open the paper bag and pulls out a tinfoil-wrapped hamburger. "If I was Nico, it'd be wicked. I just feel like a boring-ass Wikipedia."

Wes slumps on the stool. *Thanks, Zay.* He didn't need the reminder that he only has two months to make something happen. Nico's going to Stanford. He'll be over three hundred miles away—a five-hour drive on a good traffic day, which is never in California.

And here Wes is, distracted from finishing his list. Drinking tea Nico bought for him. Watching Nico and Anna laugh between the aisles.

And wait a damn minute…

Nico leans toward her. He rolls his eyes, smiles so hard. Anna's pale, thin fingers wrinkle Nico's vintage Stanford Rowing T-shirt. Nico reaches to brush the California poppy braided into her wavy hair. They laugh and laugh. Little touches are accompanied by whispers and squinty eyes. All the things from those romcoms Wes devours.

Nico and Anna?

Nico and Anna!

He's been back for less than two weeks and Wes's never noticed this. But he was gone a month and, well, that's a long time. People fall in love in less than twenty-four hours—at least that's what Reddit has taught him—so how could he not expect Nico to possibly find someone other than him to be interested in? How could he expect Nico to be interested in *him* at all, since he's never said anything?

A cold hand tightens around Wes's heart. An ache throbs behind his right eye. His hands tremble. Is he breathing? He thinks so. But his stomach's so knotted, he's not sure he's inhaling properly.

Anna and Nico. Nico and Anna. AnnaNico.

Eyes closed, Wes braces one palm flat on the counter.

Just breathe. Just breathe.

"Here."

Wes blinks one eye open. Ella waves a sheet of paper in his face from across the counter. Despite his current state, it's not an advertisement for a shady clinic that specializes in possible heart defects and therapy for crush-related anxieties.

"What's this?" he asks, scanning the paper. His vision finally recalibrates. It's an email addressed to Mrs. Rossi. There are a lot of bold and italicized words.

He snatches it from Ella's loose grip.

"What is this?"

Ella clears her throat. "A month ago, I found this while cleaning Mrs. Rossi's office—"

"You were snooping," Wes accuses.

"Technicalities."

"No. Invasion of privacy."

Ella ignores his claims. "Read it, Wes."

He does. Wes reads it once, then again. He reads until all the words start to make sense. His eyes refuse to leave one section of the email:

"...due to the lack of profitable revenue delaying timely property payments, the Tea Leaf and Coffee Cup House is extending an offer to settle all properties and rights listed in the current proprietor's contract in order to renovate the existing space into a brand-new expansion of our current super-licious franchise..."

Wes pieces together a few key points: One, Mrs. Rossi is behind on property payments for the bookstore. Two, some first-grader-named coffeehouse franchise wants to buy her out. Three, the aforementioned coffeehouse really needs to terminate their promotions consultant because "super licious" is not a word and poor marketing. And finally, this place, his childhood home, the space he's felt most himself, is going to be shut down. Permanently.

"This can't be right," he whispers.

"It's right there in writing." Ella stabs her index finger at the paper. Her nails are painted dark purple. Wes has no clue why he focuses on that, other than the fact that he needs a distraction from an impending meltdown.

"What's up?" Zay asks between bites of burger.

Ella seizes the paper back from Wes and thrusts it at Zay. "Read and tell boy genius over here what it means."

Zay studies the email with squinted eyes. Over his shoulder, Cooper reads too.

Wes's palms are sweaty. His heart beats at an odd rhythm.

Thump. Pause, *thumpthump.* Double *thump,* pause.

Sweat dribbles down Wes's temple. His throat's dry. He reaches for the tea, but his hand's shaking; his vision is blurred by a thin wall of dampness.

Wes will not cry. He's an *adult*. Managing situations like this is a part of growing up.

"Looks legit," Zay says, frowning.

"Tea Leaf and Coffee Cup House?" Cooper says slowly. "Bogus name."

"It's atrocious," Ella groans. "But real."

"No. She would've told us," Wes says to the counter. Making eye contact with anyone would unleash the tears he's fighting. He doesn't even blink. "Mrs. Rossi would've said something."

"Well, she didn't," Ella snaps. "She didn't say a damn thing."

Wes wants to scream. He wants to stand up, heave the stool over his head, and shatter one of the storefront windows. He also wants to curl up in a corner so he doesn't puke. His head's fuzzy, as if he's swimming but drowning.

Thing is, Mrs. Rossi's kept this a secret. From him. From the one person who spends more time caring for this bookstore than he does for his own future. Once Upon a Page, for better or worse, has been his past, his present, and it's always hung neatly in the photo Wes has had in his mind of what his future would look like.

When Wes finally looks up, Ella's rubbing her temples. "I need a drink."

"You're underage," Cooper murmurs as if it's a secret.

"Thanks, Obvious Police." Ella turns to Wes. "She gives me all this shit about being late and not caring… but *this*." She pokes the paper again. Wes's heart lurches. "She's the one who doesn't care. How could she not tell us?"

That cold hand tightens around Wes's chest. But his mind manages to backtrack. "Wait. You knew about this." He squints at Ella. "You knew while I was gone. Every time we talked, you never mentioned it."

Ella sucks in her bottom lip.

"And since I've been back, you haven't said a damn word. You brought up all that Book Attic bullshit, but not this." His breaths are clipped, but he lets the anger rise. "How could *you* not say anything? You know how much this place means to me."

"I didn't want you to have a breakdown."

"Mission unaccomplished then."

"Wes, you—" Ella cuts herself off, looking away. "You can't handle things like this."

"I can't?"

"No." She meets his eyes. "You. Can't."

Wes finally blinks. The first hot tear slides over his upper lip, catches on the scruff along his chin. He needs to shave. He can't believe that's what his mind chooses to focus on.

"I love you. You're my best friend." Ella reaches out for his hand, but he drags it back, shaking. She frowns. "This is reality. A fucked up one, but it's real."

Wes watches her walk away. Again. He sniffs as another stinging tear traces the tip of his nose before falling off.

"Wes? You okay?"

Zay's voice sounds muffled, distant. Wes's impressed that he can stare at Zay while not breathing properly.

"You look like you're gonna blow chunks."

Then Nico's at the counter, examining him with concern. "Wesley?"

Anna's next to him.

"Háblame," Nico whispers to Wes.

Talk to me. Wes knows that much Spanish. He also knows that, no, he doesn't want to talk to Nico. He doesn't want to talk to anyone.

He stands on shaky legs, his head spinning. *Bathroom.* He has the tiniest grasp on his bearings. Nudging past Zay and Cooper, Wes escapes from behind the counter. His feet feel heavy, but he walks. He moves as quickly as his body will allow.

"Wesley?" Nico calls out.

A fraction of Wes's brain wants to finally tell Nico, confess everything. But confessing his mind-numbing crush on Nico won't save the bookstore or fix this newly splintered piece of his future. The internet didn't need to teach Wes what he already knew about love; it doesn't solve all of life's problems.

Instead, he says, "Give me some space, Nico. Damn. I'm fine."

It's the biggest lie he's ever told Nico, but Wes is so done.

CHAPTER EIGHT

A QUICK BUT FRANTIC GOOGLE search on his phone informs Wes that he's either just survived a heart attack, acid reflux, or a possible panic attack. Further research on WebMD and a brief YouTube tutorial eliminate the first two ailments.

Deep breath in. Deep breath out.

He's been reciting this to himself for three minutes, eyes closed. It's helped, though his brain is still a little fuzzy. And, unfortunately, the bathroom is wearing its favorite perfume—eau de bleach.

Of all the places to hide, Wes isn't sure why he chose Once Upon a Page's crib-sized bathroom. He didn't think he could make it upstairs to the loft. It is the closest room except Mrs. Rossi's office, and Wes isn't going in there. What if he found something else? What other ugly, life-altering secrets was she hiding from him?

That underwater sensation returns. Blinking hard, he stares down at his phone.

Find an object to focus on.

The bookstore's sad bathroom doesn't have much in the way of decor. There's a sink, a mirror with a zigzag crack in the bottom right corner, one of those tropical-scent wall plug-ins that hasn't been changed in a year, flyers for previous store events, and the standard toilet with the lid down where Wes sits. Oh, and a faded blue poster of *The Great Gatsby* cover: depressing, disembodied eyes staring at Wes. He hates that book. He also hates Chaz, the former employee who pinned it to the mint green wall. Chaz, the clinical kleptomaniac who only stole nude photography books.

Pervy hipster.

Wes focuses on a bottom corner of the poster. It's beginning to curl like a Fruit Roll-Up. That corner's a rebel.

His phone directs him to: *Go to your happy place.*

Yeah, sorry Google, but Wes's "happy place" is now officially a gateway to hell.

Breathing deeply, Wes tries to locate somewhere else in his clogged brain, another place he's most himself. Every answer ends in Nico. Anywhere with him, having conversations with their eyes and laughing until it hurts.

Does he have that with Anna?

Wes finds himself on Google again. His hands shake as he searches "ways to know if your crush is not into you." What is he doing? Suddenly, he's on BuzzFeed, then Teen Vogue. He's browsing Reddit Relationship Advice. Wes finally draws the line at Quora, but not before he's compiled a new list:

Signs Your Crush Isn't Into You!!!

It's not his best work. There are only five bullet points, and Wes is already frowning at the first one:

1. If your crush doesn't laugh at your jokes, RUN!

It doesn't apply to Wes and Nico, but multiple sources suggest he pay attention to minor things like that.

The bathroom door nudges open. Wes forgot to lock it. And Anna isn't polite enough to *knock*, but she doesn't swing the door wide. She peeks her head in, ensuring Wes isn't using the toilet for its intended purposes.

Wes sighs, which is obviously an invitation Anna uses to enter, closing the door behind her. She leans against it. Wes pointedly stares at the wall adjacent to her.

"So."

"Yeah?" Wes sighs again.

"That was quite the exit."

Wes nods solemnly. He doesn't feel so bad about storming off, but more about the way he snapped at Nico. It was a definite infraction of the best friend code. Thing is, that's a direct result of crushing on a friend. The lines get blurred.

He's a horrible human being.

Correction: he's a horrible human presently trapped in a tiny bathroom with his crush's crush.

Wes's brain, ever ready to take a dive into a pit of fire, zones in on how cute Anna is. She's a surf goddess, all seashell bracelets and floral wrap dress and hair unbrushed without appearing dirty. Even the bathroom's substandard lighting fails to wash out the color in her cheeks or the blueness of her eyes.

"Did you read the email?" Wes asks.

Anna nods, her mouth falling.

"Did you already know?"

Anna shakes her head.

Wes figured she didn't know. It wouldn't make sense. Why would she train to manage a store that wouldn't be around at the end of summer?

"If Mrs. Rossi hasn't mentioned this to any of us, maybe it's not final?" Anna suggests.

Wes rubs his forehead. It's conceivable. Mrs. Rossi's a fighter. "Yeah," he whispers, trying to believe every one of those four letters.

"Um." Anna's fingers twist the ends of her hair, as if she's nervous.

"What?"

"You were kind of hard on Nico, don't you think?" she says.

Wes inhales loudly through his nose. He's attempting not to be impatient with her, but *Hello, Nico has a thing for* her, *not Wes*. It's number two on his new list:

2. If your crush shows signs of being into someone else, ABORT!

"It's fine," he says. Those two words are becoming his favorite lie.

"He doesn't seem okay."

"We've argued before."

Another fact. Usually, their beefs were over meaningless things. Once, they argued over a photo Wes posted on Instagram. Nico yelled, and Wes shouted and he swore Nico fractured his thumb when he punched his bedroom wall. It was ugly. It was also two months after Nico's father died. Wes hadn't recognized that Nico was stumbling through the stages of grief.

He hadn't realized that the photo, of Wes and Nico and his sisters on the beach, also included Mr. Alvarez in the background, laughing with his tongue out.

Wes whispers, "We'll be fine."

"Are you sure?"

"Aren't you two," Wes pauses when he notices he's eye-level with her breasts. Jerking his head up, he says, idiotically, "Aren't you two, like... you know?"

Anna arches an eyebrow, confused.

"A *thing*?"

"Uh, no." Anna's shoulders shake as if she's restraining a laugh. "Nico's cute in a very book-nerdy way, but I'm not into him."

"You're not?"

"No, no." She pulls fingers through her hair, detangling the ends. "There's this girl…"

Wes sits up. He doesn't know what it is that excites him when someone's anything other than straight. Maybe it's because people are taught that straight is the default, which makes him an exception. An unnatural exception according to a few too many politicians on television. How do people still think like that? How are people still holding on to immoral values and ignoring the fact that sexuality and gender are fluid?

"Oh, I didn't know." Wes plays with his own curls.

"Yes, I'm bisexual. Sorry I didn't put it on my application."

Wes blushes. "No, I mean, uh   "

"I'm kidding, dude." Anna's laugh is this smoky, raspy noise that takes a few rounds to fall in love with. "Also, Nico's not into me either."

Huh. Strike one, BuzzFeed.

"You weren't worried, were you?" Anna inquires.

"What? No." In a failed attempt to be nonchalant, Wes hugs his knees, *pffting* at Anna's insinuation. "I'm just looking out for my BFF. I screen all applicants that could turn into potential love interests."

"Uh huh. Sure thing."

Wes cocks his chin. There's no way Anna can see through his façade. He's too smooth. He says, "Yeah, well, good talk," while Anna stares at him as if he's full of shit.

It's okay. She's not the first person to solve life's mysteries while he flounders.

When she leaves, Wes's thumb hovers over the delete option on his new list. "No," he whispers to himself, locking his phone. Anna and Nico might not be a thing, but that doesn't mean Wes doesn't need this list too.

It's a fail-safe, that's all.

AT TWILIGHT, THE SCENE AROUND the Santa Monica Pier is euphoric. From Wes's view on a bench, he can see the deep blue-black water stretching toward endlessness. In his peripheral vision, the arcade's blinking neon lights are fuzzy pinks and blues. The *slap-crack* from the air hockey table is as loud as the screams from the West Coaster, the pier's rollercoaster. The lights twinkling off Pacific Park envelop the area in a hypnotic glow.

Wes inhales deeply. Sugary cotton candy, fresh churros, sundrenched wood, briny sea water—everything comes at him at once. He smiles.

Anna's the one who suggested they come down to the pier. Cooper, Kyra, and Nico agreed to tag along. Zay had a family dinner. Wes doesn't want to think about where Ella probably is. They haven't talked since she crushed his reality with that email.

Nearby, a couple leans against the railing that overlooks the beach. They're attempting to take a selfie while kissing. It's awkward and adorable. Wes is uncomfortably jealous.

He looks at the famous Route 66: End of the Trail sign everyone poses in front of. A father hoists his daughter onto his shoulders while someone snaps a picture on their phone. Wes wonders if, in ten years, that daughter will remember this moment beyond photographic evidence on social media? How does the brain decide what memories to keep permanently and which ones to copy-and-paste when needed? Which ones do people delete in order to create space for new ones?

Wes stares at his Chucks tapping against the wood beneath. The pier's a century old. It's probably in millions of tourists' photo albums. He ponders whether the architects imagined this incredible structure being nothing more than someone's phone screen wallpaper. Endless history exists here. It's a landmark in Santa Monica's story. On some levels, Wes thinks the same of the bookstore.

Will Once Upon a Page earn a Wikipedia page after it closes?

His brain works in mysterious—also, destructive—ways.

Wes pulls one leg to his chest and rests his foot on the edge of the bench. Down the pier, Nico stands in line at a food cart. Wes hopes he gets funnel cakes. He also hopes he's doing a stellar job at being covert while staring at how soft Nico looks in his glasses with flat hair and an ash-gray hoodie. He amazes himself at being able to pine while the world is on fire.

"Hey. Aren't you that guy from the bookstore?"

When Wes lifts his head, he isn't expecting much. He's definitely not expecting a guy that's easily three inches taller than him with tan skin and sharp features. He's beaming at Wes, one side of his mouth higher than the other.

"Uh." Wes shrugs. "I guess?"

The guy laughs. He pushes fingers through his dark hair. It's long on top, as if he could pull it into a topknot. "Oh, right. You don't know who the hell I am. Sorry."

Wes's brain short-circuits, staring into this guy's charming brown eyes. "I'm not really good with faces," Wes says. "A lot of people come through the store." An obvious lie. "Should I know you?"

"Nah. I've never been to the bookstore."

"Oh." Wes raises an eyebrow. "So…"

"I follow coopsarrow on Insta," the guy explains. "He posts a lot about the bookstore and you."

"Uh huh." Wes exhales.

Note to self: remind Cooper what "digital consent" means.

"Coop's good friends with my cousin too. He's big time in their community."

"Their community?"

"Yup." But the guy doesn't clarify, so Wes supposes it's something he'll have to ask Cooper about.

"So, I'm famous?" Wes jokes. He can't wait to tell Leo and his parents he's ditching college to be a social media influencer.

"Santa Monica Escapades all day." That laugh returns. Strangely enough, Wes is falling in love with it.

"Manuia." He extends his hand to Wes. "Everybody calls me Manu, though."

"Manu," Wes repeats. He likes Manu's grip; strong and purposeful. Not at all like a creepy Instagram stalker. "I'm Wes," he says, then feels like an idiot because, duh, of course Manu already knew that. "Officially. I'm Wes, officially."

"Officially Wes," Manu says, beaming.

Wes smiles nervously. He considers complimenting Manu's wardrobe choice: a tight, vintage Gameboy T-shirt. But just because Wes is a total nerd doesn't mean he's advertising it to attractive strangers.

"I've been meaning to come by the store," Manu continues. "My cousin says it's great."

"Yeah. It's sweet."

"Maybe I could get a tour?"

"From Cooper?"

"Well. I mean, sure. If you're not, like, around?"

"I usually am," Wes says. "Actually, I'm always around these days."

"Good to know."

Wes considers Manu. His thumbs are hooked in the front pockets of his jeans. He's almost leaning in Wes's direction, as if he might sit down, as if he's possibly waiting for Wes to *offer* him a place on the bench.

Wait. Is Manu flirting?

"So, yeah," says Manu. "Maybe I'll drop by sometime?"

"That'd be dope."

"Dope," Manu repeats and, if the lighting was right, Wes could swear Manu's cheeks were darker. But it's hard to tell from his position on the bench. Should he be asking Manu for his number? Or Instagram name? Could he slide into Manu's DMs?

Is Wes cool enough to slide into his own DMs?

"I guess I'll see you around, Officially Wes." Manu gives Wes a small wave, then hesitates before spinning on his heels to walk up the pier toward Ocean Avenue.

Perfect. Puberty hit like a tornado at thirteen and, five years later, Wes still hasn't grown a pair.

"Was that guy just flirting with you?"

Wes is startled when Nico flops down next to him; his throat barely contains a yelp as their shoulders brush.

Get it together.

"Doubtful," Wes replies, slouching on the bench.

Nico hums, picking off an edge of golden funnel cake that isn't piled with powdered sugar. "Looked like he was."

"He wasn't."

"Not your type?"

He's not you. Wes really hates the way his brain works. "We were just talking. He's a friend of Cooper's. It's nothing."

"Are you sure?" Nico asks, chewing. His mouth pulls a little south, as though he's concerned or disappointed.

What would he have to be disappointed over? Wes's inability to go after a semi-sure thing rather than having to create a plan just to ask his best friend out?

"Don't worry," Wes says, exhaling. "He won't be stealing your permanent position as my plus-one to all future formal events."

"Good." Nico tears into more funnel cake, chewing with his mouth open.

How is he gross and attractive at the same time?

Defeated, Wes stares down the pier.

A man strums his guitar for passing tourists. His case is open, slowly filling with crinkled dollars and shiny coins. Eventually, a raspy voice accompanies him. It takes Wes a second to realize it's Anna. He didn't know she could sing. He didn't know she'd be so bold, but here she is, singing Adele like some indie pop artist trying to gain cool points.

Wes spots Cooper whooping from the small audience forming around them. Kyra's next to him, a dreamy expression softening her face.

"Wesley, I—" Nico doesn't finish. He peers out at the water, nose wrinkled.

"I'm sorry about earlier. About…"

"Losing your shit?"

"Losing my shit," Wes confirms.

"I get it."

"You do?" Wes can't curb the surprise in his voice.

"The bookstore means a lot to all of us, but it means *everything* to you. It always has. You've been in love with that place since day one."

Wes has. Since the moment Calvin walked him through that glass door, around the cardboard stand advertising his mom's newest book, to the comics corner. He sat down, cross-legged, with Wes and let him have at it for two hours. He never said a word. Not until he asked Wes which one he would like to take home.

"All of them!" Wes wanted to eat, sleep, and daydream on that gray carpet.

"It's like a breakup," Nico says to the ocean.

"Sorry. I don't know that word," teases Wes.

"Lauren Walsh," Nico reminds him. "Angela Barry. Khalia Pressley."

"Okay. Point made."

So, Wes had a little bit of an issue with rejection in middle school. He failed to master the art of "no" whenever a girl asked him out. They were all fictious arrangements: holding hands in the halls; kissing on the cheek after class; writing the most dramatic poems via texts. And every girl would break up with him after two weeks.

It never bothered Wes. He didn't recognize who he really wanted to date until much later.

"Anyway," Wes says. "It's worse than a breakup. It's like a—"

"Death?"

A chill crawls over the back of Wes's neck, seeping down his spine. He doesn't want to compare losing Once Upon a Page to death. Not to Nico.

"I get that too," whispers Nico. "Either way, it's like someone reaching into your chest and ripping out half your heart. How do you survive with only half a heart?"

Wes doesn't know.

Nico's fingers are white from picking at his funnel cake. He raises a chunk. "Want some?"

Hesitation claws at Wes. He leans forward, and Nico pops the greasy, doughy piece into Wes's open mouth. He chews slowly, grinning. Nico matches his expression. They're twin white-bearded friends on a bench in the middle of a neon-lit pier while Anna sings Adele's melancholy "Someone Like You."

"Hey," Nico says around another bite. "Peanut butter, orange soda, or High Mountain oolong?"

Wes wants to laugh at these ridiculous choices. First of all, Nico knows Wes isn't going to choose that artificial abomination this world calls orange soda. Second, he knows Wes has recently developed a love for oolong tea thanks to Kyra and Brews and Views' ever-changing menu.

But Wes says, "Peanut butter," because it's his go-to snack.

"I knew it," Nico says, like always.

Wes isn't in the mood to call him on his shit, not after the day he's had.

"You're so predictable." Nico nudges Wes.

Did you predict I'd fall in love with you?

Wes's brain is a disaster. He can't take his eyes off the way Nico's index finger pushes his glasses up his nose, leaving a white streak behind. He's licking sugar from his thumb. It should be gross—*it is gross*—but Wes's heart refuses to use that as motivation to just say what he's supposed to say.

Stick to the plan.

"Gents, I must say…" Cooper leans over the back of the bench, his face swooping in between their shoulders. "… this is becoming the best summer of my life."

"All sixteen years, huh," Kyra says. She's arm in arm with Anna as they stand behind Cooper.

"There's no age on souls," says Cooper, smiling lazily. It's not hard to deduce he's stoned.

"It's a pretty wicked summer." Nico slings an arm around Wes's shoulders.

"Did we all miss the part about being jobless and one of this city's greatest monuments being shut down?" Wes asks, his throat tight.

"Isn't a monument something people build in memory of a person or place?" Kyra inquires.

"Thank you, Google," huffs Wes.

Teasingly, Kyra nudges the back of his head. "Shut up."

"Don't give up, young son of Queen Savannah," Cooper says. "It's not over. We're in the endgame now."

"Did you just quote *Infinity War* to me?" Wes says, offended.

Cooper's mouth stretches as if it's made of taffy.

"He's right," Anna agrees. "If Mrs. Rossi hasn't told us, then maybe there's still a chance."

Okay, they're both stoned.

"Can we not talk about this right now?" Cooper requests. Wes couldn't agree more. *Let's never talk about Once Upon a Page being shut down. Ever.* "Junior year is on the horizon. Another one hundred and eighty days of math and science-y stuff. I just want to chill with my friends. My homies. My peeps."

Wes thinks Cooper's the kind of kid who never checks his Halloween candy before ingesting.

Before he knows it, words are being tossed around—something about hashtags and selfies—and Wes is squeezed between four people on the bench as Cooper plops into his lap. Phone extended, Cooper shouts, "Say 'peeps not creeps,'" and then a flash. Another flash.

"Wicked," Cooper says, dethroning from Wes's knees.

Wes's phone buzzes in his pocket. With Nico on one side and Anna on the other, he has to wiggle to reach it.

New notification from coopsarrow.

He's tagged everyone in the post.

The selfie's respectable. Pacific Park shines in the background. Cooper must've used a photo-editing app to remove the flash's red-eye effect. Kyra and Anna are smiling goofily. Cooper's beaming as if he's physically walking on clouds. Nico's glasses are crooked; his mouth gapes, white teeth blinding.

And there's Wes, staring at Nico, mega heart eyes included.

"Hashtag love it," says Kyra as she double taps her phone.

"Ultimate squad," Cooper announces. "We're just missing El's Bells and Zay."

Wes can't take his eyes off how he looks at Nico in the photo. It's so obvious. How could Nico not see it?

Hashtag Best Friend Crushes are the Worst.

CHAPTER NINE

RETURNING HOME AFTER LEAVING THE pier, Wes is surprised to find Ella sitting on the green sofa, feet under her, phone squeezed between her hands and dark trails down her cheeks.

"Hey," he says cautiously, nudging the door closed with his foot.

Ella's eyes are wide and glassy. "Sup."

"Okay." Wes toes off his shoes, moving guardedly as if she's a velociraptor ready to claw out his organs. Ella's not that scary—thirty percent of the time—but she never cries. He's certain she *has* cried, probably as an infant, but he's never witnessed it firsthand.

She sniffles. Her nose is red.

"Ella?"

She exhales loudly, clearly annoyed by the way Wes is tiptoeing closer. "Chill out, super-geek, I didn't just fail to raise a hell demon to run for mayor while I exact revenge on the girl who left me for dead."

Wes snorts. Last summer, provoked by a book snob obsessed with a certain poorly written vampire saga, Ella and Wes binge-watched the entire *Buffy the Vampire Slayer* television series online. It's an hour's drive from Newport Beach to Santa Monica, so Ella spent weekends on the green sofa after her shift downstairs at the bookstore. Faith, the rebel slayer, was an instant favorite of Ella's. Wes leaned more toward Willow because, hello, lesbian witch. But they both agreed season four never happened.

Ella turns her phone over and over between her hands. "Mom called."

Oh.

Wes has met Victoria Graham on three occasions. Each time, she barely spoke four words to him. She's not a mean person, simply someone fully focused on her priorities. Wes isn't one of them. Victoria is a striking woman with reddish-brown hair, wide shoulders, and an affinity for anything pastel. And her words cut faster, harder, more lethally than anything Ella's ever used to fend off strangers brave enough to look her in the eye for more than five seconds.

The tension between Ella and her mom is something Wes learned early in their friendship to observe but never ask about unless prompted. Ella claims that, when she was little, Victoria would fawn over her cheeks and chubby thighs. But somewhere between nine and ten, things shifted. Victoria stopped pinching Ella's cheeks and started "suggesting" Ella join a soccer team or a volleyball club. Ella should try flirting with the boys from the football team instead of hanging with the art club kids. Listen to a little more fun pop music instead of brooding goth rock.

"Are you—" Wes pauses, rubbing his chin. *Choose your words carefully.* "Do you want to punch something?"

Ella sniffs, wiping snot from her nose. "Always."

"Cool," says Wes, dropping down next to her. "Not me?"

"You're basically bones and curls. It'd be disappointing to break you without trying."

Wes eases an arm around her stiff shoulders. "Did she say something?"

"She always says something."

"Does she want you to come home?"

Ella's laugh is this sad, pathetic thing. "No, she's quite fine without me there to tarnish her image. Why have a daughter in person when you can just as easily FaceTime her to expound your disappointment in her? Technology's the best."

Wes hums. Is it selfish that he wants to talk to his own mother? Despite her constant word vomit about writing and publishing and Twitter, there's something about the sound of his mom's voice that Wes needs once a day. It's a comfort.

With all the madness of the day, they haven't spoken. She messaged him about depositing money into his bank account for groceries, but that's about it. Wes does the math. Savannah might be still awake, writing.

"I can't wait until summer's over and we're moving onto campus," sighs Ella. "It's like, for the most part, I'll be done with them. Four years or more where I'll be focused on becoming my own person."

"You've always been your own person."

"You know what I mean."

Wes does. But he also hates thinking about the end of summer. It's this loud, unavoidable countdown in his head.

In September, he'll be at UCLA.

In September, Nico will be at Stanford.

In September, Wes is supposed to step out of being a teenaged slacker and become this instant adult who has career goals, relationship goals, money goals. So many goals. He's supposed to study hard, graduate, get a six-figure job. He's supposed to prove to the world that he's responsible and capable of solving things with next to zero stress, but that's all he sees in adults—stress and money problems and failures.

Who wants that?

He should probably tell Ella all of this, but when she says, a grin in her voice, "We're gonna kick ass at UCLA," he falters.

"Go Bruins," Wes replies, trying to drum up as much enthusiasm as possible. Absentmindedly, his arm tightens around her. Ella snuggles in; her head rests on his collarbone.

"Oh god, you reek of the hell spawn," she mumbles.

"We were at the pier. Anna, Kyra, Coop…"

"Nico?"

"Yeah."

Ella snort-giggles. "So I missed the crew."

You did. Wes doesn't say it. Thing is, he and Ella fight occasionally. Most friends do. But they don't do apologies. Well, Wes does sometimes, but Ella definitely doesn't. He thinks it's against her emo-punk code.

"Coop thinks we should…" Wes struggles to finish. It's been on his mind, what Cooper said at the pier. Fighting for the bookstore. How they're in the endgame and all that. "He thinks we shouldn't just give up."

Ella wiggles a little on the sofa, but she doesn't say anything.

"I dunno. I kind of think, maybe he's right?" Wes continues. "I have no clue what to do, but maybe we should consider it?"

"Consider what?"

"Doing anything other than rolling over and letting this rank coffee franchise just take over our turf."

"*Our turf?*" repeats Ella, mockingly. "Gee, Wes, do you want to put together a petition and hold a rally too?"

Wes slides his arm off her shoulders. "I don't want to just sit around and lose everything."

She's silent again, curled on the sofa. Her hair falls around her face, blocking Wes's view of her expression. But, softly, she says, "Fine." Before Wes can jump on the sofa and fist-pump, she adds, "But we're not discussing any of this with Mrs. Rossi."

"Okay," Wes agrees. It's not the perfect solution, but it's a start.

LITTLE TONY'S BIG SLICE IS nearly empty when Wes arrives after closing the bookstore. The family traffic has vacated the premises. Couples sit at round tables while a few solo diners eat pizza, swiping greasy fingers over their phone screens. The bookstore crew has already snagged a corner booth near the back. It's a tight fit with six people but it works.

"Is this an intervention?" Cooper asks as Wes slides into the booth.

"What?" Zay peeps over his plastic menu.

"Listen. I know some of you…" Cooper glances at Ella. "…don't approve of my musical choices, but I'm getting better."

"You played Peter Gabriel today." Ella glares back. "I didn't even know what a Peter Gabriel was until today."

Cooper frowns. "But you let him…" He points at Zay. "…play Nina Simone for an hour."

"Don't bring Nina into this," Zay warns, but he's beaming.

"This isn't about your questionable music integrity," Wes interrupts. He pats Cooper's unreasonably tall hair. "You're doing better, though."

"We clearly have very different definitions of that word," Ella says, plunking her paper straw into a glass of Dr. Pepper.

"Is it about finding new jobs now that we're all about to be unemployed by the end of the summer?" Zay asks.

"We're not gonna be unemployed," Wes argues gently.

"I was overqualified for the job, anyway," Ella proclaims. "I'm the most equipped to be successful out of all of us."

"Bullshit." Zay guffaws.

Ella balls up a napkin and flicks it at him. It bounces off his nose. He sweeps it off the table.

"It's not about that," Wes says, resting a hand on Ella's before she can assault Zay with more accuracy. "We're not looking for new jobs."

"Then what's this about?" Nico asks.

Wes is sandwiched between Nico and Ella. Little Tony's minimal staff means their table hasn't been fully cleaned from the previous customers. Nico's repeatedly sticking and unsticking his fingers from the Formica's surface. He and Wes switched shifts today so Nico could take his sisters to the beach. The smell of salt and sun and sweat lingering on his clothes and skin distracts Wes. Ella clears her throat.

"Right." Wes wasn't point-five seconds from burying his nose in Nico's collarbone. He owns his weirdness, but that's probably going too far. "The email said Mrs. Rossi is behind on her property payments. I've been thinking it's because the store's not bringing in enough money."

"It's not as busy as it's been in the past," Ella agrees.

"Corporate capitalism," Anna says, scowling. "Online convenience has continuously made it financially impossible for brick and mortar establishments to remain afloat. The limitless ability of online corporations to provide cheap deals on product without skimming a high percentage off the producer has nearly eliminated independent providers' potential to compete. It's destroying the traditional business market."

Wes blinks at Anna. "Who the hell are you?"

"I'm a business major."

"Yeah, but." Wes shakes his head. "You never talk like that at the store."

Anna's expression never falters. "Just because I *don't*, doesn't mean I *can't*."

Huh. Wes really needs to work on spending less time pining over Nico and more time getting to know his coworkers.

"You also smoke up with Cooper on lunch breaks," Zay points out.

"I'm a business major *and* an environmentalist." Anna exhales contentedly. "Green is good."

"Green is life," Cooper affirms.

"Back to the bookstore," Ella says, sounding exasperated. "We need to figure out ways to increase revenue, or it's going to end up just like Book Attic and that Barnes and Noble."

"And Page-Turner over near my neighborhood, too," Zay adds.

"They closed Page-Turner?" Ella asks, eyebrows raised.

"Yup."

Wes refuses to be fazed. Page-Turner was an obvious Once Upon a Page rip-off. They even had a neon sign in their front window that read, "Read More Books," except the lighting in the "K" burnt out. "Read More Boos" was an accidental marketing dream around Halloween but hardly brought in any traffic the rest of the year.

"So…"

A sigh accompanies the bored expression of their waiter as he stands over the table. Constantine, the restaurant owners' son, is a lanky dude with a perpetual sneer and shaggy, brooding-hero hair. He attends the University of Southern California, which makes him an automatic enemy. Kyra goes there too, but she gives Wes free tea.

"What'll it be on your pizzas tonight?" Constantine asks, staring at the wall behind their booth rather than anyone at the table.

Wes's crew have been regulars around here since he got his first paycheck and blew it on comics, a pair of sick Adidas, and a whole Little Tony's thin crust pepperoni pie.

"Hawaiian," Anna says cheerfully.

"Mushroom and onions," Ella insists. This time, Zay chucks a balled-up napkin at her. She deflects, and it tumbles onto the floor. Constantine's irremovable scowl deepens.

"What're your vegetarian options again?" Cooper asks, flipping over the laminated menu.

Clearly annoyed, Constantine rubs his temples.

Under the table, a warm hand cups Wes's knee. He can feel the soft skin through the hole in his jeans. In his peripheral vision, Nico's smile shines. "Extra pepperoni for us."

For us. Wes glows. It's so much easier to date Nico in his head. In his imagination, they're still best friends and boyfriends. They play video games and go to the same college and make out a lot. It works. There are no complications. He doesn't have to make any loud, bold confessions.

He turns his head, unable to steady the grin on his mouth. "No jalapeños?"

"You hate them."

"That's never stopped you before."

"I'm being thoughtful."

"What a concept." But Wes is grateful. He's weak when it comes to spicy things.

In each corner of the restaurant, speakers are attached to the walls. Billy Joel's humming overhead. The rich scent of marinara and melting cheese and the right hint of herbs escapes the kitchen. It's all very East Village—at least, that's what Wes's mom says. He's never been to New York City or anywhere outside of California, except his recent trip to Siena.

"Okay," Constantine squawks over the undecided chatter about pizza toppings. "You're getting two extra-pepperoni pies. It's decided."

"But—" Cooper begins to protest, but Constantine cuts him off.

"Can you all agree on drinks?"

"Beer," Ella says firmly.

"Coke," Wes quickly says before Constantine officially loses his shit. "A pitcher is cool."

"Uh," Cooper raises his hand like a second-grader asking for the bathroom pass. "Do you carry bottled mineral water?"

"Oh my god," Ella mumbles, face-planting in her hands. She lifts her head, turning to Constantine. "Can we also get a basket of those killer breadsticks?"

Constantine, broad shoulders tight, inhales deeply, then plasters on a fake grin. "Anything else, princess?"

"Uh."

"No? Perfect." Constantine huffs before stomping away from their table.

Ella looks around the table, confused. "Anyone know what *that* was about?"

Anna stares at her phone, shrugging. Wes and Nico pointedly refuse to make eye contact with Ella. They know, but they're not saying. Zay, the brave soul, finally declares, "I think it has something to do with last Halloween when you two hooked up, and then you proceeded to ghost him."

"I'm sorry, *what*?"

"C'mon, El," Zay says. It's a shame. Wes really loves Zay, but there's no way he's going to survive repeating this story. "Last year. Amalie's Halloween party down in Venice? You and Wes dragged me—"

"Invited, and you accepted," Wes corrects him.

Zay rolls his eyes. "Anyway. We went. There were Jell-O shots consumed. The music sucked. Wes was Green Lantern—"

"Again," Nico teases under his breath.

A compulsory blush doesn't stop Wes from whispering back, "John Stewart is a legend. I stan."

"You were…" Zay waves a hand at Ella. She's wearing black, black, and more black, per usual. "…you, I guess."

Ella lurches back, offended. "What does that mean?"

"Point is, you got hammered and made out with Constantine on Amalie's parents' bed. You two exchanged numbers, but you never called."

"Whoa, Ella," Cooper says, scandalized. "How could you?"

"*I didn't*," Ella says, firmly. To Zay, she screeches, "You lie!" Then she asks Wes wordlessly, eyes huge and daunting, *Did I?*

Wes nods once.

"How could you let that happen?" Ella smacks his shoulder.

"I was buzzed?" Wes offers pathetically.

"We got into this massive game of strip beer pong, which didn't go to well for us," Nico says. "That Green Lantern costume is kind of one-dimensional, so..."

"It's dope, and you know it," Wes argues.

"It is, but one layer of clothing in any game where you have to remove an article of clothing when you lose isn't helpful," Nico states.

"True that."

Wes doesn't remember that entire night, but he definitely recalls Nico standing nervously, scrawny arms trying to cover his chest, in a pair of cornflower blue boxers. It's a nice, hi-def image he's used appropriately.

"How are any of you my friends?" Ella's hands cover her face. Her muffled voice is mortified. "Con-Constantine? *Seriously*?"

"Can we get back to saving Once Upon a Page?" Wes requests. "We need money."

"Oh. Are we going to, like, cyber-rob some wealthy Fortune 500 billionaire from Silicon Valley who's too greedy to share his wealth?" Cooper bounces in his seat.

"What?"

"I just read this book about a group of teens who hack into one of the character's deadbeat dad's stacks because he refuses to help pay for her college tuition," Cooper explains, phone out. He's Googling something.

"Um, no?" Wes replies.

"Dude, are you one of those dark web hackers?" Zay asks, hiding his own phone. "Is the Wi-Fi in here secure?"

Cooper has this almost-evil gleam in his eyes.

"We're not doing that." Wes shakes his head. "We need to come up with some ideas to help boost sales in the store. You know, promotional things. Ways to attract more customers."

"Like, community events? Book signings?" Anna offers.

"Exactly," Wes says eagerly.

"But we only have until September," Ella adds, finally snapping out of her Constantine-shaped dark dimension. "According to my research…"

More snooping, Wes wants to interject, but Ella's actually being *helpful* with this, so he doesn't

"… that's when Tea Leaf and Coffee Cup House plan to begin renovations and officially take over property payments."

"We can do this," Wes says.

"Us?" Nico twirls his index finger around at the table. "In less than two months?"

"Yes. It'll be work, but we can."

Yeah, Wes sounds like a self-help book. *Six Ways to Save Your Dream Slacker Job*. But he believes every word of the wishful thinking he's spitting out.

"Each of us needs to come up with a promotional idea. Then we'll plan it out. Kyra can help," he says adamantly.

Across from him, Zay shrugs. "I'm down. I've helped with fundraising ideas at my church."

"I'm in," says Anna.

"Yes! Save the bookstore. Damn the man." Cooper thumps a fist on the table.

"This is going to be so bad," Ella says under her breath, but Wes ignores her homegrown pessimism.

He stares at Nico, attempting to maintain a smile. "Come on." He squeezes Nico's shoulder. "You kick ass at group projects."

"You were the worst lab partner."

"But we didn't fail."

"No thanks to you." Nico closes his eyes. "Fine. I'm in."

Wes silently screams. He's not a born leader, but he knows something's happening. It's all very adult. *Adult-ish.* "But we can't tell Mrs. Rossi about this. She has enough on her plate."

Since Wes's return, she's been in the store less and less. Yesterday, she only worked half a shift, claiming the flu. She was ghostly pale when she left. Wes thinks it's the stress of watching her business collapse on top of her. She deserves a break.

"Isn't that kind of wrong? It's her store, after all," Zay says.

"No. It'll mean more if we manage to save the bookstore *for her.* She'll know how important she is to this community," Wes insists.

"Whoa. Are we going rogue? Like that one *Star Wars* movie?" Cooper looks ready to burst. "Can we come up with a cool group name? Like Chronic Club?"

"This world's future is in very capable hands," Ella mutters.

Constantine returns with two pitchers of Coke, a stack of plastic cups, and a basket of garlic breadsticks. He hovers for a minute, staring at Ella. She crunches into a breadstick, avoiding eye contact. "Pizza will be up shortly," Constantine says curtly, then disappears into the kitchen.

"Awkward," Cooper says, snickering.

"Shut up," Ella says between bites.

Zay pours; Anna passes. Wes savors his small victory. They're all in.

Ella raises her cup. "To you losers," she says. "Let's kick some ass while we still have time."

"Cheers!"

"To friends," Wes says, cup still raised. He half turns to Nico. He hopes having the courage to save the bookstore won't take too much time away from planning to tell Nico how he feels.

"To friends," Nico repeats with a smile that doesn't reach past his cheeks.

Maybe people like Wes only get one summer miracle.

CHAPTER TEN

DESTINY INTRODUCED ITSELF TO WES on his eighth birthday. Its name was *Blackest Night*. Until then, Wes had a childlike appreciation for comic books. When he read them, he always closed his eyes at the end and imagined himself flying or shattering a brick wall or saving someone from the villain. He saw himself, occasionally, in the pages, but mostly he just loved the idea of wearing a cape and kicking ass.

The *Blackest Night* crossover series centered around the Green Lantern Corps fighting off undead heroes and unifying enemies and allies alike for one goal: saving the universe. Yes, the series was dark and twisty, and he fell asleep with the lights on so many times Calvin almost banned him from reading the newest issues. But Wes found something else in those books: emotion, conflict that reached beyond good and evil, inner struggles to be something great when all you want is to survive.

Though their expression of it is sometimes radical and inappropriate, Wes understands the love his mom's readers have for her books. Books are an escape. They're a trapdoor into emotions and feelings and how the smallest events can be the most life-changing.

For eight months, Wes lost himself in those comics. At the end, he found himself, too.

Yes, at the age of almost nine, Wes decided comic books were life-changing. Even without superpowers, Wes realized he could be a hero.

He just had to figure out how.

IT'S A TUESDAY, THE DAY before the newest comic books come out. It's also new release day for novels. Ella's hard at work—also known as chewing grape bubble gum while staring blankly at nothing—putting together a new window display to attract customers. Cooper mans the front counter. Mrs. Rossi is in and out of the office, entertaining customers for short bursts. And Wes is meditatively gazing at his chapel of heroes and capes, mentally mapping out where to feature all the newest titles being released tomorrow.

Once, Wes thought of asking Mrs. Rossi to buy an iPad to make this a little easier. He can't do that now. Once Upon a Page needs every dollar and penny and wish on a falling star it can get.

"You look intense. I mean, I've seen you do this whole…" Cooper points at Wes's corner. "…comics thing before. But today you look like a Jedi master conjuring the Force."

"I don't think they conjure the Force, Coop."

"Well, whatever they do, you're doing it."

Maybe Wes is. He just wants everything in the store to be perfect so that it'll still be around after summer's over.

Everyone agreed to spend a few days thinking of solid ideas for promotional events. Wes is still nervous. He knows he can scramble together some things, but he needs help.

"This is such a moment," whispers Cooper. "I need this on my feed."

Wes pivots in Cooper's direction. "Hey, do you think maybe the store needs a social media page? An Instagram? Maybe a Twitter account?"

"Bro." Stars explode in Cooper's eyes. "Yes! Hell yes. Do you know that's the first thing I asked about when I applied for the job?"

Wes isn't surprised.

"Mrs. R said the store had a Tumblr." He makes a sour face. "But this place needs more."

"Do you want to…"

Before Wes can finish, Cooper shouts, "Uh, are Goo Goo Dolls the greatest band of the '90s?"

"No, they're most definitely not."

Again, Wes isn't shocked by Cooper's statement. Two days ago, they argued Blind Melon's place in early '90s alternative rock canon—Wes for, Cooper against—so he's lost all trust in Cooper's musical ear. But Cooper's already absorbed by his phone, his tongue between his teeth.

"Coop?"

Cooper raises his head with an eager smile. He's such a puppy.

"Do you know a guy named Manu?" Wes rubs the back of his head, trying to contain his nerves. He hasn't been obsessively thinking about Manu since the pier, but he's crossed Wes's mind once or twice. Sometimes, Wes is a realist. It's good to have a backup plan. Life's a fifty-fifty gamble. So he's aware that this Nico thing might not fall in his favor.

And Manu was cute and interesting and seemed to be into Wes.

"Manuia?"

"Yeah."

"Manu is awesome," Cooper says, almost as enthusiastic about him as he is about anything involving a hashtag. "Dude always leaves the nicest comments on my posts. His cousin, Devon, is sweet too. You know she's going to be the starting setter on the Irvine women's volleyball team. She's *seventeen*, Wes. What a dream."

"Wow."

"Manu's dope," Cooper continues. "Devon's dope. All my mutual followers, including you, are dope."

"Uh, I met Manu. The other night on the pier. He seemed—"

"The best?"

"You could say that."

"He's most def someone you should hang with. I support this," says Cooper.

Is Cooper slyly trying to make a love connection? Or is he just eager for all his friends to be friends with each other? Wes can't decide.

He chooses his next words carefully. "He also mentioned you and Devon are in some kind of secret group? Or maybe, like, an after-school arts and craft community?"

Cooper tenses, staring down at his phone.

Wes shouldn't have asked. It's none of his business. It's just that Cooper's become this weird little brother that Wes feels protective of. That's Wes's problem—he gets too attached to people and things. He wants to make sure Cooper's not involved in anything illegal or harmful or, say, a teen drama fandom where all the actors are twenty-eight and playing high schoolers.

"You don't have to, like..." Wes paces around his words. "I think that's cool if you're part of a supportive group or whatever."

"They're so supportive." Cooper scrolls through his phone. He turns it around for Wes to inspect. "It's this book group for ace teens."

Wes blinks, eyebrows raised high.

"So, like," Cooper glances around the bookstore. It's practically empty. Ella's in a daydream, staring out the window. A few people graze the aisles. Mrs. Rossi's office door is closed. "So, I'm aroace." He bites his lip, whispering, "Do you know what that is?"

"Of course."

"Oh. Cool." Cooper nods too many times. "Well, that's me. I don't really talk about it because, like..." His voice dies as if someone's cut his vocal cords.

"People don't respect who you are. Or they don't understand, so they pretend it's not real? They have no concept that there are more identities other than just straight, gay, and lesbian?" Wes offers.

"Exactly!" Cooper's eyes are wide and glassy. "It happens *everywhere*. All the time."

"I'm sorry."

Cooper shrugs. "Don't be. That's what this group is for."

Wes examines Cooper's phone. His group has their own Instagram page: an entire feed of teens sitting on the beach or in coffee shops or in bookstacks sharing laughter and joy. There's a picture of Cooper, in front of a volleyball net with an orange, yellow, white, and blue flag draped across his shoulders. Next to him someone waves a gray, white, and purple flag. Dark, wind-wrecked hair hides most of her face except for her giant, infectious grin.

Wes points to the photo. "Devon?"

"My demi ride or die."

Wes continues to a photo of Cooper standing in front of a parade, flanked by two older people with his crinkled blue eyes and matching T-shirts. "Your parents?"

Cooper's shoulders relax. He drags a hand through his hair, but it doesn't lose its epic shape. "They're the best." He rotates his phone to stare at the image. "They didn't get it at first either. I'm not sure they fully understand now, but they're super supportive. They spend a lot of time on Google, then ask me questions when they think I'm okay to answer them. That's the best part—they don't force me to explain things. They make it casual, which is nice."

"That's great."

Blushing, Cooper lowers his phone. "I know I'm lucky because not everyone in our group has that at home. I feel bad about that."

"Don't," Wes says. "They have you. They have this group. That's important too." He raises his hand, then waits until Cooper nods his consent before dropping his palm on Cooper's shoulder. "Thank you for trusting me with this, Coop."

"You're Wes Hudson." Cooper's still red-faced. "Heir to the Savannah Kirk throne. King of Great Comic Book Land. The Bookstore Savior. Defender of—"

"Okay, thanks, Coop," Wes interrupts, laughing. He turns back to the comics corner. "Dreams" by the Cranberries floats through the store with its euphoric vocals and bass-heavy melody. He taps his foot to the drumbeat. Then, over his shoulder, he says, "Do you think maybe you could send me Manu's IG handle?"

"Consider it done." Cooper's eyes lower as he taps away.

Exhaling, Wes allows his shoulders to sink.

A backup plan, that's all Manu is.

It's 2:15 p.m.

Wes only notices because his phone chimes with a message from Leo. He ignores it. He hasn't even thought about the fact that Nico will arrive in forty-five minutes.

Today doesn't feel like *The Day.*

Wes is almost finished reorganizing the comic book shelves when he collides with someone. Not someone—Lucas, who apologizes repeatedly under their breath with their head lowered.

"No. It's my bad," Wes says, smiling even though Lucas isn't looking. "House rules—always apologize to the cool people for nearly giving them a concussion."

Lucas's head jerks up and their mint green eyes grow round.

"You okay?" Wes asks.

Those forehead wrinkles and teeth pulling at a chapped bottom lip don't sit right with Wes. He can smell the anxiousness pouring off Lucas.

"Uh." He pivots back toward his corner. "Lucas, right?"

"Ye-Yeah."

"Do you wanna help?" Wes offers.

"Me?" Lucas's voice is a bit of a squeak, a broken noise.

Wes extends an arm toward the comics. "Why not? You probably know the best ones anyway."

"No way," Lucas says, awed. "You're here all the time."

"Which also means I get in my own head too much about what's cool and what not."

Lucas *pffts*, and it's the first time Wes has seen a slice of their personality. He likes it.

"Save this holy place before I wreck it, please," Wes insists.

Slowly, with their head still partially lowered, Lucas follows Wes.

It takes ten minutes before Lucas mellows. They still talk more to their shoes than Wes, but a couple of dad jokes and letting Lucas take the lead opens things up. Eventually, they find a groove. Lucas fixes something. Waits for Wes's opinion. Wes gives a thumbs up, a mild suggestion, then they move on. It's hard to relinquish control over the spacing and shelving and placement, but Wes knows he needs to.

Of course, Wes deducts twenty cool points because Lucas is absolute trash for Marvel characters, but the way Lucas fawns over the last Wonder Woman issue earns a few checks in the good column.

"Who's your favorite?" Lucas asks, carefully rearranging the Spider-Man titles.

Wes appreciates the meticulousness. "John Stewart."

"The Green Lantern?"

Plus three points.

"Yup."

"He's badass," Lucas concurs "Much cooler than that Hal guy. Ryan Reynolds ruined that for everybody."

"Word."

Lucas isn't little, but they're definitely undersized. Wes easily reaches over their head to adjust a stray *Runaways* graphic novel. He steps back to admire the spread of Superman issues Lucas has just worked through. He nods approvingly, enjoying the way the freckles across Lucas's cheeks and nose stand out like dark constellations against the spreading crimson blush.

"You hang around here a lot," Wes observes, softly.

Lucas shuffles their dirty Nikes over the carpet. "Is it weird?"

"Nah. I did the same thing before I started working here. Me and my best friend."

"'That guy?" Lucas does a poor impersonation of someone skateboarding.

"Yeah, that guy."

Lucas digs the toe of their shoe into the carpet. Blond fringe hangs right into green eyes. Shoulders taut again, Lucas exhales through their thin nose. "Freshman year wasn't what Netflix made it out to be."

Wes can relate. High school on television looks so much easier than it is.

"It's bad enough I hate science and history, but then I didn't really know anyone," says Lucas. They tug on the tassels of their hoodie, making one side of the string longer than the other. "And the people I knew... *changed*." Lucas's mouth is somewhere between a pout and a frown; their green eyes are shiny. "I guess I did too, but not like them."

Wes remembers that evolution from sharing one class with the same faces for years to being shuffled around to a different room every fifty minutes with a new set of strangers. Freshman year, he didn't have a single class with Nico. And the kids he knew the year before were too busy trying to survive to acknowledge Wes.

The thing about high school is, everyone's trying to fit in somewhere. They're either trying to stand out or blend into the walls; they become something else. That survival instinct kicks in and people become cruel. Sometimes, it means they taunt others so no one else notices their flaws. Wes was no exception. It was difficult enough with all the questions he'd get— "Where are your parents from? No, I mean, *where's your dad from*?"—anytime someone saw Calvin. Coming out junior year did him no favors.

"Hey." Cautiously, Wes rests a hand on Lucas's shoulder. The tension gradually retreats under Lucas's hoodie. "You're welcome here anytime, okay?"

Lucas is five-foot-seven-ish, so they tip their chin to look Wes in the eye.

"Anytime," Wes repeats with a heap of assurance. Under his palm, Lucas's shoulder rises and falls with their easy breathing.

"We're not gonna, like," Lucas peeks around the store, "talk about our feelings now, are we?"

Wes barks a laugh so loud, Ella jumps.

"Because feelings are gross."

"So gross," Wes concurs, pulling his hand away.

"Lucas?"

Wes peeks over his shoulder. Standing in the bookstore's doorway is a short woman with brown hair turning gray at the roots, faint shadows under her eyes, and Lucas's round face. She has on wrinkled pink hospital scrubs; her small hands clutch a purse and a shopping bag.

"Hi, Mom." Lucas waves weakly.

"Sorry to interrupt." Lucas's mom gives Wes a quick, curious look. He grins in that nonthreatening way. He figures, the way Lucas talked about school, she's extra protective of them for good reasons. "We have our appointment," she says to Lucas.

The corners of Lucas's mouth inch up. Lucas twists halfway around to Wes, cup their hand around their mouth, and stage-whisper, "Codename: therapy," in the geekiest way possible.

Wes can't restrain his laugh.

"Also," Lucas's mom lifts the shopping bag, "I got, uh. You know."

Wes isn't prepared for the tiny squeak that leaves the back of Lucas's throat. Their eyes bunch up; their full, endless smile shows their teeth and the true roundness of their cheeks.

Lucas says, under their breath, "My new binder." They're a full shade redder than Wes thought was humanly possible.

"Nice," Wes says, fist-bumping Lucas.

Before Lucas bounds over to their mom, Wes says, "Hey."

Lucas turns around; their eyebrows hide under their fringe.

"I could use some help with this." Wes flags a hand at the comic book corner. "We can do this again. Same time next week."

Another squeak crawls out of Lucas's throat. A new sheen of wetness brightens their eyes when they blink. "Seriously?"

"Be here," Wes says, the way Mrs. Rossi did when she first hired him.

Lucas fist-pumps, then scampers to their mom, talking excitedly as they disappear out the store.

"Aww." Ella stands a few feet away, arms crossed, smirking. "Wes, have you gone soft? You never let anyone play with your toys."

"It's true, bro," says Cooper.

"Ugh. Don't agree with me," Ella demands. "People might think we're friends."

"Aren't we?" Cooper's voice cracks.

Ella rolls her eyes, but her acting range is limited. Wes can spot the tiniest of grins trying to fight past her thundercloud expression.

Wes stares at the empty doorway. Warmth circulates through his veins. He must ween Lucas off their love for Deadpool and Fantastic Four, probably introduce them to the magnificence that is Static, but he's okay with that.

It's one more reason Wes needs to save Once Upon a Page. For kids like Lucas who need it as much as he does.

CHAPTER ELEVEN 🛹

From: Leo
Leeann said you're going dress shopping tomorrow. Thanks!
Received 3:40 p.m.

From: Dad
English? They have Introduction to Graphic Fiction!
[link attached]
Received 4:16 p.m.

In Wes's mildly unbiased opinion, Venice at sunset is one of the dreamiest views in the world. The sun splinters behind the horizon, stretching its fading rays into the sky, dyeing it a fiery tangerine pink. To Wes's right, the ocean echoes its evening lullaby. Crashing waves sing like a choir. A warm breeze carries the tune all the way to the boardwalk where a carnival of musicians and joggers and peddlers create a flotilla Wes navigates through.

He's halfway to Muscle Beach with no destination in mind. Leo lives nearby, in an apartment tucked into a quiet neighborhood. Wes contemplated stopping by. It's the considerate thing to do, right? But Leeann's at work, and that means it'd just be Wes and Leo and the television doing all the talking for them. *No thanks.* Plus, Wes's already seeing Leeann tomorrow for dress shopping. She bribed him with Mexican food and smoothies, not that Wes required the extra incentive. He loves Leeann-time, especially when it doesn't include his brother.

Wes roams the boardwalk with one earbud in and his phone pouring out the perfect soundtrack of mellow guitars and introspective lyrics—Red Hot Chili Peppers' anthemic *Californication*. 1999 isn't his favorite year in music, but this is one gem he can appreciate.

His mind is on a constant loop of, "How can I save Once Upon a Page?" and he needs a way to escape the deluge.

Left and right, people on bikes and skateboards maneuver around him as he strolls. He glances at his phone. He responded to Leo's text with a thumbs-up emoji an hour ago. Wes still doesn't know how to reply to his dad.

Thanks?

Okay.

Do they offer a Can't Figure Out How to Talk to My Parents About My Future course, and what are the prerequisites?

Wes locks his phone. In times like this, maybe not responding is the best response? Avoiding things has worked out for him so far. Kind of.

"Springsteen, anyone?"

In the sea of artists selling original works and activists shouting about a better future, a white man stands hugging a beat-up acoustic guitar. A beanie sits lopsided on top of his wild hair. Smears of dirt cross his cheeks and forehead. Friendly blue eyes look out on the decent-sized audience he's acquired. In a throaty voice, he says, "Any requests?"

Wes pauses to watch.

Songs are shouted from everywhere, but one clear voice yells, "What about 'I'm on Fire'?"

The man adjusts his guitar. His faded green army jacket nearly swallows his thin frame as it flaps with the breeze. "I knew you were a good group." His warm smile is minus a few teeth, but that only makes Wes want to shuffle closer.

It's a slow, moody song. The man's voice is hypnotic. Every lyric comes with a deepness that says he's fought too many wars. He's lost more than he's won.

Wes doesn't know much about Springsteen except that, when Calvin maneuvered through the kitchen, singing while working through new recipes to roll out at the restaurant, his phone always rested on the counter, playing Springsteen. Wes loved hiding around the corner, listening as Calvin tried to imitate Bruce's growl about being born to run. He loved the smell of herbs and the sizzle of oil and the music.

As the man's broken voice hits a peak, Wes's heart *thump-thumps* to the melody. It's the magic of Venice. Every night's a free show. Everyone walks around here with their issues on display like an exhibit. It's a gallery of scars.

Out of tune but willing, the crowd joins the man on the chorus. Wes does too, only softer. Something clogs his throat. He doesn't want to overanalyze it.

After dropping five dollars in the basket at the man's feet, Wes follows the progression of the crowd down the boardwalk. On his phone, "Scar Tissue" kicks in with its dulcet guitar riff. He walks along the bike path toward rock walls decorated in colorful graffiti. Sand dirties his lemon-yellow Pumas as he treads to the oceanfront skate park.

Venice Skatepark is this legendary structure built on the sand with two shallow bowls, one for amateurs and one for the fearless, along with rails, stairs, and platforms where skaters test new tricks. The ledge surrounding the main bowl is always crowded with burnouts and slackers and friends. Inside the bowl, people glide and wipe out equally.

Wes finds prime space near the railings. Phones are out everywhere, capturing the best tricks and epic fails. Too scared to scuff up their equipment, kids with new boards and shoes bullshit around the edges. But the homegrown, adrenaline-hungry talent swoop in, merciless, willing to risk more damage to their boards or scars on their bodies to impress anyone watching. These are the ones without any money or any fucks to give.

One boy, long and lean, with a mop of curly blond hair, hits a sick kickflip, then rockets into the bowl with enough force to soar his board over a parked bicycle on the other side. He lands perfectly.

The fans erupt.

"Sweet pink boxers, Colton!" yells a guy from Wes's side.

Colton, lip-piercing glinting, flips his friend off. He tugs down his T-shirt in a losing effort with his sagging jeans.

Another boy, Latinx with a buzzcut, his clean board exposing his inexperience, drops in, then instantly wipes out.

"Holy shit."

"Wow. That just happened."

Nearby, a pack of girls in flannel shirts with cigarettes and sneers, and whisper to each other. One of them yells, "Come on, Juan! You got this."

Juan, dusting himself off as he stands, smiles through defeat. But he grabs his board, climbs the bowl, and goes again. Wes respects his moxie. He didn't lie down and give up. Wes, on the other hand, would've still been down there, waiting for an ambulance or Nico to rescue him.

Unlike Wes and all these rookies who stole their moves from YouTube videos, Nico's a natural on a board. Sure-footed and brave, he's more than earned the respect of everyone around here, from the newest to the crews that have grown older but no less ambitious about their craft. There are a few jealous, racist assholes who call Nico "basic Mexican trash," but he's above feeding their ignorance. He just carries on the way Mr. Alvarez taught him to.

"Call me Martín," Mr. Alvarez would insist in his kind voice.

Wes never could. It's weird because Wes has exactly zero problems calling his mom Savannah in public.

"Sure thing, Mr. Alvarez," Wes would always say as Mr. Alvarez laughed.

He misses Mr. Alvarez's laugh, nasal and high like Nico's. Nico has his dad's strong jaw and narrow shoulders too.

It's been almost three years since his death. He'd always walk into a room smelling of weird chemicals that made Wes want to gag. He'd kiss Mrs. Alvarez on the temple and whisper something in Spanish, and she'd always warn him to wash his hands before going to pick up one of Nico's twin sisters. It was a joke. Mr. Alvarez was the most hygienic person Wes's ever known.

"I don't get it," whispered Nico two nights after his father died. "He was so careful. So clean. It's unreal, dude. Like… how?"

Wes still doesn't know. No one sat him down and explained what happened in the laboratory that morning. Nico never talks about it. "Freak accident," Leo muttered over breakfast one morning while their parents whispered in the hallway.

Wes remembers sleeping on Nico's bedroom floor for a week after the funeral. Not because Nico asked him to. Wes just needed to be close, fingertips away from his best friend. It felt as if he couldn't do anything else to help Nico.

There's no manual for how to help someone you love deal with death and grief, at least none that Wes has found.

It's messy. It's lonely. It's gone today, then back tomorrow. No amount of hugs and prayers and "are you okay?" fixes grief. To be honest, Wes doesn't think grief is something to be "fixed" or "get over." It's there for a reason.

A short burst of wind descends upon the skatepark. Wes is wearing his dad's old, blue UCLA hoodie. He tugs the zipper higher, then shoves his hands into the front pockets. He pries himself away from the carnage of two more skaters wiping out on the smooth bottom of the bowl.

The Strand, a bike trail that runs along the shoreline, is lit marigold by the industrial lights towering higher than the palms. Wes follows the path toward Santa Monica. On his left, a group of college-aged kids spread blankets across the beach. The flashlights on their phones move like dancing stars as they search through coolers.

In a year, maybe that'll be Wes? Coming home on the weekends with Ella to spend a day at the beach after they visit Mrs. Rossi and the bookstore. Because, in a year, the bookstore will still be around. Maybe he can coordinate those trips with Nico's planned bimonthly visits to his family.

Someone's Labrador is parked on the edge of the sand with its tail wagging.

Wes pauses. He tugs out his phone and unlocks the screen. It takes him a few tries, but he manages to capture at least three high-quality photos that show the juxtaposition of the dog's gold fur against the black ocean.

He texts all three versions to Nico.

Instantly, his phone buzzes. Two new messages. Unfortunately, they're from Cooper.

He's about to pocket his phone when it vibrates in his palm.

It's a Pinterest photo from Nico.

Against a plain black background with bold white text, the image says, *"If you can't stop thinking about it, don't stop working for it."*

What does that mean? Is Nico referring to saving the bookstore? Or is he talking about something else?

To: Nico
??? 😐
Sent 8:41 p.m.

Nico's gray text bubble fills with ellipses. Then it disappears.

Wes has no clue, and no time to decode Nico's weirdness. But his phone emits a *doo doo-doo-doot* noise and the screen lights up. Obviously, discussions of the Pinterest kind need to be held over FaceTime.

But, when Wes finally answers, it's not Nico's face on the screen. It's an upside-down view of a pair of tiny nostrils. Breath fogs the lens before things go sideways. Images blur across the screen like one of those documentary-style horror movies. All the shaky visuals make Wes want to hurl. He hears giggles and bare feet padding on hardwood floors.

"Hey! Sofía!" Wes can hear Nico's frustrated voice as the screen finally pauses on a giant Lego castle erected on a glass coffee table. "¡Tranquila!"

After a little maneuvering and more laughter, Nico pops into the screen's view. "Wesley," he says too fondly. "Perdóname."

"Having fun?"

Nico puckers his lips. "I turned my back for two seconds, and Sofía convinced the twins to finish my orange soda. They're on a mad sugar high right before dinner."

"Wes! Wes!" He can hear the twins' matching pitchy voices, but they're out of frame. "Come over!"

Nico groans, head tipped back. Now Wes has a view up his nostrils. They flare, then shrink to normal size as Nico says, "Your fans have been asking about you since I got home."

Expeditious amounts of heat surge into Wes's cheeks. His mouth is stretched wider than the Pacific.

Deep wrinkles shrink Nico's eyes as he says, "Wanna come by? Mom's making gorditas."

You little shit.

In the annals of their history, Sundays at the Alvarez house were Wes's favorite. They'd catch the Big Blue Bus from Santa Monica to UCLA, walk the campus and dick around Westwood for a few hours, pretending to be college students with goals, before coming home to Mrs. Alvarez's freshly fried gorditas.

"¡Gordita de chicharrón!" Wes loved the way Nico would shout whenever they walked back into his house, sun-warm and exhausted.

Some Sundays, they'd skip the Big Blue Bus for beach time with Sofía and the twins, Isabel and Camila. They'd build structures almost as tall as the Lego tower on the Alvarez's coffee table. The twins would always bring their Barbies to live in the sandcastle.

"It's a *fortress*," Nico would clarify. "It's to protect them from the invaders, Wesley, because aliens are obsessed with anything created by Mattel."

After dinner, Mr. Alvarez would lead them all into the living room, Wes included, for all his favorite, age-appropriate sci-fi movies. Nico would burrow into Wes's side, one of the twins would sleep across their laps, and they'd crack quiet jokes about the cheap special effects or corny acting throughout the film.

When Mr. Alvarez died, Sunday dinners became rarer. They stopped visiting UCLA too. By senior year, Nico decided Stanford was the college for him.

"They have a highly ranked medical school."

Nico didn't have to tell Wes the reason he wanted to study medicine was because of his father. Because, for whatever reason, he thought becoming a doctor meant he could save others from Mr. Alvarez's fate.

"Wesley?"

Wes jumps. In the small square at the bottom corner of the screen, his eyes are cartoonishly big and his mouth is wide enough to drive a SUV through.

"You okay?"

No. Wes's been so zoned out, he's walked for five minutes in the wrong direction. *Shit.* His stomach growls like a starved tiger.

"Do you want to come over?" Nico asks again. He's shifted to somewhere quieter. Wes can just make out the navy and white stripes on Nico's pillowcase and the nose of the skateboard deck from their infamous bloody-eyebrow incident. He recognizes the colorful calavera design.

Wes really wants to be there inside the Alvarez's beach house, but he knows he can't. Not tonight. His head's in a messed-up dark hole. He can't risk ruining all his plans to tell Nico about his nuclear-sized crush on him because of a dinner invitation. BuzzFeed's *Crushes 101* quiz doesn't exist for him to scrap his list over gorditas and orange soda.

"Rain check?" Wes requests. "Totally forgot to do laundry today."

"No clean underoos?"

Wes pulls his phone back enough for the lens to capture him flipping Nico off.

"You'll disappoint your fans."

"I'll make it up to them," Wes promises.

"And me?"

Wes is almost certain it's wishful thinking that makes him hear the hope in Nico's voice. It's not there. He sucks in a breath, then says, "Of course."

Nico mumbles something quietly in Spanish, then their video feed fuzzes out. Wes has just enough willpower to pocket his phone and not call Nico back. This isn't the Big Moment.

"Tomorrow," Wes says to the sky.

"Tomorrow's not promised," a dark-skinned Black girl with pink and purple braids sings as she passes him.

And Wes is about to reply with a very Ella-worthy sarcastic barb, but he turns the wrong way and face-plants into the sand, as one does.

CHAPTER TWELVE

"WHAT ABOUT THIS ONE?"

In the full-length mirror, Leeann turns and turns. Her bare feet sink into the cream-colored shaggy rug. The bridal salon's dressing area is separated from the main floor by French doors. A long white sofa sits against one of the powder blue walls opposite the mirror. It's currently occupied by two girls on their phones, typing away and occasionally snapping photos of Leeann as she shows off another dress.

This current selection, a ball gown with a sweetheart neckline, beaded bodice, and flowing white skirt, is number four. The other three hang ignominiously on hooks near the closed doors.

Wes slouches deeper into one of the comfy armchairs a few feet away. Head tilted, he examines Leeann as she spins; the skirt flutters like a cloud. Before he can respond, Tiffany says, "It's... cute."

"Cute?" Leeann's mouth droops.

"Very cute," Tiffany amends in the least convincing voice Wes's heard all morning.

Tiffany is Leeann's former college roommate. She has voluminous, soft-looking curls and wide, engaging, brown eyes. Wes supposes, as a bridesmaid, Tiffany's obligated to be sensitive of Leeann's dress choices as she hasn't uttered a single "I hate it" since they started browsing for potential gowns two hours ago.

"It's kind of boring. Very TLC-friendly." Grace Chen, Leeann's older sister, has zero problems voicing her opinions. Her auburn-tinted dark hair is swooped into a clean ponytail, amplifying the sharpness of her cheeks and the arch of her thin eyebrow. She's taller than Leeann and, even seated, she's all legs and arms and neck.

"That's not a bad thing," says Leeann, still frowning in the mirror.

"Maybe we can do less cute and more HBO After Dark," Grace suggests. "It's your wedding, baby sister. Be glamorous and bold."

"Thanks for your honesty," Leeann mutters.

"That's what I'm here for," says Grace, eyes glued to her phone again.

"Don't listen to her," Tiffany insists. "It's a good dress."

Grace sighs. "I hope we're not settling for 'good' now."

Quietly, Wes snorts. This unintentional sitcom has been thoroughly entertaining.

"Wes?" Eyebrows raised, Leeann looks at him in the mirror. She has the same cheeks as her sister, but Leeann's eyes are softer and seem effortlessly friendly when they're focused on someone. "What do you think?"

Wes shouldn't be surprised by Leeann's inquiry—this is not the first time today his opinion has been requested—but he can sense Tiffany's curious stare and Grace's judging one pin him to the chair. He's certainly not an authority on wedding dresses. More than once, he's had to Google things like "A-line" and "Basque" and "Who the hell is Queen Anne?" His own wardrobe doesn't extend past sweatpants, hoodies, and graphic T-shirts. He wears shoes for *comfort*, not attention. But this is important to Leeann, so he's attempting to be thoughtful and constructive with his views.

"Uh…?"

Okay, attempting *might've been an embellishment.*

In the mirror, Grace sizes Wes up. "Are we sure we want…" She peeks down at Wes's electric blue Pumas. "…*his* opinion?"

Her phone case is bedazzled in pink jewels outlining a Hello Kitty. He doesn't think she has room to discuss opinion levels.

The corners of Leeann's mouth quirk, showing off twin dimples. Her shoulder-length hair is twisted up in a messy bun so she can access the dress's neckline and how her bare shoulders look. "Yes," she finally says, raising an eyebrow that matches her sister's. "That's my brother — your future brother too—and his kickass thoughts matter the most."

A flush burns Wes's cheeks.

"O-kay," mumbles Grace.

"I think..." Wes pauses, rubbing the back of his neck. He considers Leeann's reflection. "It's not over the top. It's not unnecessary and, what did you call it? HBO After Dark?" Wes pointedly waits until Grace scowls before continuing. "Because that's not you. It's kind of a princess vibe, but definitely the princess who has no problem stepping up and ruling the kingdom and ending anyone who challenges her."

Leeann chortles. Soft, loose pieces of hair escape the bun and fall around her cheeks. She's wearing minimal makeup, and everything about her is a dream. That's probably the magic of precisely chosen store lighting and object spacing. Wes is certain Jessica, Leeann's personal dress attendant, sells everyone a new dress and a share of whatever pyramid scheme she's pushing with this kind of lighting.

"Thanks," whispers Leeann.

"As future maid of honor, I hope you'll at least listen to me when we go veil shopping," Grace says with a huff.

"Girl, bye. There's no way you're maid of honor over me." Tiffany puckers her lips.

"I'm her *sister*."

"I'm her best friend and the one who introduced her to Leo."

Hand over her eyes, Leeann groans as they squabble. Wes doesn't envy her at all.

Sneakily, he snaps a few photos of her in the dress. He doesn't plan to show Leo—that would require some form of communication—but maybe he'll text them to Savannah. Then, he swipes away all his notifications except one. Nico's updated his Instagram with a new post. It's from a few hours ago; a shot of the morning sun still kissing the ocean's surface. Pinkish blue skies float above the darkened silhouettes of palm trees. Wes recognizes that view without peeking at the tags.

"Have you two decided on a date yet?" Tiffany asks. She stands behind Leeann, helping fix the dress's tangled skirt.

"Not an exact date, but a month." Leeann puffs out a breath to get hair out of her eyes. "May of next year."

"May? A little cliché, don't you think?" Grace says, tapping away at her phone.

"Nope," Leeann replies cheerily, as if she's grown accustomed to fending off her sister's judgment. Wes should study her tact, then use it to vanquish Leo. "We didn't want to do something too soon. Leo's getting ready for the LSAT. Then he's starting law school." She brushes invisible lint from the bodice. "Plus, Wes starts UCLA in the fall. We wanted to give him a chance to adjust to campus life."

Wes sits up, stunned. They picked a wedding month partially set around him? It's a kind gesture—and something completely unexpected coming from his brother—but... Wes doesn't know if their life choices should be based around his very uncertain future.

"Whatever you want," Grace says, as if she's opposed to *everything* Leeann wants. She stands, elbowing Tiffany as she passes. "Come on. Let's go shop for possible maid of honor dresses."

"For me, right?" Tiffany grabs her purse.

"Sure thing, sweetie," Grace replies tightly.

Leeann saunters over to the armchairs. She carefully sits on the edge of the empty one and presses down the tulle skirt.

Tulle. Another word Wes had no definition for before today.

Leeann bends toward him. "We're thinking of asking your dad to help with the catering," she whispers, as if it's not just the two of them in the room now.

"Dad would love that." A small, weird lump crawls into Wes's throat.

His parents have never chosen favorites. But there are days when Wes's mind plays this wicked game with him. He was born at an odd time for his parents. His dad was opening his first restaurant on a negative bank account and a giant hope. His mom's first book was being published. And along came Wes, interrupting the chaotic flow they were living in.

Leo established his independence at a young age. But Wes still hasn't. Maybe that's why his parents butt in even when he doesn't ask them to. Maybe that's why his dad suggests possible majors and his mom deposits extra money into his bank account without him asking for any of it. He feels like a *child*, but maybe they do it because he's never shown them he could be an adult.

Leeann's small hand covers his on the chair's arm. "Leo hasn't picked a best man yet."

"Does he even have any friends?"

"Yes." Leeann giggles. "He has a lot of friends." When Wes puckers his lips, she adds, "Okay, a handful. Like three. Including me."

"Shouldn't be hard then."

Leeann squints at him, nose wrinkled. "Wes."

"What?"

"I think he wants you to—"

"Yeah, no," Wes interrupts her. "He doesn't want me as his—"

Leeann holds up a finger. "Leo's stubborn and petty and an awful loser."

"Are you reciting your vows? Because I think you nailed it."

Leeann rolls her pale brown eyes. "What I'm saying is, he's difficult, but he loves you."

"You have a pretty interesting definition of love."

"I do!" Leeann's hand slides away from his to cover her snort-giggle. "But I have to! I'm marrying a Hudson, *duh*."

"Good point."

Leeann wipes at her eyes, then shakes out her hands. She struggles to maintain a serious expression as she stares at him. "Consider it, please."

Being Leo's best man would be… Wes shudders. One, it'd be against all Wes's principles. Two, Leo would be even more annoying. His parents would be delighted, and Wes certainly enjoys seeing Leeann happy, but it's Leo.

"Fine. If he asks," Wes's lips go numb, but he manages to stammer, "I will."

"He *will*." Leeann's confidence is shatterproof. Wes learned a long time ago not to bet against her, but that was because she kicked his ass in a marathon of Monopoly that stretched through three days and two different locations. She's ruthless about two things: board games and Leo Hudson.

"Now," Leeann reaches forward, patting Wes's curls, "I have one more dress to try on…"

Wes groans.

"… then I promised you Mexican food and smoothies."

"Sounds rad." Wes checks his phone. Three hours until his shift starts. "Can we be quick? Not that I don't love spending time with you and all of this." He twirls his index finger around the room. "I have to meet someone before work."

"A boy?"

"None of your business," Wes counters, voice cracking.

"Could it possibly be a very single, extremely funny, stupidly handsome boy that you've known forever?" Leeann teases.

Wes inhales, but doesn't reply. It's official: His future sister-in-law has topped Mr. X-Files.

THE FIRST TIME WES CAME out was a complete accident.

Being sixteen on a Thursday evening in the summer meant Wes and Nico had three options: video games, going to a movie, or staying in to stuff their pieholes with pizza while watching Netflix films about being a sixteen-year-old in the summer. Wes voted option two. Nico hopped on Wes's laptop to Google start times. But, per usual, Wes forgot to close out a few of his last tabs. It wasn't porn, thankfully. He'd been researching LGBTQIA+ youth support groups in the area because, yeah, Wes *planned* on coming out.

But not at that moment. Not on the green sofa with a bag of spicy cheese puffs between them and Leo FaceTiming his girlfriend down the hall.

There it was. A Google listing of nearby support groups for queer youth. On the screen, in a smaller window, was Wes's newest list:

The Five Best Ways to Come Out!

Nico peeked at Wes through his eyelashes. Wes didn't breathe for a solid minute. The articles and the few movies he'd watched in the dark when everyone else was asleep warned Wes that coming out was a big deal. It didn't matter if it was planned or came up unexpectedly in a conversation. They also warned Wes that, no matter what, he'd always be coming out. It never happens just once. But most of the webpages promised, when the time was right, it'd be worth it.

So, he finally said it: "I'm gay."

He didn't cry—not immediately. He also didn't look Nico in the eyes when he said it.

Nico's response?

He plucked the bag of cheese puffs from between them, scooted closer, and then curled both arms around Wes. Even at sixteen, Wes was substantially taller and wider than Nico, but he felt so small in those arms. He buried his face in Nico's shoulder. The dry kiss Nico pressed to his forehead did trigger tears. But Wes was okay with that.

"Thank you, Wes," Nico whispered into his curls.

Wes can't remember what he mumbled back as his tears soaked Nico's T-shirt.

He remembers the street tacos Nico bought them on the way to the cinema. He remembers Nico clumsily dancing around questions during movie trailers. He remembers Nico's warm fingers squeezing his sweaty palm when Wes stumbled through the answers.

Most of all, Wes remembers those three words— "Thank you, Wes"—sounding a lot like, "I love you," when he truly needed it.

WHEN IT COMES TO ADJECTIVES that describe himself, *smooth* is a stretch for Wes.

Stealth. Incognito. Wes loves that word. For the little time he's been here, he's managed to blend in with the crowd surrounding Venice Skatepark. No one's noticed him, not that Wes is a big deal here. He's just some curly-haired biracial kid in a swelling group of people from different racial backgrounds and ages and bad hairstyles watching the local crews hit tricks, nail ollies, and sail over props as if it's any other day.

His hands are clammy. He's sweating as though he's the one risking permanent spine damage. And he's rehearsed what he's going to say so frequently that it's become *forced*.

"Wes? Are you, like, hiding?"

And there goes "incognito," devoured like fresh, bloody limbs in shark-infested waters.

Wes blinks hard against the bright sun haloing over the skatepark. Next to him, Autumn lifts both eyebrows. She's a kickass skater girl with a sick dragon tattoo snaking up one arm, straight penny-brown hair that hangs down her back, and a labret piercing. Her usually pale white skin is sunburnt. Wes maintains that she's hella cool despite totally blowing his cover.

"I'm not hiding," he hisses.

Autumn's arms are propped against the railing surrounding the main bowl. "You sure?"

"Positive." Wes *isn't* hiding. He's being covert. There's a theoretical difference. "I'm chilling."

"Oh, is that what we're calling it?"

"Yup." Wes turns back to the action.

"He's getting good air today," Autumn comments.

"Who?"

In his peripheral vision, Wes can see the *cut your bullshit* sideways glare Autumn gives him. All around the main bowl, phones are all trained on one skater. The sun is high, beating down on them. Wes cups a hand over his brow to get a better view. Effortlessly, the skater hits a flip lipside. He drops back in for a frontside air. Then, just to show off, he nails a heelflip.

The audience roars.

Behind his ribs, Wes's heart rumbles like the center of a thunderstorm. It repeats one word in its cage: *Nico. Nico. Nico.*

"He's been here for hours," Autumn adds.

Wes knows. The Instagram photo was his giveaway.

"Ugh. I hate him," Autumn says with no heat behind her voice. "He makes the rest of us look like such posers."

"Nah," Wes says, only half serious. Unintentionally, Nico does make the rest of these goons look pathetic. But he can't help that he's gifted. And being skilled at anything shouldn't be hidden away. No one should lessen who they are for anyone. That's how the world stays balanced—everyone has at least one gift and at least one flaw.

"It's all good," says Autumn. She tugs down the brim of her snapback before flipping her own board up. On the underside, it's decorated in skulls with a Sailor Moon sticker slapped in the center. "One day, I'm gonna show all these dudes up."

Wes watches her hop the rail, dropping in for her own round of applause. She's not lying. One day, Autumn's going to be famous.

On the opposite side of the bowl, Nico goofs around, hitting lazy tricks while chatting with the other skaters. His green board shorts contrast nicely with his denim shirt. The shirt's first four buttons are undone.

Absently, Wes licks his lips, which, of course, is when another skater yells, "Yo, Alvarez! Yo' *boy* is here!"

Trey, with his cornrows and arms inked in fading tattoos, shoots Wes a slick smile. Wes squints back. He hopes the implied *you're a dick* in his glare is well-received.

"Wesley," Nico says, breathless after he crosses the bowl, board in one hand, the other stretched to ruffle Wes's curls. Nico's not wearing glasses today, only clear contacts that lighten his irises to a nice shade of copper. "I've got this vibe today."

Wes does too. *Today's the day.* He's already decided on which of his date ideas he's going with—the beach one.

Nico's extra bouncy as he sidles up to Wes. "I'm just… I'm vibin.'"

"Maybe you're high?"

"High on life." Nico exhales slowly. "And this."

"This?"

Nico shrugs, refusing to explain.

They lean against the railing together. Their bare forearms brush as they breathe. Wes watches Nico staring at the swaying palm trees in the distance. The words bubble up, but he swallows them down with a wince.

Not yet.

He wants to wait until there are fewer distractions.

Across the bowl, a guy with wavy blond hair and owlish brown eyes steals glances at Nico. He's got that classic Californian glow, with a scattering of freckles and moles across his nose and long neck. It's Colton.

"Looks like someone's digging your vibe." Wes knows he's breaking all kinds of crushing-on-your-best-friend rules. But he can't shut his mouth.

Colton doesn't try to hide it. He nods his chin upward in that *what's up* motion.

Nico shrugs nonchalantly. "I noticed."

Wes cranes his neck. "And?" What the hell is wrong with him? This is where Wes should be executing his plan. Why is he trying to encourage this instead? Nico clearly isn't reciprocating Colton's weak flirting. He's too busy studying the other skaters hit their aerials and ollies.

"So…?" Wes exhales softly.

"He's cool, I guess." Nico shrugs again. "We've hung out."

"You have?"

"Yeah."

Something cold and uncomfortable moves through Wes's chest. In his back pocket, his phone is heavy. It taunts him with the list he created in Once Upon a Page's bathroom:

Signs Your Crush Isn't Into You!!!

2. If your crush shows signs of being into someone else, ABORT!

"I'm not really into playing games though," Nico adds. "I want more than a trip to In-N-Out Burger and a little hand action in the back of his mom's minivan."

"Oh." Wes's shoulders loosen. *Wrong again, Reddit.* But his mind shifts into a new thought. "So, you've..." Why are his cheeks so hot at the prospect of using the word sex with Nico? He clears his throat. "Is Colton, like, the only one you've done *stuff* with?"

"No." Nico's eyebrows droop. "Two others before him. It was all pretty low-key."

"So not, like." The golf ball-sized lump in Wes's throat expands. "All the way stuff."

Nico tips his head back, laughing.

Wes fakes a laugh too.

"Nah. Nothing like that," says Nico, still chuckling.

"Cool, cool."

Nico stares at Wes for a long moment with scrunched eyes. "Want me to walk with you to the bookstore for your shift?"

"That'd be nice."

Nico shouts farewells to most of the skaters. He waves at Colton, something Wes wishes he didn't notice, but then Nico's arm drapes around Wes's shoulders as they walk through the sand toward The Strand.

Once they've cleared most of Venice, Nico drops his board and hops on. He rolls slowly next to Wes, only kick-pushing every few feet. Comfortable silence floats between them. The sun is against their backs; the waves crash and sing to their left.

"I've been thinking of some cool ideas for the bookstore," Nico says once they're closer to Santa Monica.

"Yeah?" Wes tries not to sound too eager. "Are you gonna share?"

"Nope. Waiting to hear everyone else's ideas first."

"Just in case yours are inferior?"

Nico gasps, taking offense, before flipping Wes off. A nice sheen of sweat shines on his brow. Wind catches under his shirt and billows it outward.

"Nice shirt," Wes comments.

"Ha. Better than the one I wore to prom?"

Wes grins sheepishly.

"Do you remember that night?"

Wes will never forget anything about prom. Not a single detail.

The second time Wes came out, it was voluntary. It was all thanks to Nico's undeniable persuasion.

They didn't go to junior prom. Nico's mom caught the flu, so they chose to crash on his couch with Nico's sisters for movies, orange soda, and cheese on crackers. Senior prom was a big deal to Nico. Wes, on the other hand, didn't feel as though he'd miss much if they skipped it again. He had zero interest in poorly posed photos in rented tuxes. He hates dancing to generic rock ballads or hip-hop songs that require profuse amounts of dry humping. And there weren't many out guys at their school. If they were out, they had older partners or straight friends who wanted to be their dates.

Nico glides down the boardwalk. He's coordinated enough to skate and grin cockily at Wes. "Admit it—I killed that promposal."

He did. Not at any point, in any world did Wes think Nico would ask *him* to be his prom date. At first, Wes thought it was a cruel joke.

Three weeks before prom, in the middle of the senior hallway, most of Santa Monica High's marching band came stomping through before the start of homeroom. They were performing, of all songs, Jason Mraz's sickeningly sweet "I'm Yours." And there was Nico in a white T-shirt with Wes's fifth-grade class photo on it, in front of the band, holding five shiny gold mylar balloons spelling: P-R-O-M-?

It was mortifying and hysterical and every level of epic.

"Your family was really cool about you coming out," Nico continues.

"My dad baked a cake with rainbow sprinkles!" But that wasn't as bad as Savannah crying for a solid ten minutes after Wes came out. He knows he didn't have to. He could've easily gone to prom with Nico as friends. They *did* go as friends, but Wes knew it was time. Nico had built this bridge that finally allowed Wes to meet his family in the middle.

"Leo's reaction was the best," Nico reminds him.

"Because everybody wants to come out to their older brother and get a punch in the shoulder as a welcome."

Nico almost falls off his board laughing.

Wes pulls at his earlobe. "You looked great that night."

"Really?"

"Really."

Wes's has never said it, but standing in his pre-cranberry-juice-stained tux next to Nico, who looked like a twenty-first century Richie Valens with his white jacket, blood red tuxedo shirt, and a few locks of curly hair falling from his perfectly styled pompadour, was major.

"Ugh." Nico scrunches his face. "But Chainsmokers, man."

"Chainsmokers," Wes repeats, groaning.

When the DJ called for the last dance, Nico took Wes's hand, spun him around and then they shuffled under the spotlight to a forgettable Chainsmokers song.

It never seemed to bother Nico that, shortly after prom, students thought he was gay too. Those rumors quickly died when Nico kissed Tabby Gomez at a graduation party, but still. He never let the jokes embarrass him. It was as if he'd been happy to be called Wes's boyfriend.

Wes likes to hold on to that delusional dream.

They're less than a mile from Once Upon a Page when Nico says, "¡Tienes una sonrisa muy bonita!"

After all these years around the Alvarez family, Wes's Spanish is still very limited. He has no clue what Nico said, but he loves the way Nico looks at him afterward.

A shrill beep rings from Wes's back pocket. He tugs out his phone. His alarm is going off with a reminder: TELL HIM!!!

Wes hesitates. This isn't the ideal setting BuzzFeed advised him about. He's sticky with sweat and not wearing his lucky T-shirt. *Teen Vogue* would be disappointed that Wes hasn't organized a flash mob or at least a marching band to accompany him but that's fine.

He just needs to do it.

Wes just needs to...

"Watch your step, Wesley!"

On cue, Wes trips on a crack in the pavement and repeats his epic face-plant from last night. In the distance, he can hear Nico cracking up.

Obviously, today's *not* the day.

CHAPTER THIRTEEN 🛹

WES DOESN'T CARE HOW ANYBODY spins it: Physical Education sucked. Four mandatory semesters of sweat and team building activities like dodgeball just to graduate? Hell no.

But there was one positive to his gym experience: long-distance running. He was freaking boss at that.

Running always gave him a clear head.

Ella's still snoring in Leo's bedroom when Wes slips on a pair of red Pumas. He tugs on a loose tank top with palm tree designs on it, and an old pair of Santa Monica High gym shorts. Earbuds in, Wes jogs down Ocean Avenue.

He takes off with no destination in mind.

After two hours, he ends up at Tongva Park. He stops to stretch his legs on a wooden bench. He hasn't gone on a run since graduation. His calves burn, but he feels good.

The sun's a gold gem in the center of a clear blue sky. Wes inches over until he's under the shade of a curved palm tree. The giant leaves spread above him like a green roof. He pulls out his phone to check the time. 1:37 p.m. Less than a half hour until his shift at the bookstore starts.

Leaning over, elbows on his knees, Wes pulls up his notes app. He needs to double-check his ideas before he meets with the others today. He scrolls past all his other lists but pauses over an unfinished one.

His heart lurches; his breath stalls.

Wes & Nico's Ultimate Guide to UCLA Greatness

1. Catch the Big Blue Bus until Nico gets a car. Get a license, Wes!!!

2. Visit Los Angeles County Museum of Art. Take selfies in front of Urban Light like a true basic tourist.

3. Eat @ Fat Sal's deli!

4. Study at Espresso Profeta. Learn to like coffee—all the cool college kids drink ICED COFFEE!

5. Ice cream sandwiches @ Diddy Riese.

6. UCLA Planetarium. Kiss Nico under the stars!

Wes blinks away the sting in his eyes. There it is. The plan he made sophomore year just before Nico's life went into a tailspin.

Why do I still have this?

His thumb hovers over the delete option. It's a pipedream now. But Wes closes the list, keeps it tucked in his phone's memory like a hope.

Today is about Once Upon a Page. He refuses to let some cheap Starbucks knockoff come into his territory and take over. There's no way he's letting his comic book sanctuary be demolished and turned into a bar where someone can order fifty different versions of the same damn latte. No one's writing their amateur bestseller in the same spot where Cooper reads crappy novels. Freshmen will not invade his space to sip Frappuccinos and compare selfies.

He'll deal with his other issues later.

By the time Wes has reviewed his list to save the bookstore, it's 2:09 p.m. He's late for his shift, but at least the tightness in his chest has loosened. Besides, it's only a two-minute walk from here to Once Upon a Page. He pockets his phone, reties his shoes, and stands. His eyes scan all the places the sun touches—the batches of mountain aloe nearby, the pebble pathways that wind all around the park, monster palm trees reaching green hands into the sky.

Today's too pretty to waste. I'm already late. Might as well enjoy it.

With a quick stretch of his hamstrings, Wes jogs in the direction opposite from the bookstore.

"YOU'RE LATE," ANNOUNCES ELLA BEFORE Wes has one crimson-sneakered foot through the open doorway.

The irony of Ella Louise Graham, notorious tardy employee, calling him out isn't lost on Wes. But he ignores her.

"A book drive," he says, strolling into the partly vacant bookstore. Most of the city's population is clogging Third Street Promenade, as he observed while stopping by a smoothie shop nearby. Lateness might as well come with a banana-orange-strawberry-peanut butter concoction.

Ella, dressed in a sleeveless Debbie Harry T-shirt and black tights, sizes him up. "Nice legs."

Mrs. Rossi has never implemented a strict dress code, so Wes didn't bother changing between his jog and showing up at the bookstore.

"A book drive; that's my first idea to save this place," he says, turning away from Ella.

Ella pops her gum. "Weak, but not terrible."

Anna leans against the front counter; her hair is spun into a braid-bun hybrid. "What's that?"

"We'll head down to the pier and boardwalk with some stock." Wes crosses around the counter and flops onto his favorite stool. "We can hand out flyers and discount codes. Sell some of the more popular books."

"I think we'll need permits to sell the books out there, though," Zay notes from the carpet. He's surrounded by a pile of books. Wes can see formulas and numbers and, nope, he doesn't want any piece of that.

"We can do that." Wes unlocks his phone with one hand while slurping his smoothie. "It can't be that hard."

"I'm pretty sure an adult's signature is required," Zay remarks.

"Cool. I'm eighteen," Wes starts, but Ella cuts him off.

"Eighteen does not equate adultness. It's only a marker used to enforce rules, not mental maturity."

"Maybe you could ask Leo for assistance?" Nico appears from between the aisles, stepping around Zay before sitting next to Wes. "He could help with a lot of this."

"Yeah," mumbles Wes, but contacting Leo is the last thing on his mind. "Has anyone else come up with ideas?"

Cooper hops onto the counter next to Ella. Surprisingly, she doesn't explode. But her dark, cold glare says she's considering it. "An author appearance," he says, hands spread above his head as if he's highlighting some invisible marquee. "People love the chance to meet anyone famous."

Wes nods. Los Angeles is full of notorious names. Mrs. Rossi used to host book launches and writers' clubs and author signings before Wes came along. Back when she had a little more pull. Now, the only bestselling author popping in is Savannah Kirk.

"Who do we know?" Zay asks, confused. "Besides Wes's mom. No offense, bro."

Wes shrugs as if it's nothing. But it's true. Savannah Kirk isn't due home from Italy until late August. They need immediate star power.

"I'll find someone," Cooper vows.

"Cool," Wes says, adding another item to his list. "What else?"

"We could host a kids' book corner," Nico suggests. The warm pressure of their elbows pressed together is a mild distraction for Wes. He stares at his phone while trying to focus on Nico's voice. "Once or twice a week, we could host a book reading. Parents are always looking for ways to entertain their children. Plus, it means they'll drop loads of money on the books their kids won't stop screaming about."

"We can dress in character." Anna claps animatedly. "Kids love that!"

"You won't make three grand off costumes and children's books," Ella says flatly.

Wes cocks his head in her direction. "What do you have?"

The corners of her mouth curl. "Speed booking."

"What the actual fu—"

Again, Ella cuts Wes off. "We get on Instagram. Twitter. All the networks." She nudges Cooper. His face brightens. Ella continues. "We hit up all the singles. Or the ones who happily pretend to be single on social media. We offer a one-night event where they come in here with their favorite books and participate in quick, one-on-one rounds of getting to know someone else. We can do an entry charge plus sell books."

"So, like speed dating but with books?" Anna questions.

"Exactly."

"Wow." Zay's mouth hangs open. "That's kind of brilliant."

Elbows on the counter, Wes leans forward. "Who are you, and what've you done with Ella Graham?"

"Eat shit," Ella says. "I'm the only one who cares enough about this place to come up with true money-making ideas."

"I like my idea," Wes whispers to his phone.

"Me too." Afternoon light peeking through the front window gleams off the lenses of Nico's glasses.

"Thanks." Wes offers him his white Styrofoam cup. "Try."

Nico doesn't hesitate. Their fingers brush as Nico grips the cup. He slurps, then rubs his temples, shivering. "Brain freeze."

They laugh together.

"Oh." Cooper snaps his fingers. "An open mic night! People can come in and read their favorite book passages. Or take their favorite quotes and turn them into a song."

"I like that." Anna swipes her phone screen a few times. "Kyra can help. Get the coffee shop involved. They might let us borrow their space."

"Is this an excuse for you to read poems about Wes's mom?" Ella inquires.

"Coop. Gross." Wes shudders.

"What? Not cool." Cooper's face wrinkles. "All my sonnets are about Angie Thomas."

"Yo. I respect that," says Zay, fist raised in the air.

Wes's thumbs blur across his phone's screen.

The Bookish League: Saving Once Upon a Page

1. Book Drive—Text Leeann to ask Leo for help.
2. Storytime—Buy costumes.
3. Author Meet-n-Greet—Find someone other than Mom.
4. Speed Booking—Leave up to Ella. Notify local authorities.
5. Open Mic Night—Talk to Kyra. Don't let Cooper read poetry.

"This is awesome. I'm already getting content ready for the bookstore's social media accounts." Cooper twists on the counter, holding his screen in front of Wes. "We officially have an Instagram, Twitter, FB, Snap, VSCO." He scrolls through each page.

Wes is impressed. @OnceUponaPageBookstore is live.

"Let me know when we get verified," Zay says, shifting to his knees before standing. He dusts off his army-green joggers. "I'm gonna go hit Kyra up for an iced coffee. Anyone in?"

Anna quickly follows while fixing loose pieces of her blonde hair. "Coffee and Kyra. Yes."

"I need to head out too," Nico says, packing up a few books in his drawstring nylon backpack. He tucks his skateboard under one arm.

"Hot date?" Ella asks, strategically talking to Nico while staring at Wes.

Wes bites his thumbnail to refrain from flipping her the bird. But he anticipates Nico's response. Mrs. Rossi usually schedules Nico for longer, later shifts.

"If you count babysitting a date, then, yeah." Nico sniffs, pushing a hand through his hair. "Mom's got a business dinner with clients."

Mrs. Alvarez is a bilingual consultant for an insurance firm. According to Google searches, it pays well. Occasionally, she drives into the city or to places like Malibu for client meetings and consultations.

"I promised my sisters we'd play that new dance game on Xbox."

"*Disco Dance Revolution Xtreme*?" Cooper says, awed.

"That one," confirms Nico in a flat voice. "Anyway, I'm on little monster patrol for the night."

The twins are seven now, which makes Sofía nearly nine years old.

"It's a shame you have to work," Nico says, chewing the inside of his cheek while looking at Wes.

"Yeah."

He wouldn't mind finding an excuse to sneak Nico out to the beach to execute his plan. Then they could spend the night sipping juice boxes and marathoning Pixar movies with the twins passed out on the floor, Sofía tucked under his arm, and his own head pillowed by Nico's shoulder. It's the perfect boyfriend scenario.

But Wes has a shift to work. And a bookstore to keep in business.

"Next time?"

Nico reaches out to tug on a few of Wes's curls. "Eres el major, Wesley." He shuffles from behind the counter and fist-bumps Zay on his way to the door.

"Wait!" screeches Cooper. He holds his phone above his head, beaming. "Major notification just received."

"What alien language are you speaking?" Ella snaps.

Cooper continues to wave his phone around. "So, my buds Jimmy and Savvy hit my DMs about this kicking get-together happening two nights from now. Beach bonfire. Tunes. Fellowship. Cool peeps community outreach at its finest."

"First of all, no one calls themselves Jimmy in this decade," Ella says. "He sounds sketch."

"He's cool."

"Coming from you, that's confirmation of this person's shadiness," Ella declares.

"There'll be booze." Cooper wiggles his eyebrows. "And choice selections of herbal refreshments."

Ella closes her eyes and sighs. "Fine. Where?"

"The Howls," Cooper sings, eyes lit like a field of stars.

Wes drops his head into his folded forearms. *The Howls*. First off, it's the most vapid name he's ever heard. Generations ago, a group of pre-college freshmen found a location off the beach that was hidden by rocks and scrub. They called it The Howls because, when the wind hits just right, it sounds as if the ocean is emitting this haunting song. Secondly, it's not that much of a "secret." Adults know about it but choose not to give the kids who convene there hell because it's harmless and no one's been killed yet.

But it's notorious for its summer parties hosted by people without the kind of pull and fake IDs to hit up real clubs, the ones who would rather spend summer getting wasted than think about the future—the intoxicated Wes Hudsons of the city.

Cooper glances around their small circle. "So, are we all in?"

Zay shrugs. "Sounds harmless."

"That's what all the murder victims in horror movies say," Wes mutters.

"If Kyra goes, I'm in," Anna says. Wes gets that. They're both young college girls. If he was Anna, he doesn't know if he'd be caught without backup on the beach at night with a bunch of slacker teens like them.

Cooper's phone chimes, and his face lights up again. "She's in."

Something warm passes over Anna's face.

"Wessssssss?"

Wes isn't really in the mood for sand in his shorts and pretending to care what song the dude with the guitar is singing. Also, navigating conversations about college with strangers is the worst. It doesn't matter. He's not going without Nico, which is the most unlikely thing to happen because…

"Sweet. I'm down," Nico says.

Wes's face falls. It's not as if Nico doesn't party. They both have, occasionally. But they were the two teens most likely to skip those things for a night at the movies and burritos after.

"Wesley?" Nico blinks at him.

"Uh." Wes's truly perfected this deer-in-the-headlights thing. His shoulders droop as he says, "Sure. Sounds dope. I can't wait."

He's become a first-rate liar.

CHAPTER FOURTEEN

THE FIRST SIGN THIS IS going to be a terrible night: Someone's singing Ed Sheeran in an off-key, raspy voice.

From above the rocks, Wes surveys the scene with narrowed eyes and crossed arms. The tuneless singer is a white guy with unkempt brown hair, the beginning of a five o'clock shadow, and an unzipped red hoodie that shows off his bare chest. He's sitting at a firepit, surrounded by a small group dressed in enough flannel and denim to be an American Eagle ad. Slowly, others join their band from different parts of the beach, enchanted by the flames and bad pop covers.

"Beer, here. Beer, there. Now we've got beer everywhere," shouts some frat-bro-wannabe with a giant cooler resting on one of his wide shoulders. The gold, curled script across his oversized sweatshirt says, "CAL," and Wes's not surprised.

The Howls is notorious for drawing this kind of audience.

"At least it's a nice night," Anna comments, standing next to Wes.

The outline of the crescent moon is sharp as the blade of a scythe. In the distance, the pier's still-lit Ferris wheel spreads its colors over the inky-black ocean. The wind rips its familiar whine; some of the people laugh while others seek shelter under heavy blankets.

Cooper runs up beside Anna. "It's gonna be great." He giggles, a clear indication he's partaken of a shared joint with Anna on the drive over.

"That's what all the white guys who know they're going to survive a horror movie say," Zay points out. Against the chill of another breeze, he tugs down the cuffs of his orange hoodie and hugs himself.

Cooper rummages through his backpack. "Dude, I brought rolling papers and some of Laguna's finest," he says as a peace offering.

Zay high-fives him. "Okay. Let's do this."

"We don't even know anyone here," Wes argues.

"What? I know *loads* of people here," Cooper says.

That doesn't comfort Wes.

"I do too." Kyra pops her head between Wes and Anna's shoulders. "Few of Trojan's coolest. I know two girls from the coffee shop are here." The light from her phone shines blue across her face. She's wearing a denim jacket over a pink crop top.

"They seem harmless," Ella says.

Wes loses all his allies before they set foot on the beach.

Bits of the party spread out across the sand. A new fire sparks a few feet away; people gather around. Embers pop through the flames to float upward like fireflies.

Nico nudges his way into their line. He bumps Wes's shoulder. "We don't have to stay long," he promises. "An hour, tops. After that, we can vacate if you want."

It's hard for Wes to deny Nico's offer. He wants to, badly. But he doesn't. Besides, Ella drove. The walk back to the loft isn't long, but there's no good lighting around here, and he's wearing a navy blue hoodie with dark jeans. It's not ideal for strolling alone at night near the Pacific Coast Highway.

He concedes with a soft, "Okay."

As the group begins to shuffle toward the manmade dirt path to the beach, Cooper hops in front. "Wait!" He holds his phone high. "We have to get a groupie to commemorate tonight."

"Nice SAT word, dude," Zay says through a laugh.

"Thanks."

"What did he just call me?" hisses Ella.

Wes snorts, elbowing her back. Before he knows it, they're all crowded around him and Zay, the tallest of their group. Cooper, sans selfie stick, tries to angle his phone to capture everyone in the frame. But Cooper's arms, like him, are short. Anna intervenes. She snaps off a few shots that are all awful.

"No, turn off the flash," Kyra instructs.

"Everyone shift to your left," Cooper shouts.

"Oh my god, I look like a vampire," Ella groans.

"Accurate." Wes receives a hard elbow below his ribs.

"Over here." Anna swings the phone around. Their heads follow like a hawk tracking its prey. "With the moon in the background."

"Yessss. Natural lighting," Kyra cheers, head resting on Anna's shoulder.

"Here." Nico reaches up, cold fingers holding Wes's chin. "Tilt that way."

Nico's wedged into Wes's side. Unconsciously, Wes's left arm hangs limp across Nico's shoulders. Then, their warm cheeks are pressed together. All Wes can hear is the wind and Nico breathing near his ear and Anna's manic countdown.

It's an out-of-body experience when he looks at the final photos.

Cooper's in front, giving a peace sign. Half of Zay's curly 'fro is cut from the frame. Kyra's laughing in Anna's neck. Ella is all scowl and frown. And Nico's beaming, face pressed to Wes's who looks… so *happy*.

"No filters," Kyra warns as Cooper begins messing with his phone. "Don't you dare whitewash me."

Anna gleefully drags her away from Cooper, arm in arm.

"I need a bath in holy water after standing next to you too long," Ella grunts, marching down the path. "And a lot of alcohol."

Wes pats his jeans. Thankfully, he has Ella's car keys.

Nico and Zay briskly follow Ella.

"And posted." Cooper flashes his phone for Wes to view.

He's right. In the photo, they look like the perfect car wreck.

ELLA APPEARS OUT OF NOWHERE. "Here. Drink."

Wes has been casually monitoring the party from the edge of the crowd. With the ocean to his back, everything in his view is cast in orange and red. There are people of all ages at The Howls: teens with acne and too much energy; college kids with their big words and booze; even a few who look older than Leo, talking about jobs and sharing whiskey, lamenting about their glory days.

Ella shakes a bottle of hard lemonade in his face. She knows Wes hates beer.

"Is there an alternative?"

"No." She presses the cold, wet bottle to his palm. "You need it. You have that whole Stressed Wes face. I know you're overthinking this bookstore thing."

"I'm not." At least, not in the panicked way he was a few weeks ago. But it's created its own residence in his mind next to the future and Nico. He's excited about their ideas. It's just hard for him to trust the others to want it as bad as he does, no matter how enthusiastic their words might be.

"I'm fine," he says, gripping the bottle's neck.

"This is what you always do." Ella shakes her head. "This is why I hate telling you things."

"What's that supposed to mean?"

Ella doesn't explain. She chugs a beer; amber liquid slips from the corners of her mouth. She belches, head tilted to stare at the sky. "Just take a night off from being all Stressed Wes, okay? We could all use a break."

She drifts away, intercepting a crowd of teens wearing all black and too much eyeliner.

Wes twists the cap off the bottle. He contemplates drinking. Why not, right? But Cooper and Zay are somewhere, blitzed out their minds. He can't find Anna or Kyra. Nico *hates* driving at night, especially without his glasses. And Ella's only mission is to get trashed. He'll be the only sober driver.

Two girls with matching lime green hair pass him. "Hey." He stretches out the bottle toward one. "Cheers."

"Thanks," one slurs, winking at him.

As they walk away, Wes hears the other girl say, "Cute. Kid's juice."

Whatever.

Small groups break out around The Howls. Wes can pick out Zay's heavy laugh in the noise, though he can't see him. A cluster of college kids stands closer to the rocks. Kyra's big curls and Anna's wind-tossed blonde hair are outlined by the fire's dancing orange flames. Wes considers joining their troupe, but then realizes he'd probably have nothing to add to their conversations.

Cal Guy sings another song. The Pixie's "Where Is My Mind?" Wes wants this tool to get swept away by the tide.

Down the shore, Wes spots Nico talking with people he doesn't recognize. Red Solo cup in hand, he looks so at *ease*. He's a social multitasker, laughing at something one person says while nodding at someone else.

Nico won't have any problems meeting new friends at Stanford. He'll fit in. Over time, someone new will replace Wes.

Breath caught in his throat, Wes turns away.

Maybe he *should* have a drink. Mellow out. Think of anything other than the fact that he's on a beach and not executing his plan because the timing's off. Again.

A colossal, giggling monster stumbles past him. Well, not a monster. The heavy shadows make it difficult for Wes to identify that it's two people, one piggybacking on another. Cooper's perched on a tall Asian girl's back as she trudges through the sand. Her face, soft with a round nose and a thick lower lip, is familiar, as if Wes has seen it more than once.

Then it clicks: *Devon*. Cooper's BFF. Manu's cousin.

They carry on: Cooper shouting, Devon galloping. They manage a few more feet before eating sand. Wes laughs into the crook of his elbow. Then he pulls out his phone.

Is it kind of creepish to log on to Instagram to see if Manu's posted any photo evidence or maybe a live story of himself at The Howls?

As of last week, he and Manu are online mutuals.

Wes is formally *allowed* to casually scroll through Manu's Insta while standing in the middle of the beach at night with the smallest morsel of hope that he's here.

They've spent the past week liking each other's old posts. Some mornings, Wes wakes up to four different notifications—all from @manus808. They leave single-word comments under each other's captions. "Love." "Sweet." "Wow." Occasionally, Manu drops an emoji, like a palm tree or the blushing face.

Once, Wes tapped the red heart emoji, then quickly deleted it. What was he thinking? Everyone knows full commitment is required when using that emoji. Things haven't escalated to that level.

Manu's last post was two days ago.

Wes slides his phone into his back pocket. If he's here, maybe Wes will stumble into him the way he did on the pier. It'll happen organically. Then they can talk, face-to-face, like adults. Except, with no Manu or Nico or Ella, Wes realizes he's all alone.

Is that what being adult is? Making all these mature executive decisions that result in loneliness?

Wes staggers down the beach.

"You look lost."

Planted on the sand closer to the shore, Wes watches the water slither up to his feet. He's not sure how long he's been sitting when Zay plops down next to him. Ten minutes? Thirty? His whole life?

Wes shrugs lazily. "I'm cool."

"Brooding," Zay says.

"Placid." Wes groans. He hates that word. He doesn't know why he said it.

But Zay laughs, then coughs into his fist. "Tranquil."

Wes likes this game. He likes that Zay, despite all the fun and noise and bad singing, is willing to play along. He whispers, "Desolate," to the ocean.

Zay's elbow touches his. "That's heavy."

Without looking, Wes slowly nods.

"Where's your sidekick?"

"Who?" Wes knows who Zay's referring to, but he's willing to act ignorant if Zay obliges.

A rolling grin pushes Zay's cheeks upward. "Okay." And Wes has never been more thankful for the way Zay changes the subject. "I'm meeting with the school's academic advisor."

"What? When? Tomorrow?"

"No. The first day of school."

Wes's eyebrows feel permanently stuck at the top of his forehead.

"My momma emailed a bunch of people. I don't know." Zay runs a hand through his hair. It's so thick, his fingers disappear, and all Wes can see is his wrist. "Since UCLA doesn't have an early admissions option, we're going to discuss ways for me to jump headfirst into things. Maybe extra course loads."

"Is that what you want?"

"I mean," Zay pauses, pulling at a few tangled curls. "I want to go to UCLA. And I want to be ready."

"But?"

Zay tips his head back. Closer to the shore, the moon stretches a soft paw over them. Wes always forgets Zay's the younger one. He's so mature. In extreme situations, Zay's the friend Wes wants around. He doesn't panic. He doesn't curl up into a weak, mewling ball. Zay simply handles shit.

"No buts," he finally says. "Not yet, at least."

"You're gonna kill it."

"You are too." Zay elbows Wes's bicep. "You were made for blue and gold."

"Uh huh."

Wes studies him. His eyes are droopy from smoking up with Cooper. There's a faint, dark line across his upper lip from not shaving. Legs pulled to his chest and arms on his knees make his orange hoodie bunch up around his throat. Though they're around the same height, Zay seems smaller—a reminder that despite being mentally prepared for his future, Zay's physically seventeen.

"Do you ever feel... not ready for the future?" Wes lowers his eyes, blinking. "Or you're always changing your mind about it?"

Zay's quiet. The waves roll and crash. Gulls shriek. Cal Guy has launched into the Killers' greatest hits. Wes can hear his own heartbeat in his ears.

Thudthudthumpthump.

"Sometimes."

"Why are we even doing it? College, I mean."

"Because some of us don't have the option," Zay whispers.

Wes lifts his eyes.

Zay rubs a hand down his face. "For some of us, college isn't going to swing the job opportunity door wide open but it's going to crack it just enough for us to stick a hand in. To remind people that just because we're not white doesn't mean we're not smart. Or capable. That we're just as qualified as that person who dicked around during school, got drunk, and made a lot of bad choices that money made go away."

He tugs up his sleeve and jabs at the back of his left hand with his index finger. "This is what people see."

Wes knows he's talking about his skin color.

"Mom's an executive at a nonprofit. Momma has *two* degrees and travels all over the west coast giving TED talks about the power of being who you are. About standing in the strength of standing out. It's exclusively speaking to people of color." Zay scowls at the sand. "I haven't had a new phone in almost two years. My shoes? I pick them up at after-market sales. Both of my moms are smart as hell and still only get so far up the ladder before someone reaches down to pull up another person without any melanin in their system."

"Yeah," whispers Wes.

"*We*," says Zay, wiggling a finger between them, "have to fight twice as hard."

Wes appreciates that just because he's often seen as passing and people don't always connect him to Calvin, Zay makes it a point to include him in discussions of race and privilege. He doesn't lay any guilt on Wes because there are some prejudices they won't share. They're still united.

"I have no clue what's gonna happen in the future," Zay says. "But having a degree gives me more of a chance. It's not a guarantee. Nothing is. It's just a backup."

"Are you doing it because of your moms?" Wes asks.

"A little bit." Zay's nose wiggles like he's fighting off a sneeze. "You?"

"Yup."

"I wonder if all kids feel that way?" Zay smiles sadly. "Especially POC kids. Like we owe our parents for putting up with this fucked up world so we can have a future."

"It's in our DNA."

"The struggle continues."

Wes sighs at his shoes.

"Damn, Wes. Why are you so deep?" Zay pulls back, face scrunched.

Wes squawks, almost falling over.

"I came over here for a laugh." And Zay does laugh, hoarsely. "Your mad sad vibes are killing my high."

Wes shoves him. "Welcome to adulting, my dude. *Everything* kills your high as an adult."

"Slow down. You're only eighteen, not Mrs. Rossi's age," Zay says, standing. He shakes sand off his jeans and hoodie, then scrubs it out of his hair. "I'm gonna head back. You staying?"

Nodding, Wes turns back to the water. *Alone again*. This time, Wes doesn't mind. He just wants to empty out his brain and let the tide drag all his jumbled thoughts into the dark waters.

But that's not happening. Someone's standing over him.

"Wesley?"

CHAPTER FIFTEEN

"WESLEY CRUSHER," NICO SAYS, BEAMING.

He's replaced Zay next to Wes on the sand. His legs stretched out in front of him, one hand braced behind for support, Nico leans against Wes. He doesn't smell like Zay did—smoky sweet mixed a mustiness from the weed. Nico's scent is sweat and citrus and the sugariness of rum. Long strands of Nico's flat hair lie across his forehead.

Wes's heart beats like a summer storm—wild and unpredictable. He's simultaneously cold from the breeze but warm from Nico's proximity. It's too much and just enough.

Nico whispers, "Missssssed you." He's tipsy, but not incoherent.

"I didn't go anywhere," Wes chokes out.

"You *did*," Nico argues, then chuckles. "Stupid Italy. Gone, gone, gone."

Voice breaking, Wes says, "I'm here now."

"You are." Nico rests his temple on Wes's collarbone. The breeze carries the sigh he expels into the night.

Cautiously, as if the wrong move could disrupt this, Wes curls an arm around Nico's lower back. Nico's body tenses, then relaxes. Wes's chin is perched on the top of Nico's head. He revels in the fact that Nico's hair isn't stiff and gross with sand.

It takes Wes a second to identify the song Nico's humming.

"Frank Ocean?"

"My boy Frank," Nico confirms with a smile in his voice.

The breeze sweeps over them. Nico shivers. Reflexively, Wes tightens his arm. Nico's warm breath skims the side of his neck. If he turned slightly, he could press a kiss there. And Wes knows exactly why he's thinking about that.

This is the perfect place to tell Nico. But the vibe isn't right. Nico's intoxicated. And Wes doesn't want this thing he's been holding inside for so long to slip out when Nico can barely hold his head upright.

Nico. Nico. Nico.

He mumbles something in Spanish into the collar of Wes's hoodie.

"What?"

Nico jolts a little, jarring Wes. "Nothing." He shifts back, staring up at Wes. His lips are shiny, as if he's just licked them. There's a similar sheen across his eyes. "No es nada. I think I'm drunk."

Wes's eyebrows draw inward. "What did you say, Nico?"

"Nothing."

"Nico…"

"You're my best friend. Bestest friend." Nico squeezes his eyes shut, then blinks them open. "I want… you're my friend."

Friend.

Wes hears that word loud and clear. It's been attached to him for years and years, but it's never stung like it does now. In his mind, Wes can see his list in perfect, hi-def quality.

Signs Your Crush Isn't Into You!!!

3. If your crush constantly refers to you as a friend, THEY MEAN IT!
4. If you always ask, "Does my crush like me?", FALL BACK!

"Is that what you—"

"No, no. It's not." Nico hiccups, then shakes his head. "I'm drunk. I'm messed up. No es nada." He grabs the hem of his red sweatshirt, uses it to wipe his face. There are no tears there, only sweat.

Wes curls his fingers around Nico's wrist. Under his fingertips, Nico's pulse is a slow thump.

"Wesley." Nico swallows. Wes studies his Adam's apple, then the way his lips move as he whispers, "I'm tired."

"I'm sorry."

"Maybe I should go."

Maybe you should. Wes's breaths are shallow. He's checked off two more items on his list. It's a huge, screaming, blood-red sign. But something deep in his marrow keeps dragging him in another direction. Closer to Nico.

"We'll go," he says, pulling. "Me and you. I'll walk you home." It's not that far from The Howls to the Alvarez house off Palisades Beach Road.

"No, no. You should stay. Chill," insists Nico. He pushes to his feet. He's just coordinated enough to straighten his sweatshirt and dust sand from his shorts.

"I'll go with you." Wes stands too. He wants to let Nico piggyback him, like Devon and Cooper, all the way to his house. Then he wants to crawl into Nico's bed and hug him. Nothing else. He wants to protect Nico from whatever he can't say to Wes.

Screw Stanford. Screw UCLA. Screw the future. Just Wes and Nico and their protective bubble. But that's not possible. Nothing Wes wants is possible, except maybe saving the bookstore. At least he has that.

At least he still has Nico's friendship.

"Come on." Wes links their fingers together.

The slightest glint of hesitation registers in Nico's eyes, but he doesn't yank away. "What about the others?"

"Here." Wes tugs out his phone. One-handed, he unlocks it, taps on his messages, and types. "I'll let Kyra know. Anna too. We can call Ella on the way. She'll take care of Zay and Cooper."

"She won't take care of Cooper."

"You're right. But Zay will," assures Wes, leading Nico up the soft sand. The wind is heavy against their backs. That's why Wes is shivering. That's why his eyes sting. He's not going to cry.

I can't tell him. We're just friends. This is what's best.

That's what he repeats to himself the entire walk back to Nico's house.

Hands behind his head, Oz stared at the crow-black sky. Blades of wet grass tickled the nape of his neck. Avoiding his mother had become his new specialty. Moms, though nurturing, never understood teenage boys.

"Life's right there, Oz," whispered Sarina.

It was. Beyond the big, ominous stars that hung overhead. Too far away to touch with his fingertips. That's how Oz viewed his whole life before Sarina—too far away.

He was only seventeen when she died.

He was eighteen when she returned.

"Life's right there."

He loved the way Sarina talked with her entire face. Once ivy-green eyes and a button nose and a mouth softer than a peach's skin.

Oz's mother believed teenagers, especially boys, only wanted three things: control, the future, and sex.

Not Oz.

He didn't want the world. He only wanted to cradle it in his palm for a little while. He only wanted to bring Sarina back…

But not as a zombie. Oz never meant for that to happen.

Maybe his mother was right. Maybe Oz wanted to control one thing: the future. His future. With Sarina.

But maybe that's what all teenagers wanted.

—Savannah Kirk, *The Language of Dead Hearts*

CHAPTER SIXTEEN

SUMMER WEEKENDS INSIDE ONCE UPON a Page are always a strange mix of a traffic pileup and a graveyard. Mornings can be a quiet, serene landscape, mostly due to the Third Street Promenade Farmer's Market, with random customers popping in to browse but never buy. Afternoons are a hellscape of people fleeing the heat or in search of their next beach read.

Luckily, Wes has at least an hour before that crowd clogs up the aisles.

He eyes all the comic books in his favorite corner as Lucas practices arranging them.

"What about this?" asks Lucas.

Wes taps his chin, then squints for a long moment. He knows Lucas is dying for his validation. But he also knows it's hilarious making Lucas sweat.

"It's okay."

Lucas squeaks. "What?"

"Nah," Wes says teasingly. "It's great."

A hearty shade of red paints their cheeks as Lucas crumples. There's a peal of laughter from behind them. Lucas stands on their toes to get a better view. "What's that about?"

Wes peeks over his shoulder. Cooper and Kyra lean suspiciously close over the counter. "Nothing." Wes turns back to Lucas. "They're planning an open mic night for the bookstore."

"Really?"

"Yup. We're trying to do a few things to up sales. You know, bring in a bigger crowd."

"That's so cool," says Lucas, eyes twinkling. "Can anyone come?"

"What? You got some sweet vocal skills you're keeping hidden?" Wes nudges Lucas's shoulder. "I bet you rock out hard to Bon Iver."

"Yuck." Lucas sticks out their tongue, shivering. "I'm big on synth-pop. Stuff influenced by the '80s."

"That's a mood," says Wes, chuckling. "I can get behind that."

"Can you? I've heard the garbage you listen to," Lucas says. "Weezer? Ugh."

Wes points an accusing finger at Lucas's nose. "Don't disrespect the power of Rivers Cuomo."

Lucas makes a sour face.

"You're not invited to the open mic night," Wes says, chin tipped up. "You're not qualified to hang with the big dogs."

"All I see is a puppy," Lucas jokes.

Wes likes this side of Lucas, less restrained and small. He likes the way their blond hair still falls into their eyes when they laugh too hard. He likes that Lucas is wearing a white Henley with an old-school MTV logo in the middle. In fact, this is the first time Wes hasn't seen Lucas in their green hoodie. Everything about Lucas is… free.

"Hang on." Wes holds up a finger. He almost forgot. "Don't move."

Lucas blinks at him a few times, but Wes merely shoots them a surreptitious smile before trekking to the front counter.

"Shut up. Shut up. He's here," Kyra chokes out while giggling.

Wes negotiates his way around them to get behind the counter, then kneels to rummage through his backpack. He tugs out a graphic novel. When he stands, they're still chortling. He pauses, eyebrows so high they're making out with his hairline.

Kyra turns her head, wheezing.

"What are…" Wes narrows his eyes. "…you two…" He motions his index finger between them. "…doing?"

"Working on open mic night!" shouts Cooper, which sends Kyra over the edge, collapsing on the counter, face mashed to the woodgrain as she howls.

"A likely story." Wes crosses his arms.

"Fine, fine." Kyra lifts her head. She wipes at the tears hanging on her long eyelashes, then clears her throat. "Because of this dork…" She stabs a finger in Cooper's direction. "…we might've been brainstorming ship names."

"Ship names?"

Wes knows what shipping is. Being quite fond of certain LGBTQIA characters in the X-Men comics—Wes's only Marvel weakness—has led to many searches for alternative romantic storylines between his favorite queer characters when the writers either kill one off or dissolve the relationship for no apparent reason.

Anyway, he's read his share of fanfiction: good, bad, and weirdly sexy. The internet is a strange, magical place.

"Yes. Ship names," Cooper confirms. "For you and Nico."

Time-out. Pause the game. Pump the brakes.

"Me and Nico?" Wes feels embarrassment's vise-grip on his vocal cords. "Me. And. Nico?"

Cooper's eyebrows furrow. "It's obvious—"

"*Obvious?*" This is where Wes will die, behind the front counter at Once Upon a Page. At least he'll go out in his favorite place in the world—with the voice of a thirteen-year-old who's been caught by their mom looking at inappropriate Google searches.

"Wes, come on," Kyra implores. "We've all seen the heart-eyes you've been tossing Nico since day one. You're like that Patrick from *SpongeBob* GIF where he's kicking his feet back and forth. Big, gooey eyes with that sweet smile. It's gross."

No. Wes most certainly is not that GIF. He has supreme levels of chill about Nico in public. No one knows his dark secret, except Ella, with whom Wes shares an airtight friendship. She's not a narc.

"It's not true," he replies firmly.

Kyra puckers her mouth, clearly unconvinced. "Anna knows. Zay knows. Ella knows. Anderson Cooper and I know." She lists every name on a finger. She lifts her other hand, flexing another index finger. "Gemma, the pink-haired girl who only works weekends over at Aerial knows."

Wes glares at her. He can't believe this. Betrayed by his own kind.

"I know!" shouts Lucas.

"You know nothing," Wes yells, his pre-puberty voice reinstating itself with a vengeance.

Kyra's moved onto her second ring finger. "Mrs. Rossi knows."

No. That's impossible. Not Mrs. Rossi. N-O.

A sharp pang hits Wes's chest. His spine locks.

"It's not as if you treat it like privileged info." Kyra shrugs. Her cardinal and gold USC sweatshirt has been shredded into an off-the-shoulder crop top. It smells of dark roasted coffee. The overpowering scent is the only thing keeping him conscious.

"You two looked kind of cozy the other night," Cooper comments. "At The Howls."

They didn't. They were only talking.

"And you disappeared," Kyra points out.

Yeah, so Wes could walk Nico home. They held hands, but only to balance Nico. That's it. No kiss goodnight. Only a long, silent hug before Nico stumbled inside.

"We're just friends," Wes says, his voice as deflated as it was in his head that night.

"Hear me out." Cooper clasps his hands together. "I think I have the perfect ship name. Nesley."

"Like the chocolate company?" Lucas asks, suddenly right next to Wes.

"Almost. The first letter of Nico's name and then the end of Wes's name. N-E-S-L-E-Y."

"I like it," Lucas says, way too into this very unfunny game.

"I liked Weco," Kyra huffs.

"It sounds like a gas station," Cooper argues gently. He pivots toward Wes. "How do you feel about it?"

Wes feels the same way he feels about Oasis's music— absolutely nothing. A knot forms behind his skull. His right eye twitches. His fingers curl inward, squeezing to manage the shaking spreading from his shoulders to his forearms. He's only blocked from releasing his wrath upon Cooper by a raised voice escaping one of the aisles.

"Just tell me what book you want? Pick one. Any of them."

It's a man with a blond beard and thinning hair wrecked by his large hands. He's a giant compared to the young girl beside him, whose face is splotchy with wet, round cheeks. She's biting the black polish off her thumbnail while he paces. They have the same pair of downturned brown eyes; his are rimmed red while hers are glassy.

The rest of the store quiets under the weight of their tug-of-war.

"Cassie." He rubs his forehead. "It's not that hard. Grab any book you want."

"I don't know which one I want!" She hiccups. The threat of more tears is imminent.

"Just..." He waves a hand around. "There are so many. Grab whatever you want. We're going to be late for lunch."

Cassie sighs wetly at the ceiling. "I've read most of them."

"I know," he grumbles.

"Why are you rushing me?"

"I have—"

"You just don't want to miss golf with Mr. Leeson," she snaps.

"Cassie, sweetheart, he's a very important client," the man says through his white-strips-bright teeth.

"They're all important," whispers Cassie, dejectedly. She sniffs hard.

A thick vein throbs along the man's forehead. He sucks in his cheeks, looking ready to unleash another complaint, but someone in the doorway cuts him off.

"Hey!" Ella yanks off a pair of big, dark sunglasses. Hair knotted into one long braid she flicks off her shoulder, she strolls into the bookstore. She stops in front of Cassie. The man, whom Wes presumes is her dad, glares at Ella. Cassie looks at her Doc Martens, then scans Ella. Her eyes bulge when she realizes Ella's wearing the same boots.

"Excuse me, miss, but—"

Without looking, Ella holds up a finger to cut off Cassie's dad. "Sorry, Pops, but it sounds like this badass future rock star needs my assistance." She smirks at Cassie.

Cassie's mouth twitches up nervously before blooming into a full smile.

"I'm Ella," Ella says, up-nodding.

Cassie sniffles again. "I'm Cassie."

"Okay, Cassie. This is pretty simple," says Ella, pushing at the sleeves of her black leather jacket. "We're gonna play a little game." Behind Ella, Cassie's dad huffs, arms folded. Ella ignores him.

Wes parks it on the countertop. He loves when this happens. Ella might be an undeniable slacker, but when it comes to customers— especially teens—and books, she's a fairy godmother. Her bibliophile skills know no end.

"What do you like to read?"

"Uh." Cassie mashes her left foot onto her right. "Fantasy." She peeks over Ella's shoulder at her dad. He's still scowling, but it's starting to soften around the edges.

Quietly, Cassie adds, "Dark fantasy."

"Favorite author?"

"Leigh Bardugo."

"Favorite book?"

Mouth open, Cassie pauses as if considering the question. Then she says, "*A Darker Shade of Magic*."

Ella nods, an eyebrow ticking upward. Her approval's showing. "Strong choices." She points behind Cassie, two shelves down. "Let me introduce you to a friend of mine named Holly Black."

"Okay," Cassie whispers, trailing behind Ella with her father in tow.

The magic of Ella Graham is limitless.

Cassie and her dad return to the front counter with four books and a handful of buttons. Cassie's face is luminous as a halo of gold. Her dad drops one of those heavy, black credit cards on the woodgrain and shakes his head. But, on the way out, he circles his long arm around her wide shoulders, pulling her close to kiss the top of her head.

Ella replaces Wes on the counter. "Another hard day's work."

"You just got here," Cooper says while flipping through the CD collection.

Before Ella can eviscerate Cooper with her comeback, Kyra says, "El. You act tough, but you love this place."

"I do not," Ella replies flatly.

"You do. You love these customers. You love changing people's lives," Kyra says.

"Shut up." Ella pushes her bangs back, which only highlights the tiny curl at the corners of her mouth. "I have a rep to maintain."

"Besides…" Ella's mouth finally succumbs to a soft smile as she stares at the empty doorway. "Us big girls have to stick together."

Wes considers calling out Ella's nonchalant façade but doesn't. Maybe she sees a bit of herself in Cassie. Maybe that strain between father and daughter is relatable in ways she doesn't talk about often. Ella can pretend her heart's made of goth rock music rejects all she wants.

When it comes to Once Upon a Page, she's a softy. She loves it here as much as Wes does.

Maybe more.

COOPER THUMPS A HAND ON the counter.

"I'm telling you—Pop-Tarts are the superior any-meal pastry."

Lucas wrinkles their nose. "Incorrect. Evidence shows that Toaster Strudels are exceptionally better in taste and overall effect."

"What? You're bananas."

"It's true."

Cooper *psshs*, waving a dramatic hand at Lucas. "False statement. Toaster Strudel requires too much prep and practiced execution to be an any-meal, on-the-go snack. From perfected frozen-to-hot completion, in which the middle is cooked to the same heat as the outer edges, to the flawless crosshatch application of the icing. It's too complicated. A five-year-old could create the perfect Pop-Tart. It's just facts."

"Which lowers the Pop-Tart's overall approval rating," Lucas counters. "Simplicity doesn't always equal quality."

Cooper smacks a hand over his eyes, groaning.

They've been at it for, according to the time on Wes's phone, no less than thirty minutes. That's enough time for Anna to come in for her shift, Kyra to pop into Brews and Views to grab a tea for Wes and a chocolate croissant for Anna, and Ella to take two breaks from helping Wes reshelve books.

It's been chill since Cassie and her dad exited. The handful of shoppers, Cooper's been able to manage while breaking down the science of Pop-Tarts for Lucas. Mrs. Rossi's office door is ajar, but she's not there. She called it quits an hour ago. But it's not as though she's been on the floor interacting with customers anyway. Mostly, Wes's caught her looking over paperwork, occasionally pinching the bridge of her nose or rubbing her temples.

It's left a mucky feeling in his stomach.

We need to raise money for this place ASAP.

Wes's phone buzzes. He has five notifications staring him down: a calendar reminder about checking out potential floral shops with Leeann, a text from Leo he hasn't bothered to read, two texts from Calvin he's definitely avoiding. Honestly, Wes doesn't know how to reply to him anymore. All these suggestions about college stress him the hell out.

Then there's an Instagram notification from @manus808. He commented on Wes's last post. Wes is saving it for his break, which he hopes is soon, because he could kill at least two carnitas tacos and a MexiCoke from Taco Libre right now.

"I've got news from Zay." Ella's perched on the counter with her phone raised.

Wes pauses, a small book stack in his arms.

"He's possibly lined up an author to do an event here."

A wave of excited nausea hits Wes's stomach. He rearranges the books under one arm. "Who?"

Ella's mouth puckers, a move Wes recognizes as hesitation. Then she says, "Morgan Weatherford."

Wes's arm goes slack. He falters, almost dropping the books but catches himself.

Morgan Weatherford? Hell. No.

"Who?" Cooper asks, head tilted.

"You know. *The* Morgan Weatherford." Ella flaps a hand around. "He wrote *Heir of Dragons.*"

"Oh." Cooper drags out the "H" forever, rubbing his chin. "Dude's ancient. Didn't that book come out like eight years ago?"

"And yet..." Ella waves her phone in Cooper's face. "...that book still sells like mad. They even made a movie."

"Not a good one," Lucas says, frowning.

This is why Lucas remains in Wes's friend club. Lucas gets it. Morgan Weatherford blows. He's a subpar author who writes the same tired girl-princess fantasy, where some rando guy is her only agency and helps save her kingdom, that men have thought they could pull off for decades. Problem is, the people with power—also privileged men—have been boosting guys like Weatherford for just as long. The patriarchy at its finest.

Plus, Weatherford was a total dick to Savannah when she asked for a blurb for her fifth book. Wes has never forgotten watching his mom restrain tears while explaining it to his dad at her birthday dinner a few years ago.

"No," Wes says firmly.

"Zay says that's all he can find," says Ella. "We need someone. Soon. We don't have forever to save this place."

"We don't have long at all," Anna says, appearing from the back, a stack of papers in her hands.

Holy Shazam, is everyone creeping Mrs. Rossi's private things?

Wes doesn't have much room to complain, since he's organizing this entire plan behind Mrs. Rossi's back, but still.

"September sixth. That's it. That's all we have," Anna says, flipping through the documents.

A scream is crawling up Wes's throat. He shuts his eyes. *Deep breaths.* He can fix this.

"There have to be other options," he says, voice strained. "It's freaking L.A."

"Yeah, on mad short notice too," Ella argues. "Zay's trying."

"He can try harder!" Wes demands. Ella lifts an eyebrow; her mouth is flat. Wes isn't going to fight about this. Zay can do better. They all can do better to keep Once Upon a Page open.

"We still have at least six weeks," Wes continues. "There's time."

Everyone's quiet. Ella exhales heavily through her nose while tapping away at her phone. Someone else's phone buzzes on the counter.

"Oh! Sorry to ditch, but I'm having fajitas with Mom," Lucas announces, pocketing their phone.

"Sweet," says Wes. He accepts Lucas's fist-bump.

"Yeah, I guess. She's really on this quality time thing." Wes can see through Lucas's nonchalance. They love spending time with their mom.

It makes Wes miss his own mom. He needs to FaceTime her tonight. Maybe he'll catch her during breakfast. Savannah's always extra chatty over brioche and espresso.

Wes wishes he could ask his mom for ideas to save the bookstore. But he can't. If she knows, she'll call Mrs. Rossi.

"Thanks for the book," Lucas says, holding up the graphic novel Wes had stashed in his backpack. *Blackest Night.* Wes special ordered a copy for Lucas.

"It's my favorite," Wes says.

"I know." Lucas beams.

As Lucas high-steps it out the door, Nico glides in, kicking up his board. "I think I've nailed it." He grins animatedly, unsettling his glasses on his nose. He has an iPad in the hand not holding his skateboard.

"It took me most of the night…" Nico drops his board behind the counter, then parks it next to Ella. He taps the iPad's screen awake. "…but I think I came up with some artwork to advertise the open mic night *and* children's story time."

On screen, Nico swipes through a few fully colored sketches.

"Siiiiick," Cooper says.

"I'm marginally impressed," Ella agrees.

"I tried to come up with multiple options." Nico's thumb drags across the screen. "Then I had to format and resize so Coop can throw them up on Insta and Twitter." He opens a gallery with all the designs.

"This is perfect, bro." Cooper claps his hands together. "Send them my way when they're ready. I'll be sure to tag you. Gotta get those follower counts up."

"I'm just trying to keep this place alive, dude."

"Word." Cooper squeezes Nico's shoulder.

Wes leans in for a closer inspection, careful not to press too far into Nico. A calculated distance. That night at The Howls still haunts his thoughts. In one way or another, he's crossed off every bullet point from his **Signs Your Crush Isn't Into You** list. The universe has firmly told him, "No, this isn't happening." He's accepted that.

Well, ninety percent of him has accepted it.

A beastly sound erupts from Wes's stomach.

Nico peeks over his lenses. "Have you had lunch?"

"No."

"Wesley," Nico says in that protective warning voice that Wes appreciates.

"It's been busy."

They both glance around at the scattering of customers in the store. The only noises come from Ella's gum popping and Anna's love for Alanis Morrissette any time after three p.m., when she can growl lyrical profanity without too many judging eyes.

Nico passes Wes the iPad. "Burritos. On me." He hops down from the counter. "MexiCoke?"

"*Please.*" Yup, Wes isn't beyond begging. He repositions in Nico's spot on the counter as Nico gathers his skateboard. Adobe Illustrator is still open on the screen. He scrolls through the bookstore designs. Underneath is a gallery of other sketches and doodles. Most of it is original art. Sick graffiti tags and a few realistic portraits. Wes recognizes Mrs. Alvarez and Sofía, but much younger, when Sofía only came up to Wes's kneecap and Mrs. Alvarez didn't have an irremovable sadness behind her smile.

"Hey." Wes pinches the sleeve of Nico's black T-shirt when he passes. "You're drawing again?"

Nico peeks at the iPad. "Sometimes."

"These are really good."

"Nah. They're shit. I'm just messing around."

"No," Wes insists, tugging harder on Nico's shirt. "This is incredible. You could get into art school with this stuff."

Nico doesn't respond, which Wes guesses is an invitation to continue, though Nico's eyebrows shift inward.

"You know, UCLA is one of the top five art schools in California," he says, pointing at the image of Nico's mom and sister. "You could learn a lot there."

Nico's eyes narrow.

Shut up. Shut up.

But Wes doesn't. "You could kick it around here. Be at home with your sisters, study art. And…"

Be with me.

Holy hell, that ten percent of himself that hasn't accepted he and Nico aren't going to work is still getting in the way. He's so selfish. Is he trying to convince his best friend to stick around Santa Monica to pursue an art degree for Nico's benefit or his? He doesn't even have an airtight argument. Nico's already been accepted into Stanford. What's he going to do? Call the admissions office and cancel? Who cancels on Stanford?

"Stanford is a top five art school," Nico says. His cheeks are hollowed, showing all the tension behind his jaw. "It's also where I'm going to study medicine because of my family, in case you forgot."

"I didn't," Wes says, his voice small.

"Then drop it." Nico snatches the iPad from Wes's loose grip. "Art school isn't for me. Art school won't bring back…" Nico nudges his glasses up, wiping at his eyes. "Mierda. Forget it."

"Okay," whispers Wes. But he knows he won't.

He stares at Nico's back as he pushes out the door. Briefly, Nico looks over his stiff shoulder. Wes's mouth opens, then closes. Nico disappears. Wes knows he won't be back with a burrito and a MexiCoke.

He knows he's royally fucked up.

CHAPTER SEVENTEEN ✐

"So, I told him..." Leeann pauses to take a sip of her green iced tea.

In true hot-tea-only elitist form, Wes frowns at her.

Leeann *ahhhs* at him because she's aware of his vehement disdain for iced teas. She continues, poking her phone screen awake: "We have to finalize the wedding party in the next two weeks. I love your brother with all my heart, but he's such a slacker when it comes to the finer details of this wedding thing."

Chin propped against the meat of his palm, Wes hides a smile behind his long fingers.

Leo, a slacker? In what world?

"I'm sure Grace and Tiffany will be thrilled when you finally choose a maid of honor," he says.

"Assuming they're in."

"Assuming they're in," Wes repeats, laughing.

"I dunno." Leeann picks at her everything bagel, careful not to get the chunky avocado she's spread all over it on her fingers. She chews, head tilted, looking thoughtful. "I should just have one of those Mad Max, post-apocalyptic duels for that spot. I love my sister, but I think Tiffany might win."

This morning, Wes witnessed Tiffany verbally take down a florist who wasn't prepared with a selection of sample flowers for Leeann despite an appointment scheduled two weeks ago. No offense, Grace, but Tiffany would slay that contest.

Leeann wipes her hand on a brown paper napkin, then dives back into her tea. "I'm kind of dreading the menu planning next month.

You think Grace is bad? Wait until Mei Chen critiques a caterer on traditional spring rolls."

Wes has never met Leeann's parents. They live in Oakland. But he can't imagine anything worse than Grace—except maybe Leo.

He plays with the crystalized sugar on top of his blueberry muffin. His Darjeeling sits near his left hand, growing cold. Kyra keeps shooting him death glares from behind the bar. It's a special white tea, the coffee shop's featured Brew of the Week, but he doesn't have it in him to enjoy it.

Usually, it would've been Nico handing him a cup of tea, not Kyra.

Nico.

It's been a solid two days since Wes said the stupidest shit imaginable and Nico stormed out of the bookstore. To Wes's surprise, Nico returned with a burrito for him. They didn't talk about it. Nico restocked shelves; Wes bummed around the front counter. But he still can't shake it.

"So." Leeann jabs at the melting ice in her cup. "Are we going to talk about what's got you so distracted, or would you like to discuss how I was dropping hints about the wedding party to see if your lazy brother finally got the balls to ask you to be his best man?"

"He hasn't."

"Huh." Leeann's got her phone in one hand, tapping away. "Noted."

"Stop," Wes pleads while pawing at her phone. "I really don't feel like dealing with Leo at the moment."

"Fine." Leeann lowers her phone. "But we're talking about whatever's got your brain all fuzzy. I swear, Hudson men are like Fort Knox."

Wes doesn't disagree. Truthfully, he isn't up for discussing Nico. Something in his brain keeps reminding him that Nico's the last thing he should be thinking about. Not when there's the bookstore and UCLA and certain doom the moment he answers one of his dad's texts.

"How do you know this is what you want?" asks Wes.

"This?"

"Yeah, like." Wes circles his hand around his head, as if that explains anything. "Life. You're only twenty-three. How do you know you want to get married? To be in love? To drink green iced tea of all things?"

Leeann's hair flies in front of her face when she snorts.

Wes continues. "How do you know you want to be a pediatrician? That you wanted to go to Pepperdine? That, every morning, you know what the hell is going on and still don't have a meltdown?"

Leeann blinks at him a few times, then shrugs. "I don't."

"You *don't*?" Wes's screechy voice alarms a couple as they walk in.

"No, I don't." Leeann scoops hair behind her ears. "Not always."

Wes face-palms into both hands. The fortune cookie lied. His horoscope misrepresented his future.

"I take everything one step at a time. And even then, I sometimes trip. I've made some awful decisions, before and after meeting Leo," Leeann says.

Wes nods into his hands. He knows Leeann's not perfect—her love of iced tea proves that—but as far as great examples go, she's the closest this world has to flawlessness.

"I almost went to Ohio State." Leeann grins when Wes peeks from behind his fingers. "I know, right? O-freaking-hio."

Wes mouths *Wow* at her.

"I didn't always get along with my parents. And Grace was the epitome of a perfect daughter. I wanted to scream all the time. I had to get far away." She clears her throat. "I didn't know what I was going to study or who the hell I'd know out there. But I was going."

"What happened?"

Leeann stares down into her cup. "Perfect little Grace had a pregnancy scare. My parents flipped the F out."

Wes loves that, sometimes, Leeann refuses to use actual swear words while talking. She says she's preparing for a life in childcare. Admirable, but still funny as fuck.

"My mom begged me to reconsider my plans." She shrugs again. "It was the first time I felt like she cared. Like, if *anything* happened to me, she'd never survive it. I dunno—it made me feel loved. Morbid, right?"

Wes shakes his head. "Sounds like most of us."

"My mom spent weeks with me curating a list of schools on the west coast," Leeann says. "My dad, the dentist who never vacations, took an entire week off. He drove me up and down the coast."

Wes watches her shred the napkin into tiny brown snowflakes, forming a pile in the center of the table.

"I didn't like Leo when I met him," she continues, softer. "In fact, he tried his shot with my roommate and missed. I felt so sorry for him, but I didn't think I was in his league. He knew what he was going to be from day one."

Even though she's not looking, Wes nods.

"But then, outside the library, we got to chatting." The brightness of her expression dwarfs the afternoon sun streaming through the giant front windows. "He's got no game. Like, none."

Wes grins victoriously. The Calvin Hudson disaster-flirt gene is strong in both his sons.

"I asked *him* out." She snorts. "You only live once, right? I didn't think he'd fall in love with me."

When their eyes meet, Wes wiggles his eyebrows as if to say, *Come on, you're a ten.*

passing cars pop on, briefly blinding Wes. The first few drops dot the pavement outside the parking garage they're standing in front of.

"Wait for what?" Manu asks, eyebrows furrowed.

Wes gasps. If he'd had three more minutes, he could've pulled out his phone and typed up a quick list before running all the way here:

Top 5 Reasons Manuia Is the One.

But he didn't have time. Honestly, he doesn't know if there are five reasons. More importantly, does he need more than one?

You're not Nico.

At a certain age, crushes stop being fun. They stop being these things that people secretly write about in diaries or online journals or in their next great fanfic story. Crushes become this damning thing: the ultimate hill one must climb. Because once someone gets over a crush, they can see what's on the other side.

Thing is, maybe there's nothing there. Maybe life truly is just a *Choose Your Own Adventure* and picking the wrong next step is the only way to get somewhere. Anywhere.

Wes is stuck between an amazing guy in front of him and an old crush behind him.

"I get it," Manu says, sighing. He brushes a hand over his hair again. "No hard feelings. It's cool."

"It's not," Wes finally wobbles out.

"But it is," Manu says, smiling sadly. "Not to lay on the inspirational quote of the day from a Zen IG account or anything, but: 'The heart wants what it wants.' Hashtag Emily Dickinson."

For a second, Wes imagines Nico liking that quote on Pinterest. Then he hates himself.

Manu steps forward. "Listen," he says, sincere.

Wes tries to. Rain splats on his cheek, his eyelashes. It tags his costume as if the sky is playing a game of paintball and winning. Wes's chest heaves, betraying him, as Manu's hand touches his cheek.

"At some point, you get over someone." That sadness edging Manu's mouth almost reaches his eyes. "But I hope you don't miss out on the rest of the world waiting for that to happen."

Wes shivers. Manu's thumb brushes rain from just under his right eye. Except, Wes isn't certain that precipitation is what's wetting his cheeks.

"Call me, if—" Manu pauses, shaking his head. "Wait, we didn't exchange numbers."

It's a depressing reality Wes hadn't realized. He never bothered to ask for Manu's number so they could communicate like real people instead of two online entities sharing metadata and likes. This was never going anywhere.

"DM me if things change," Manu finally says.

"Okay," Wes says, hoarsely, fighting off that tremble in his voice. He inhales the scent of summer's first storm.

Manu leans closer, then hesitates. He searches Wes's face for permission.

Wes nods.

Manu's lips taste like coffee and powdered doughnuts and finality. He pulls away first. Wes tries to memorize the moment, eyes closed. His first kiss with a boy in the middle of the afternoon where anyone could see. A cooling, wet thumb strokes the apple of his cheek, then Manu's gone.

And Wes lets the rain soak him through.

STANDING JUST INSIDE THE BOOKSTORE'S entrance, Wes drips a puddle onto the beat-up carpet. A handful of eyes are on him. He notices Ella has joined the others.

"What happened?" she demands.

Wes shrugs, incapable of making his throat work.

"You just let him go?"

He nods, biting his lip. The sour flavor of rain tickles his tongue.

"Why?"

Wes sniffles. He uses the back of his wrist to wipe water from the end of his nose. His shoes are squishy. He didn't jog back to the bookstore. He walked. Slowly, shakily, without caring about how soaked his costume would be by the end.

"Wes," she says, shaking her head. She's disappointed in him, which is one hell of an ironic moment coming from Ella Graham. "You're ruining your life waiting for—"

He cuts her off. "It's already *ruined*, El."

It's pouring outside. The rain splattering on the pavement is marginally louder than Wes's voice. It's louder than Zay as he reads to the children still gathered around the carpet. It's louder than the murmuring from the parents who are now staring at Wes, hands over their mouths as they whisper to each other.

He's too much of a mess to give a shit.

"This…" Wes waves a hand around the bookstore, then smacks it against his own chest. "…isn't something you can fix with a half-assed effort. You can't just roll over whenever you want and decide to deal with reality. It's here. It's always been here."

"I don't—"

He interrupts her again. "*You do*. Don't feel like dealing with the reality that the bookstore is closing? Show up late. Don't want to deal with the possibility of heartbreak by having feelings for someone? Hook up, then ghost them."

He's seething, chest inflating too quickly. "Can't handle the pressure that maybe, just maybe, there are some issues with your parents you have to face head-on or they'll never be fixed? Camp out at your best friend's spot for the summer, then pack up for college in the fall. Boom. Mic drop. Peace out, life-givers; it's been real."

Okay, Wes is a certified, dog-faced asshole for that one. Raging against the machine comes with casualties. Unfortunately, that includes one of his closest friends.

Ella blinks and blinks at him. She doesn't say anything. Maybe she's mentally plotting where to hide his body.

"Ella. Wesley." Nico wedges between them, his voice a low warning. "Let's not fight."

Two of the parents have their phones pointed at them. Great. Wes's meltdown will probably be a viral hit in a few hours. Another set of parents are already escorting their children from the story time circle toward the front door. Before they can escape, Cooper yells, "Have a page-turning day!" with as much charm as a guy dressed as Dogman can spare.

Nico turns to Wes. "¿Estás bien?"

Something is stuck to Wes's shoe. He shakes it off. It's a semi-glossy cardstock flyer for next week's Speed Booking. Ella and Kyra are supposed to pass them out near the pier tomorrow.

Reality hits Wes like a runaway train. Next week's too late. Next month, there won't be a Once Upon a Page. It's over. Leo called the time of death a week ago, and Wes has steadily ignored the fact that the cold, lifeless shell that once housed his teen dreams is all but buried.

"No. I'm not okay." Wes stumbles back from Nico. "Things aren't okay; thanks for noticing." After a deep, unsteady breath, he chokes out, "And *we're* not okay either."

Nico's eyebrows climb his forehead. "¿Que?"

"We're not okay," Wes repeats, anger crawling into his voice. He squints to stop anything from leaking out his eyes. "I've been trying to…" He doesn't finish.

"Trying to what?"

"Never mind."

Wes almost says it. But he's become such a pro at giving up, the words are like cotton candy in his mouth, dissolving instantly. And the one time he fights, the one time he demands the universe give him what he wants, he fails.

He failed Once Upon a Page. He failed Mrs. Rossi. The truth is like swallowing glass.

"Wesley," Nico repeats, firmer.

Who was Wes kidding? He can't save the bookstore. He can't make Nico see him a certain way. Life isn't a shortened-for-content, perfectly cast, movie version of his favorite book.

"I'm leaving," he finally whispers.

There's no waiting for protests from Nico or Cooper. He doesn't make eye contact with Ella. He pretends Anna isn't standing next to Lucas, wearing a banana costume, looking like a real-life sad-face emoji. Shoes squishing, he slams out the bookstore's front door.

No one follows him.

Wes makes it as far as the stairwell leading up to the loft before falling to his knees, dry-heaving and crying at once.

He's so done.

CHAPTER TWENTY-TWO ✐

WES HAS BROKEN RULE NUMBER one.

For three days, he's called out sick for his shifts. In reality, he's perfectly healthy, but he can't be inside the bookstore. Not after his Tony Award-winning breakdown.

"I have a cold," he says groggily to Mrs. Rossi's voicemail every morning. She always calls back an hour later. He never answers. She's texted. He doesn't check the texts. Yesterday, at eleven a.m., there was a knock at the door and Wes, the burgeoning adult he is, hid in the kitchen with a blanket over his head as if it were an invisibility cloak.

Mrs. Rossi left him a Tupperware of homemade chicken soup, a gallon of cold-pressed orange juice, and a handwritten note on cartoon kitty stationary:

Eat. Drink. Feel better! Love, the Rossi family X.

Wes follows her first two instructions, but it doesn't cure anything. He's never missed a shift. He's never *lied* to Mrs. Rossi. Guilt eats him alive at three o'clock every day. He's been sunk into the green sofa's cushions while Nico's downstairs, probably holding a cup of tea, anticipating Wes's appearance behind the front counter.

But, for seventy-two hours, Nico doesn't call. He doesn't text. He doesn't update his Pinterest. And Wes feels less and less horrible about it all.

Is this what the fall will be like? No communication? One of us at Stanford, the other… who knows?

Wes is waiting for his *Survival Guide to Being an Adult* handbook to show up, but it never does.

For her part, Ella continues her day-to-day routine without saying a word to him. He was expecting her to pack her bags and leave, but she didn't. She also didn't set his bed on fire while he showered the other day, for which Wes is also grateful. Ella just... keeps going.

He doesn't FaceTime with his mom, though he texts. Calvin texts, too, but Wes only replies with single-word responses. He hasn't decided on a field of study. He hasn't figured out any of the mysteries of the universe.

It takes twelve DMs on multiple social media apps and a Facebook friend request to Wes's prehistoric account before he finally agrees to speak to anyone.

@coopsarrow is hard to ignore.

"So, what you're telling me is..." Cooper's hands are raised, palms out. Moon-sized eyes stare at Wes. "... no one making this movie caught the absurd illogic in this plot?"

"Nope."

"And they tried to explain it away by saying time travel isn't like *Back to the Future*, but they did *this*?"

"Yup."

"How do you ignore science?"

Wes guffaws, tipping back on the green sofa. He hasn't laughed in days. It's this strange rumble from his chest, shaking off all the mucous and exhaustion built up from emo-crying over his life. Damn, he's missed it. "This is why DC is the superior brand," he says smugly.

"Whoa." Cooper shakes his head as if his brain is fried. The end credits of the last Avengers movie are rolling across the screen. "Mind blown."

They've been marathoning Wes's definitive list of must-see Marvel films for most of the morning. Cooper, the novice, had only seen

Infinity War because of Devon. But, due to length and continual explanations from Wes about plot points, they've only made it through two films. Wes doesn't mind. He's slumming it in a Shazam onesie with a sauce stain on his chest from yesterday's microwavable burrito. He hasn't showered in approximately twenty-six hours. His jaw is itchy with stubble. There's cheese puff grime in his cuticles.

Yeah, this is adulting at eighteen.

At least he remembered to brush his teeth this morning.

Cooper cracks a yellow can of Red Bull and chugs. The kid's got a lead stomach. He burps, then says, "So, for continuity purposes… are we going to talk about it?"

Wes tosses one of his mom's throw pillows at Cooper. He catches it one-handed. He's got major hand-eye coordination skills too.

"No," Wes yells at the ceiling.

"But you don't even know what 'it' is."

Wes guesses it's either what happened at the bookstore or Nico or Ella. Maybe it's Manu. He's done a daily check to see if Manu's unfollowed his Insta account. He hasn't. Wes is sad and grateful about that. At the end of the day, he wants to be Manu's friend. But the idea of initiating that conversation with Manu makes him nauseous.

Cooper stares at Wes expectantly.

He takes a slug of his own Red Bull before whispering, "Fire away."

"Well," Cooper says, grabbing a handful of cheese puffs from the bag. "What's the deal with school?"

"What do you mean?" Wes can't knock the surprise out of his voice.

Cooper shrugs one shoulder before stuffing the cheese puffs into his mouth. The dust paints his lips orange. "Everyone else is talking about it except for you." He chews and chews before downing the rest with a gulp of Red Bull. "Anna's going to be finishing up her degree. Ella plans to brainwash the next generation of kids into being steampunk, ultra-goth, black coffee drinking, rage-against-the-system leaders, which I'm totally not against."

Wes snorts before stealing back the bag.

"Nico's all Stanford trees that and med school prodigy this."

It's impossible to prevent the flinch that wracks Wes's entire body. If Cooper notices, he doesn't mention it.

"Even Zay's on some graduate early so he can conquer the music industry gnarliness," Cooper continues, dusting cheesy crumbs all over his sweats. "Again, I'm not opposed. Have you heard his stuff? It's wicked."

Admittedly, Wes hasn't heard any of Zay's latest tunes. Another tidal wave of guilt takes him under. How many pieces of his friends' lives has he missed in two months of stress and anxiety?

"But not you," Cooper says softly, his expression puzzled.

"I'm… Uh." The stutter is unavoidable. "I'm *going*. You know that. UCLA, next month."

It's the only part of Wes's outline, his entire five-year-adult-plan that's always been there. But the more Wes thinks about it… Is he the one who scripted that agenda for himself?

"Yeah, yeah. Go Bruins." Cooper fists pumps the air with zero enthusiasm. "But, like. You don't *talk* about it."

"I don't talk about—"

"Yes, you do," Cooper says empathically. "Your obsession with Weezer? You talk about that. Your utter disdain for Oasis and all things Peter Gallagher? You discuss that too. You talk about your love of tea, your favorite comic books, the worst pizza toppings, how you'd direct a Green Lantern movie to erase that CGI, trashcan fire, Ryan Reynolds version from the annals of history."

"It was complete shit," Wes moans. "Ugh."

"Geoff Johns, Nirvana's musical impact on alternative rock greatness, the revolution Dr. Dre created in hip-hop," Cooper lists every topic on a different finger. "And forgive me if this one burns, but even how you feel about Nico—you whisper to Ella about it when you think none of us are paying attention."

Wes stares at his lap. His left foot wiggles anxiously.

"The things you hate, care about, or are madly in love with, you talk about," Cooper says quietly, curving forward enough that he appears in Wes's peripheral vision. Fuzzy, goofy Cooper reminding him that he's avoiding life like a hypochondriac avoids a person who sneezes.

"I..." The lie can't make it past Wes's tongue.

He *doesn't* talk about college.

"Do you want to go?"

"Yes."

He does, right? Does it matter if he's having second, third, or fourth thoughts about it? All the paperwork is done. He's been assigned a roommate—it's in his email. His parents return next week, which means it'll be a mad dash to get supplies, clothes, boxes, maybe a new laptop.

He's going. Right?

Wes scratches his scruffy chin. "I mean, I'm doing it."

Cooper rolls his eyes. "Yeah, I got up this morning at six a.m. to walk the dog. Doesn't mean I wanted to."

"But that's different," Wes argues.

"Is it?"

"It's optional," Wes chokes out.

"So, is college."

Well, duh. Wes knows that. There's such a thing as a gap year. Or not going at all. Wes thinks saving himself and his parents thousands and thousands of dollars in tuition would be the most selfless win ever. But... is that an option for *him*?

Keys jiggle in the front door. Wes can hear laughter. And then Ella and Anna walk into the loft. They're the perfect counterparts: Anna in an off-the-shoulder peasant dress as pale yellow as her hair; Ella in a black T-shirt and jeans, her dark nails cradling a cup of black iced coffee.

Wes tries to remain perfectly still, as if they're dinosaurs who can only visually track their prey with movement. It doesn't work.

"Sup, Scott Pilgrim and Brutus," says Ella, dropping her keys on the coffee table before crossing over to sit next to Cooper. Anna follows, waving.

"Wait. Which one am I?" Cooper asks.

But, despite the Michael Cera reference, Wes already knows he's Brutus. He's a traitor.

"Hi," he says quietly to Anna. Then he waves at Ella.

She slurps her iced coffee loudly, eyes narrowed.

He deserves her frosty glare. Neither of them have extended an olive branch, but Wes knows he should be the one apologizing. He hasn't quite figured out the opening act for his Wes Is a Screwup world tour. First stop: Ellaville, California.

"What're you two up to?" Anna asks, riffling through the cheese puffs while looking around the room.

This is the first time she's been to the loft. Cooper too. Wes's never invited any of his friends over other than Nico. Even Ella took at least a summer before Wes admitted where he lived. He's always kept this unconscious barrier between himself and the people he likes.

"Nothing," replies Wes. Ella continues to burn a hole through his skull with her eyes.

Cooper clears his throat. "We're discussing the future. Specifically, the future of Wes Hudson, son of the great Savannah Kirk."

"Perfect timing then." Ella smirks at Wes.

His head cocks so far to the right, it almost detaches from his neck. "Is it?"

Ella nods, finishing her iced coffee.

He squints at Cooper. Then Anna. Wes studies each of them, suspicious, before he asks, "Is this my intervention? Was this planned?"

He's spent copious amounts of time on YouTube, scanning through suggested videos when business has been slow at the bookstore. Wes knows that when someone's friends—even the ones who currently hate them— "unexpectedly" turn up for a group conversation about that person, it's a sign they're going to rehab.

"No," Cooper says as Anna declares, "Yes!"

"Coop, how could you?" Wes accuses, snatching the near-empty bag of cheese puffs from his dirty, tangerine fingers.

"I didn't!"

"He didn't," Ella confirms. She crosses her legs, hands in her lap. "This wasn't planned. But it's been discussed."

"By who?"

"All of us."

"Bullshit." Even though they're on radio silence, Wes is certain Nico wouldn't participate in any discussion like that. Zay too. Gossip in any form isn't their M.O.

"Fine," Ella huffs. "Me and Anna. Today, at Brews and Views."

Anna gives a guilty nod. Cooper sits, arms folded, pouting. It's not until Wes passes back the bag with apologetic eyes that Cooper grins, all forgiven.

"Why?" Wes asks, his voice small and distant.

"Newsflash, dude," Ella says, her eyes set into a glare that could destroy entire armies. "I'm not the fat, sarcastic sidekick in your Taylor Swift-esque love story, okay? I'm not the marginally cute friend who gets to vicariously live her fantasies through your trope-filled, cliché coming of age arc. I'm your best friend. That guarantees me, at the minimum, fifty percent of your self-growth and Molly Ringwald happy ending."

Wes laments spending an entire weekend last summer devouring the John Hughes '80s films because, according to some clueless commentator on Reddit, they were "the films of this entire generation." *Wrong*. They were mildly funny, predictable, hella racist and problematic, with some killer dialogue and tingly romantic moments.

"There's not much to discuss," Wes says indifferently.

"Ha." Cooper's smiling mouth is crusted in cheese dust.

Kindly, Wes flips him off.

"I'm thinking about going into teaching," Ella says, shaking the ice around in her cup. Their eyes immediately shift to her. "I think I could be good at it," she declares, unblinking. "You saw how I was with Cassie."

One customer out of two hundred isn't exactly a winning record, but Wes will never forget Cassie's expression when she left the bookstore.

"A school counselor," he suggests.

"Yes! You could put up all of those inspirational posters on your office walls," Cooper says ecstatically. "Aww, ones with kitties on them."

"Or I could just mount your head to the wall as a warning not to piss Ms. Graham off," Ella counters.

Cooper sinks into the sofa, face scrunched.

"Anyway," Ella turns back to Wes, "I love working with the younger generation."

"Okay. Calm down, grandma." He chuckles. "You're only eighteen."

Ella gives him a double middle finger salute.

"What about you?" Wes asks Anna. "What're you gonna do when the store closes?"

There, he's said it out loud. Two months ago, Wes would've had to lock himself in a bathroom, struggling to breathe, before he'd accept the bookstore's closing. But he's being an adult. Wes is taking this like a champ, pretending that mist that's clouding his vision and the soreness in his throat aren't there.

Anna taps her chin thoughtfully. "I'll finish school and then maybe work at a bank? I could manage a branch. I'm good with money."

She is. It's the management part Wes thinks could use some extra care. But Anna's held up well while Mrs. Rossi has been M.I.A., so he decides to let it slide.

Their eyes turn on Cooper. He shakes his head. "Don't look at me. *I'm sixteen.* I just figured out what pizza topping I like best."

"Lies," Ella says, reaching over to steal the bag. It's empty. "Just last week it took you ten minutes to decide if you wanted marinara or white sauce."

"Still." Cooper angles his body in Wes's direction. "Aren't we allowed to change our minds about things? As much as I love my parents, I'm pretty sure they have no clue what they're doing half the time."

"Well, we know my parental figures sure as hell don't know what they're doing," Ella says, eyeing Wes.

His cheeks warm. "I'm sorry about—"

"I'm not mad about it," Ella interjects. She lowers her chin and picks at her nail polish. "I think I was more pissed because someone else called me on my own shit."

They're all quiet for a moment. Then Cooper says, "My mom's quit smoking sixteen times in six months."

Anna, nodding, says, "I haven't seen my mom in seven years. She likes to bail on responsibility. And my dad's kind of a wreck when it comes to taking care of himself."

"So," Ella says, popping her gum, "All of our parents are still making bad choices."

Wes slouches. The tightness behind his ribs loosens.

"I like Kyra," Anna says, unexpectedly. Then, sheepishly, she whispers, "I really, really like her."

"*Oh*-kay," Ella sings.

"Sorry. I thought we were having one of those confessional moments."

"I mean, yeah. Sure." Ella pats Anna's shoulder. "Good for you. And her."

"I'm aroace," Cooper says, eyes bright, a soft flush to his face. He drags a hand over his hair, staining it orange. "I just thought—uh. I wanted to share that."

Ella tilts her head, eyebrows lowered.

Cooper tenses.

Then, Ella pats Cooper's shoulder too. "That's awesome, kiddo."

Simultaneously, Cooper and Wes exhale. Ella stares at Wes. "Since we're all sharing stuff, is there anything you'd like to add?"

"Um." Wes lowers his eyes while dusting cheese crumbs from his onesie.

"Fine," Ella says dramatically. Head titled back, she squints at the ceiling. "I was—I *am* mad with Mrs. Rossi. Not just because the bookstore's closing, but because..." Her voice catches. She blinks and blinks. "Because she's the closest thing I have to a mom. To a role model. And she's just giving up. I want her to fight, but she's not."

A thick wall of silence closes in around them. Cooper eyes the empty cheese puff bag. Cautiously, Anna has slipped an arm around

Ella's shoulder. Wes counts Ella's sniffs. Five. It's the only thing grounding him.

"Maybe she did," Anna says. "She's a tough cookie."

"She has to be to deal with you, El," says Wes, stretching his leg out to kick her knee.

Cooper bumps her shoulder, whispering, "That's why you're so awesome."

"Ugh. Quit trying to win cool points with me." Ella leans into him; a single tear leaves a black trail down her left cheek.

Wes clears his throat. He has no clue what he's doing. His heart leapfrogs into his throat, but he says, "I like Nico. A lot."

"I'm sorry, what?" Ella asks, craning in his direction.

"I said—"

"A little *louder*, please."

Anna giggles into her hands; her hair falls across her face. Cooper raises his phone, playing music. Anyone who's ever said The Cure's "Just Like Heaven" isn't the ultimate feel-good song is the biggest liar.

"Come on, Molly Ringwald," says Ella. "Scream it for all the losers pining everywhere."

Wrinkling his nose, Wes almost pretends he never said anything. But what for? It's not as if he's had the guts to at least say this to Nico's face. He might as well shout it to his friends. "I have the biggest, middle school crush on Nicolás Alvarez!"

"Again!" Cooper and Anna yell simultaneously.

"I love Nicolás Alvarez!"

They all crack up. When the laughter dies down, Wes's stomach is too tight for him to breathe. Ella squeezes his forearm and says, "For the record, I was always Team Nico."

They dissolve into laughter again. It's the best Wes's felt in seventy-two hours.

CHAPTER TWENTY-THREE ✎

STEAM SWIRLS IN A THIN cloud from the mug of tea sitting in front of Wes. Engraved in the ceramic is the Brews and Views logo. He eyes it suspiciously. It smells good, an earthy bold flavor. Oolong, possibly. And Wes is ninety-nine percent certain it's poisoned.

Across from him, Leo stares, one eyebrow raised, his mouth twitching impatiently.

"There's cyanide in here, right?" Wes gestures toward the mug. It was sitting at the table waiting for Wes before he arrived.

"No."

"Odorless horse tranquilizers? Arsenic? Heroin?" Tentatively, Wes sniffs, then sips the tea. He's not experiencing any instant numbness. He's not lightheaded. There could be delayed symptoms, but for now, the tea's... *incredible.*

"It's regular, boring, overpriced oolong," Leo confirms, sipping his own extra dry cappuccino. It's decaf and made with almond milk, not because Leo's lactose intolerant, but because he's just a complicated, pretentious dick.

Slurping his tea, Wes studies Leo. The first two buttons of his starched white shirt are undone; his sleeves are bunched at his elbows. He hasn't shaved. His tie's loose. Honestly, he looks a mess.

"Sup with you?"

"Interning, studying for the LSAT, and trying to ensure your fiancée doesn't have an aneurysm over your ideal wedding venue being booked *two years* in advance is detrimental to my health." Leo wipes at his foam moustache. "At least the coffee's good."

"Sorry," Wes says, sounding anything but that.

"You haven't answered any of my texts." Leo folds his arms on the table.

"Been busy. Planning a funeral for your childhood fantasies is a lot of work."

"Wes," Leo tries.

"Is that why you invited me here?" Wes asks, voice hard. "You need me to return to my wedding duties?"

"Leeann misses you," Leo says softly. "And you haven't answered any of her calls either. That's not like you."

Wes rolls his eyes. Leeann's a narc. She's sold Wes out to his own demonic kin.

"So, what? You're here to play nice?" Wes hisses, almost burning his tongue as he gulps tea. "This pretend, 'I care so much' version of Leo? You can keep it. I'm good."

"No," Leo says, low and defeated. They're seated in a far corner, close to the large storefront windows. Sunlight pours over them. The rain's finally left. In its wake, a milder August warmth has emerged. Leo squints at the people passing by outside. "I don't really know how to be the brother I should be to you."

"What?"

Leo drags a finger around the rim of his mug. "We're so different," he says. "When we were growing up, I felt like I had to protect you. We liked different stuff. Different things set us off."

He clears his throat, eyes on the table. "The kids my age would make fun of you."

Wes flops back in his chair. "Okay."

Behind the bar, Kyra's not-so-secretly watching over them. Beyoncé plays on the speakers, and she's singing along. But her eyes never leave Wes's face. She's waiting for any indication to jump in. Wes loves her for that, but he needs to hear Leo out.

"I tried to make you less... *you*," Leo says, voice dropping in shame. "I tried to make you like different things. Act a certain way. I was hard on you, hoping you'd get the hint that I didn't want to give anyone a reason to pick on you."

"Ha." Wes's forehead wrinkles. "How'd that work out for you?"

Leo exhales. "They still made fun of you. So, I thought if I pushed you far enough away, they wouldn't be able to talk shit about you. You wouldn't be around. They'd find a new target."

"And?"

"They did." Leo's eyes finally lift, soft and glassy. "But by then, the distance between us was so big, I didn't know how to bring you back."

Poisoned or not, Wes sips his tea. It burns in the way he needs. He tries not to remember what it was like to have Leo shout at him or slam his bedroom door in Wes's face. It doesn't work. He can recall every time Leo wouldn't let Wes follow him and his "friends" to the beach, every moment Wes wanted to share a new comic with Leo, but he wasn't there.

"I wasn't a good brother back then," Leo admits. "Or now. There are times when I don't know the right things to say."

"Yeah, well." The heat from the tea barely dissolves the lump in Wes's throat.

"But you're still *my* brother." Leo frowns. "I give a shit about you."

Wes snorts. But the honesty in Leo's guilt-stricken eyes is unavoidable. Wes blinks until that sheen dampening his eyelashes passes. "I know," he says tightly.

A quiet filled by Beyoncé's voice settles over their table. Wes refuses to cry. But that eight-year-old version of himself crawls out of the shadows Leo put him in, warming Wes's chest, making him wish they'd said any of this to each other sooner.

"I need a best man."

Wes sits up, shoulders drawn like a boss. "Are you asking or telling me?"

"I'm *trying*," Leo says, incredulous.

"It's a weak effort."

Leo gags; his body shifts as if he's two seconds from reaching across the table and duffing Wes on the shoulder. But he doesn't. "Well?"

"Am I allowed to quote Green Day during the reception toast?" Wes wonders.

"Hell no."

"You're a dick," Wes mumbles.

"Thanks. I'd hate to disappoint you."

A laugh floods Wes's mouth. *Who is this alien?*

"Are you gonna ask Nico to be your date?" Leo leans back, his expression relaxed.

Wes's the one choking this time.

"Don't act, bro," says Leo. He takes a quick sip of his drink. "You know you want to."

Wes face-palms, groaning. Of course Leo knows. Of course, the universe has let everyone in on Wes's secret except the one person who should know.

"I have no clue what to do," he mumbles into his hands.

"Wes," Leo says, "If the worst thing you do in this lifetime is fall in love with your best friend, then I'd say you're doing pretty damn good."

ON HIS LUNCH BREAK, WES sneaks into the alley behind Paseo Del Mar. He squats, spine pressed to the pastel pink wall, while scrolling through his contacts. He inhales deeply for courage before pressing the FaceTime button. It takes two rings before the video comes in fuzzy, then crisp.

"Wesley?"

And there he is, Calvin Hudson, droopy eyes deep brown with green flecks around the outermost parts of his irises. His hair's cut close; the shadow of a beard and mustache outline his mouth. There's a touch of gray in the black. His voice's groggy, but so warm.

"Hey, Daddy."

Damn, how long has it been since he called Calvin that? How long since he's felt this vulnerable, a man-sized shell of a body containing a five-year-old desperate to crawl into his father's lap for tea and cartoons.

"Are you okay?" Calvin looks down, probably to check the time. "Are you at work?"

"Ye-Yeah," Wes stutters, smiling with all the muscles that'll cooperate.

"Mrs. Rossi good?"

Wes doesn't know. She's taken another unplanned day off. Technically, he's in charge, but he has the slightest faith Ella and Cooper won't burn the store down in the next ten minutes.

"Yeah, she's fine."

Calvin hums; the camera shifts until Wes gets an up-close-and-weird view of him. He's always been strange about FaceTime. He doesn't understand the concept of keeping the phone still or what to do when the picture freezes and always holds the lens too close, as if it'll make the moment more personal rather than awkward.

"How's the restaurant?" Wes asks, killing time until he can corral courage.

"Good, good. But I can't wait to get back home. They'll be fine without me here."

Wes loves the confidence in Calvin's voice. It's taken him years to get to the point where he trusts anyone else to manage one of his projects.

"Did you get my texts?"

This is the point Wes's been avoiding. For weeks, he's kept Calvin on hold. Or he's skirted the subject of school. But after talking to Leo, he knows this is what he needs to do. Thankfully, Leo's got his back. He even offered to call their parents for Wes.

But Wes needs to own this.

"About that." Wes scratches his cheek.

Calvin hums again. The camera pans back as he lifts a cup to his mouth, slurping.

"Is that tea?"

"Yup," says Calvin, holding the cup higher, almost dropping his phone. The joy in his voice collapses the light-years of distance between them, as if Calvin's right here in Santa Monica with Wes, both of them stretched lazily across the green sofa with twin cups. "Thai ginger. Do you remember drinking this?"

Wes nods, eyes wet. A sleeping, curled memory stretches in his chest. Its blissful light overtakes Wes's cells. Calvin's drinking herbal tea. He's thinking of Wes.

I can do this.

"So, uh." Wes clears his throat. "Can we talk about college?"

On Thursday morning, before the ivory imprint of the moon disappears, Wes jogs down the stairwell to Colorado Avenue. From the sidewalk, he can view the unlit blue-white arch welcoming tourists to Santa Monica Yacht Harbor. The air's slightly damp and cool. Eugene's already inside Brews and Views, setting up the espresso machines for the seven a.m. crowd. A soundtrack of birds and rolling waves from the beach whispers into the streets.

It's like every other morning Wes has been here, in front of Once Upon a Page, before the bookstore opens.

But today it's different. There's a weight on his shoulders he's ready to remove. There's a hollowness in his chest that needs to be filled.

When Wes opens the door, he inhales the scent of new books and old carpet. In a few hours, the bookstore will smell like sand and ocean. In a month, the bookstore will probably reek of new paint and retail commercialism. Anna forgot to turn off the neon BOOKS sign in the window last night. The pink letters aren't the only lights glowing in Wes's vision.

In the back corner, the office shines like a beacon.

Wes's fingers drag along the shelves as he navigates the aisles. What happens to the books when a bookstore closes? Are they donated to charity? Given to schools? Put in a storage locker, where their stories grow old and lifeless in the dark?

The void in Wes's chest expands, but he carries on.

Mrs. Rossi is hunched at her desk. Her hair's more gray than pink now. Sitting on a messy stack of papers is a used copy of *The Heart of the Lone Wolf*. Mrs. Rossi's mumbling to herself; her left hand trembles as she attempts to hold a pen. "Heaven help me!"

Wes frowns, then clears his throat. "Hey?"

"Good morning," Mrs. Rossi croaks, lifting her head. She's pale; her face is clean of any makeup. It amplifies the sadness in her brown eyes, the wrinkles at her mouth. Her right hand crosses over to grip the left. After a moment, the shakes subside. "It's fine."

Wes nods. They both know she's lying.

The office chair squeaks loudly as she reclines. "You're here early."

"I wanted to—" His voice breaks. "I wanted to talk to you."

"I was wondering when you were going to finally ask."

"Ask?" Wes's eyebrows shoot up.

"Mmhmm." She brushes hair off her forehead, her hand shaking again. "I've known you for a lifetime, Wes. I knew it'd take you ages to come to me about what's happening with this place. I'm sure it's been eating you alive."

"You knew I knew?"

Mrs. Rossi tuts. "Of course I did." Her eyes close; her inhalations are long, and she exhales noisily. "You're all a hot mess. You've been running around here, having events after hours and shuffling my store around, and doing everything under the sun to save it."

"*You knew*?" Wes can't control the volume in his voice.

"Did you really think I wouldn't notice? I'm old, but I'm not naïve." She snorts. "Hell, half the time, you forgot to rearrange the bookshelves to the right places."

A tactical error. Wes shouldn't have trusted Cooper and Zay with those tasks. But his eyes narrow, and he hisses, "Why didn't you say anything? Why did you just let us—" He sucks in a loud breath. "You let us fight for this place while you just disappeared. What the hell?"

"I *let* you try to save this bookstore for many reasons," Mrs. Rossi says firmly.

Wes allows the silence to surround them. Then, voice shaky, he says, "Why?"

She shuts her eyes again. "I should've told you. I should've told all of you, but," she pauses, her throat bobbing. Wes waits. Nose wrinkled, she says, "Part of me wanted to believe that you could do it. Bring back the customers. Keep this place afloat just a little longer."

Her hands grip the chair's armrests. White knuckles. Blue veins. Age and wear and unsteadiness.

"That's not fair of me. To expect so much of everyone else." She blinks her eyes open. They're shiny brown moons. "To expect so much of *you*."

Wes leans against the doorframe. He tries to control his expression. He failed the bookstore. He failed her. But Mrs. Rossi failed him too. And that's the hardest part to digest. Ella's right—she's the closest thing to a second mom for all of them.

"I also didn't say anything because I know you. This is your home," she squeaks. The tremble in her voice is almost too much for him. "It's my home too. Decades, Wes. I've given this place decades, but I can't keep it going. *I* can't keep going."

Wes crosses his arms. His expression hardens. "But someone else could've."

Mrs. Rossi shakes her head.

It's selfish. If she's too tired to keep going, then retire. Give the reins to someone like Anna. Or one of the local bookstore managers that have been ousted by online retailers destroying the lifeline of independent bookstores.

Maybe… *him*. Wes doesn't know all the ways Once Upon a Page operates, but he knows enough.

"You're just giving up on something that means a lot to this community," he snaps. "You can retire. But you can't just let this place go."

"I *can*," she bites back. "It's mine."

"No, it's the property of some bullshit, commercialized coffeehouse now."

"You don't understand."

Those three words strike the flame over the kerosene in his chest. "How am I supposed to? I'm eighteen. Everyone expects me to just wake up and have my shit together. I'm supposed to have a plan." His chest heaves, his brain on fire. "But everything I come up with isn't good enough. I'm adult enough for expectations, but not adult enough to know what I want."

"Wes, sweetheart, it's not—"

"You gave me my first and only job at sixteen." Wes hates how pathetic his voice sounds. It's whiny. It's filled with ache. "You were the one person that believed in me. But even you didn't believe I was adult enough to handle any of this."

There's a thick pause. A few pieces of gray-pink hair fall over Mrs. Rossi's forehead. She inhales, but it looks as though it takes so much effort. Then she says, "Wes, I'm sick," in a voice that he swears comes from somewhere else.

"What?"

"*I'm sick*," she repeats. Before he can ask, she tells him, "Brain tumor," and follows with "I found out earlier this year," and finally "They think I have a fighting chance, but the statistics say otherwise. I've tried avoiding added stress. Taking more time to relax. I gave it my all but, if I hold on to this place, I'll be living the time I have left worried I did the wrong thing by not letting it go."

Wes isn't sure he's breathing or standing.

She's sick. Doctors say Mrs. Rossi's dying. Wes blinks repeatedly. Tiny black holes form throughout his body, devouring every nerve. He's numb.

"There's too much debt, sweetheart," she says weakly. "Do you honestly think I could afford to keep all of you on staff with no customers? I did it because I know how much all of you, even Ella, love this place. But I can't put that burden on someone else."

Words try to climb into his mouth, but they keep slipping on the bile coating his throat.

"I want what time I have left spent not stressing over what could be," she says, eyes wet. "I want to spend it with my husband. I want all of us to move on. And I'm sorry I didn't convey that in the right way."

Wes finally inhales.

"They promised me they'd keep a corner of the coffeehouse dedicated to books." She taps the spine of Savannah Kirk's novel. "I spent decades trying to make sure people found the stories they needed to go on. To live. To heal and to love. To fight. The least I could do is make sure there's still a piece of me in this damn space."

Tears latch onto Wes's eyelashes.

"It's just a place," she says, waving a trembling hand around her head. "It's just a bookstore. A thing."

"It's not," he tries to argue.

"It *is*. Just a possession." Her grin is an unshakable force. "It's filled with amazing memories, but we don't get to take our possessions with us everywhere. We leave those behind. But the memories—damn it, Wes, we get to take the memories with us to wherever our next road may lead."

There's a coffee mug at the edge of her desk. She reaches for it, but her hand shudders too much to grab. Wes steps into the office. He passes it to her, hands cupped around hers.

"I tried so hard," he says, choked. "I wanted to fix this for you."

Now he's the selfish one. *Poor Wes Hudson, incapable of adulting.*

"I tried," he repeats. "I'm not an adult. I can't make an impact."

Mrs. Rossi takes a long, slow sip of coffee. Then she says, "Excuse me, but are you smoking? Are you high?"

Wes lurches back, stunned. Then he cracks up.

"An *impact*? Have you not seen the change in Lucas?" she asks.

He's noticed the small things—Lucas's giant smile every time they walk through the door. The way they're more talkative. Their change in clothes. But that's not because of him, right?

"Lucas's always loved it here. But since they've started hanging out with you, they're more themselves than I've ever seen." Mrs. Rossi proudly lifts her chin. "Their mom called the other day to thank me. I assured her it was all you. Lucas might not ever have it easy, but every teen should have the right to be their true selves. We should give that to them. Always."

Wes bites the inside of his cheek, waiting for her to finish.

"I always knew you were great. After all, no average kid hangs around a bookstore."

Wes chuckles. "It was the comics."

"Whatever." Mrs. Rossi tuts again. "Stop trying to *make* an impact, Wes. *Be* the impact. For teens like Lucas. But also, for yourself."

Their silence is filled with inevitable sniffling. "We're holding onto old, broken things, sweetheart." Her warm hands grab his. Her eyes are soft, but Wes can still see the doubt edging her pupils. "I don't know what'll happen in six months. Or tomorrow. But I can't change the past. Neither can you. And we can't stay here hoping the world will make things happen for us. It's time to let go. Move on."

Wes nods slowly.

That's the thing. Some people are chained to their pasts. Some only have tunnel vision for the present. And some are so terrified by their future that they won't just let it happen. It's all real. It's all suffocating.

Mrs. Rossi is right. At some point, everyone has to move forward.

So, Wes does. He presses his store key to her desk. Then he eases his arms around her for a hug. It lasts too long. But that's okay. Sometimes, it's appropriate to hold on longer than necessary.

Neither one of them mentions how wet Mrs. Rossi's shoulder is when he pulls away. They don't comment on their damp cheeks, or the way they keep sniffling.

They just... move on.

CHAPTER TWENTY-FOUR

"You have one new voicemail."

"Buenos días, Wesley. ¿Cómo estás? It's Nico's mom. Oh, you know that already, don't you? Duh! Today's Nico's father's birthday. We're getting together, as a family, down by the beach to watch the sunset and have a small memorial for him. Please come. Around 6:00 p.m. I'm cooking dinner after. You still love my cooking, yes? Te amo."

"End of message."

The sun over Santa Monica Beach has begun its lethargic dip behind the horizon. Wes haphazardly rolls his white shirtsleeves to his elbows. He presses down the shirt's collar. Then, discreetly, he lifts one arm, sniffing. *Still fresh.* He didn't have a chance to shower after his shift.

Behind him, an ivory house trimmed in blue looks over the soft sand. Wes spent half of his high school years in that house. He knows the legs of the table on the patio are uneven. He knows there's a spare key under one of the potted spider plants. He knows the open window on the second floor is Nico's.

Wes knows Mrs. Alvarez's scent—mangoes and light roast coffee—when she finds him. She tugs him into a long hug. He holds her tightly as evening joggers and cyclists maneuver around them.

"Te extrañé," she says into his ear.

Wes knows this, too—*I missed you.* It's what she always says, no matter if it's been months or hours since they were last around each other. She steps back, auditing him. He rubs a damp hand across the back of his curls.

"You look great," she finally says.

Embarrassed, Wes stammers, "Thank you Mrs. Alva—" but she cuts him off.

"Guadalupe," she insists, just like Mr. Alvarez would. "Just Lupe, you know that."

He can't fix his lips to say Lupe. "It's good to see you," he replies instead.

"You too." She fires off a series of questions. How was Italy? How are his parents? How is Leo? She's heard about the wedding and wants all the necessary details. After Wes has rambled about how Leeann's checklists make his look inferior, Lupe talks about her daughters with this unnamable glow. She mentions Nico and Stanford, and Wes dutifully forces out a grin that his lips barely hold.

"I bet you're excited about school," says Lupe.

"So hyped."

Lupe hums. Wes suspects she notices the flatness in his tone, but she says, "Just like that Nico. Undecided," without any explanation.

"Uh. Sure."

"Come." She links her arm with his, gently pulling. "Walk with me."

They follow the bike path. She leads him onto the sand, closer to the pier and roaring Pacific Ocean. The water drifts so far up the shore, it shreds someone's forgotten sandcastle. Wes loves the way the sun looks against Lupe's already warm face.

"Martín loved this hour," she says to the ocean. "He loved the sunset. He'd talk about how this is when you knew it was okay to let whatever was troubling you go. Because the day was ending. "Don't carry today into tomorrow," he'd tell our children."

Her mouth falters, almost frowning.

She's inches shorter than Wes, just like Nico. Carefully, he leans close. A reminder. If she needs comfort, he's here.

"It doesn't hurt as much to miss him now. Not for me." She tilts her chin up; her eyes blink shut. "But I know it's still hard for Nico."

Wes is expecting tears when her eyes flutter open, but there are none.

"God, I'd never wish to lose that wonderful man, but if I had a choice, it'd be for it to happen later. When Nico was away, doing things for himself." Her mouth twitches. "He doesn't have to tell me he misses Martín. He doesn't have to explain why he's going to school over three hundred miles away to simultaneously fix something that wasn't his fault and to get away from the painful memories of it all. But I wish he was doing this for himself; not for me or Martín."

Wes can't find a place to rest his eyes. The sunset. The gold-green water. A group of teens down the shore, taking a selfie. Lupe's indifferent expression, the battle between her curled mouth and frowning eyebrows.

"Why don't you try to talk him out of it?"

Lupe laughs, both short and defeated. "You think I could?"

Probably not. Nico's too stubborn.

"When I look at him, I still see mi pequeño sol, but that doesn't mean I shouldn't let him make decisions for himself," she explains. "I've always encouraged my children to be themselves. I'm not here to dictate. I'm here to listen, support, love, and interfere when they do stupid things."

"Like chugging milkshakes while smashing an entire extra jalapeño-pepperoni pizza?" A smile teases Wes's lips.

"I don't understand you boys." She pretends to gag. "Jesus, the smell coming from Nico's bathroom that day. It was so offensive."

Wes tips his head back, guffawing at the sky.

The wind off the ocean sways the hem of Lupe's white dress. Her hair's dark, like a sky emptied of a moon and stars. It continuously dances into her face. "I just want Nico to figure himself out," she says. "He can be a doctor. Or a skater. He can be bisexual or pan or whatever feels right. He can be here or Palo Alto."

Her bottom lip trembles. One of them is three seconds from crying. Probably him.

"I just want him to do it for himself."

"I want the same for you, Wesley," she adds, pinching his wrist. "You two are so different, but so alike. It's like I have two sons."

Wes chuckles. It's easier to laugh than for him to confront the sting in his eyes and the way his sinuses are ready to explode. Honestly, he's been stuck on the top of an emotional rollercoaster for an entire summer and, at some point soon, he's going to crash.

"He loves you," she says. "You know that, right?"

"Yeah, sure. We're friends—"

"No." She shakes hair out of her face. "*Loves* you. In love."

The way she says it, so confident and pure and amazed—Wes's chest aches. He doesn't need Google to tell him what's coming.

"How do you know?" he asks, choked.

"*Please.* Nico's definitely Martín's son." Lupe smirks, eyebrows climbing her forehead. "Do you think I don't recognize the way Martín would stare at me doing the most ordinary things is the same way my son looks at you reading a comic book or shoveling food in your mouth? Ha."

They've drifted closer to the water. It almost kisses the soles of Wes's Pumas.

"It's probably killing him, knowing your time is short and he hasn't said anything."

Wes stares at her blankly.

He loves you.

"Go." She nods up shore. "Talk. Or whatever it is you teen boys do. Just don't be late for dinner."

NICO'S PLANTED IN THE SAND next to a lifeguard tower; the wooden shack is painted pale blue. He's dressed in a denim button-up and white linen pants. His feet are buried in the sand. His hair's wind-tousled. Wes doesn't know why he's observing all these things, creating a new untouchable list in his brain—**Reasons to be Forever in Love with Nico Alvarez**—instead of flopping down next to him.

He has so many issues.

"Cool sunset," he finally says, settling into the sand.

The top of the sun's still visible. Its reach over the waves keeps them gold and beautiful. From here, they can see Sofía playing leapfrog with the twins. Lupe joins them, taking turns spinning each of her daughters in circles until they fall. Nico wiggles closer until their shoulders touch.

Wes is grasping for something incredible to say. A teen romcom swoon-worthy monologue. Instead, he says, "Did you take a photo for the Gram yet?" like the geek loser he is.

"Of course." Nico unlocks his phone, scrolling through his feed to show Wes. He caught an amazing shot of the sun, large and looming over the Pacific, with the sand and a few birds and the silhouette of two people standing near the shore.

Oh. It's Wes and Lupe.

Hashtag family. Hashtag SME. Hashtag my world.

Squinting against the fading light, their eyes meet. Nico sucks on his lower lip. Wes forgets to breathe. It's a head rush. Their shoulders and knees and the edges of their feet touch.

Nico looks away first. "Do you think my dad would be proud of me?"

"Of course," whispers Wes, rocking in Nico's direction.

"Do you think he'd want me to go to Stanford?"

Wes's heart rests behind his teeth. What should he say? That he doesn't want Nico to go to Stanford. But that's not fair. That's not what Martín would say.

"Is it what *you* want?" he finally asks.

Nico stares at his knees. "I don't want to leave my sisters. Or my mom." His shoulders shake when he inhales. "I don't want to leave you."

"Yeah," Wes says softly, too much a coward to scream, "So don't go," the way his brain wants him to.

Nico sniffs. "I hope it doesn't change anything, but I think I need to."

All Wes hears is, *Because of you, Wesley. I need to get away from you.* "Okay," he mumbles, biting the inside of his cheek.

"Does it change anything?"

Straining to keep his expression neutral, Wes shrugs.

"Wesley." Nico sighs loudly. "Sometimes it's hard to be your friend."

"I'm sorry."

"You should be."

Wes winces. He deserves that. Before the summer, he was mild-to-acceptable by crush standards, an easygoing kind of pining. But for weeks, he's been on edge and frustrated and the kind of douchebag he'd never be friends with.

"It's impossible to be your friend when…" Nico pauses, nose wrinkled. "When I want more."

Yes, Wes has been difficult and insufferable and—

"What the—"

Nico cuts him off with a slow-building grin. It's all crinkle-eyed; the corners of his mouth stretch like clay. He bumps their shoulders.

"When I saw the way you and that guy looked at each other that day..." Nico lowers his head.

Ugh. Manu. Fortunately, they still follow each other on social media. In fact, yesterday, Manu messaged Wes a funny meme. Wes messaged back with a funnier GIF. They continued like that for five minutes. And it wasn't the least bit awkward when they wordlessly agreed to stop. It was cool.

"It *killed* me, dude," Nico gnaws out. "I was jealous as hell."

"You what?"

Wes has lost all concept of sentence structure. Was anything on his **Signs Your Crush Isn't Into You** list applicable to Nico?

"I'm not your mom," Nico starts, then his face scrunches. "Okay, that came out wrong. I'm not *like* your mom. I suck at words and confessions. I come up with plans in my head, but execution? No bueno."

Wes laughs at that. He could teach Nico a thing or two about lists. But also, he could sit here, be quiet, and let Nico finish.

The evolution of Nico's expression continues as he frowns at his feet. "I don't know how to say all the things I want."

Wes tries to grasp a fraction of the confidence building in his belly. "Then let me." He takes in the scene: they're on a beach, just after sunset, and it's the kind of August evening that's automatically transferred into a folder in Wes's memory under the filename *Perfect*.

Reddit, BuzzFeed, and six billion online sources would call this The Moment. It's time for Wes to throw down the gauntlet.

His mouth opens, then closes. He refined a list for this, but Wes never actually came up with what he was going to say. He was only supposed to write "I love you" in the sand, and, *bam*, happily ever-freaking-after.

"Damn it. Okay." He brushes a hand over Nico's arm. Mrs. Rossi's right—he can't wait around for the universe to make things happen. "This summer, I made a list. Well, I made a lot of lists. But this one was kind of important."

Nico chuckles. "Okay. And?"

"It was a list of the perfect ways to tell you—" He pauses.

Nico looks as if he's holding his breath. Good. Wes stopped breathing two minutes ago.

"I have the most epic crush on you," Wes finally says. And before Nico can blink, or utter a word, Wes adds, "I don't want to ruin our friendship. But I want more too. If you're sure that's what you want?"

The thing Wes should've researched is "what to do if your crush doesn't instantly respond to your confession?"

Nico's quiet for a long moment. Sweat tickles Wes's temple. His heartbeat's as noisy as every emo-pop-punk song Ella's ever played.

"Okay."

"Okay?" Wes chokes. *That's it? One word. Okay?* The internet truly set Wes up for disappointment.

"Yes, okay," Nico repeats, but with a sweetness in his voice. He shakes sand off his hand. It slides behind Wes's neck, palming it. He tugs until their foreheads touch.

The ocean's belting out anthemic songs. The kind of alt-rock summer tunes Wes lives for.

"I want that."

"Define *that*," Wes requests, hoarsely.

"More than friends, Wesley." They inhale at the same time. "I want *that*."

Wes smiles, almost leaning forward for a kiss. Instead, he says, "Sweet."

"Yeah." Nico grins back. "Sweet."

CHAPTER TWENTY-FIVE

"WELCOME TO THE FIRST..." ELLA pauses, smiling nervously while holding the microphone to her matte-black lips. "...and last ever Speed Booking Night at Once Upon a Page!"

People cheer, shaking their books above their heads. The bookstore's packed. There are so many bodies, attendees spill onto the sidewalk outside. That's where Wes is, watching from the doorway. He's surprised the police haven't shut them down.

Ella's leggings and Doc Martens match the black jersey dress she wears under her leather jacket. She stands on the front counter, breaking every unspoken rule Mrs. Rossi's ever invented. But sandwiched between her and Kyra is a third co-host for the evening: Mrs. Rossi.

After their talk, Mrs. Rossi whipped out a leftover flyer for tonight's event. She demanded that, despite the bookstore's looming closure, this event happen.

It's clear Ella dressed her—oversized Janet Jackson T-shirt with a black ballerina tutu, lips painted black, and a black bowler hat hiding her gray-pink hair—but she looks as if this is the most fun she's had in decades.

"Who's here to party?" she screams.

The crowd roars. Kyra doubles over laughing. Her hair is pulled and fastened into a sick curly mohawk. "Okay, go off then." Below her, Anna's dressed like a fairy with glitter across her face, heart eyes directed at Kyra.

"We want everyone to have an amazing time tonight, but we need to make something clear," Ella says when the room quiets. "Tonight's not about hooking up."

A group in the middle of the store jeers.

"If you meet someone you're romantically compatible with—cool. If you find a new friend—even better. Platonic relationships rock." Her eyes search until they find Wes's. "But if you find someone who knows what it's like to not be understood outside this store. Someone who gets how books can change your life. Someone you can lean on. Someone who doesn't always get you, but is willing to try, starting with a book and a few words, then…"

Ella exhales, blinking. Wes is almost positive she's wearing waterproof mascara, but he's not emotionally ready for her to cry.

"Then thank this woman," Ella says, tossing an arm around Mrs. Rossi's shoulders. "Because she made all this happen for you. For all of us." She kisses Mrs. Rossi's temple.

Okay, Wes might cry with or without Ella.

People clap, wolf whistle. Some chant Mrs. Rossi's name. It's a buffet of singles, locals, teens, and adults, all here thanks to Mrs. Rossi. And in the middle of the sea of faces and books is her husband, salt-and-pepper hair to match his moustache, broad shoulders juxtaposed with his small gut. He can't take his eyes off her.

Neither can Wes.

"Ohmygod, there's a *rock* in my eye," Kyra says, wiping her face. "I didn't sign up for this."

Everyone laughs, including Wes.

"Sorry, sorry." Ella snorts. "Emotions are the worst, man."

"Amen," Mrs. Rossi says, dabbing at her own eyes. "Let's stick to books."

"Agreed," says Ella. "Is everyone ready to get this thing lit?"

Another wave of cheers breaks out; the noise floods Colorado Avenue with more excitement than Wes can handle. He takes a few steps back, allowing latecomers to nudge inside.

"Dude!" Cooper walks up, Lucas beside him. "Are you leaving?"

"Uh." Wes rubs at his jaw. "Nah. Just making space."

"Good, because the two coolest peeps just arrived," Cooper says, curling an arm around Lucas's shoulders.

Lucas beams, rocking a bright orange and blue plaid shirt and jeans. Cooper's in a tank top, board shorts, and flip-flops, holding a Savannah Kirk book, of course. Lucas clings to a Batman graphic novel. Wes is proud of his mild influence there. Both have over-styled and product-stiff hair, so clearly Cooper's having an effect too.

"We can't stay long," Cooper announces. "This one has a curfew."

"Oh, like you don't."

Wes is elated they're friends. They don't go to the same school, but Wes is positive Cooper's going to look out for Lucas during the year. Vice versa too. And Wes called in one last favor from Mrs. Rossi—when the new coffeehouse opens, Lucas has a guaranteed job managing the book corner. They've already worked out a plan to sneak some graphic novels next to the bestselling mystery novels.

"Wow," Cooper says, standing on his toes to peek through the front window. "It's jammed in there. A cornucopia of singles waiting to hit on you." He waggles his eyebrows at Wes.

"Yeah, no." Wes laughs. "I'm totally not interested."

He and Nico still haven't mentioned their talk on the beach to anyone. Not that there's much to tell. They haven't kissed or even gone on a date. Not one hand-holding moment has occurred in three days. But that's cool with Wes. For now, at least.

"Understood." Cooper lifts his book. "I'm here to find my fellow Kirklands."

Ugh. It's the worst name for Savannah's fandom. It's so basic. So unoriginal too.

"But you, Wes," Cooper shares a look with Lucas, "Your OTL will show up any day now."

OTL. *One true love.* It's something Cooper made up. Or maybe it's a hashtag. Either way, it's terrible.

"Suuure," Wes says, but then, like out of a dream, he hears wheels grinding on the pavement. Nico glides up, hair tucked under a backward snapback, wearing black-rimmed glasses, a loose tee, and ripped skinnies.

He stops right in front of Wes. "Sorry I'm late," he says, a little breathless.

"I didn't know you were coming?" Wes replies, confused. "I thought you'd be babysitting."

"And miss this?" Nico up-nods toward the bookstore. "I'm feeling lucky tonight. Like I might find my match."

"Your match?"

Nico tugs off a nylon drawstring backpack and digs through it. He pulls out a book. No, a graphic novel. He holds up a copy of *Blackest Night.* "Think there's anyone who I might be compatible with?"

Whoa. Wes inhales sharply.

"So, yeah," says Cooper, jerking on Lucas's arm, edging toward the bookstore. "Looks like fate did you a solid."

"I was thinking we could..." Nico signals behind him, toward the pier. "...maybe head down to the beach? Grab some food? Just like, uh, the two of us?"

"The two of us," repeats Wes.

"The two of us," Nico confirms. His scarred eyebrow is lifted, waiting.

"*Go*," Lucas whispers-shouts, softly punching the base of Wes's spine.

Then Lucas and Cooper giggle as they tumble into the bookstore. They're barely out of earshot when Cooper says, "Holy fuck, Nesley's real. Wait 'til I tell my followers."

"Want a ride to the beach?" offers Nico, pointing toward his skateboard.

"Are you serious?" Wes asks. "That didn't work out for us last time."

"True that." Nico kicks up his board, taking it in his left hand. The fingers of his free hand wiggle between them. Nervous energy vibrates off him. So Wes does the bravest thing he's done in a long time. He grabs Nico's hand, threading their fingers together.

As they walk leisurely toward the pier, Nico comments, "Cool shirt."

Wes peeks down. He can't believe it. It's his lucky Green Lantern tee.

AN HOUR LATER, WES BRUSHES sand out of his hair and mouth, shaking it off his jeans. They'd decided to goof around after finding an abandoned Frisbee on the beach. Bad idea. Wes ate it no less than three times trying to jump and leap and teach his unwilling body about coordination. Nico was all cool grace, snagging the flying disc from the sky like a god pulling down the heavens—an injustice Wes will watch for as long as time gives him.

Now they stand near a food truck parked outside Palisades Park. Nico buys them churros. Wes squints against the headlights shining from cars as they pass. People move in herds all around them. Music exits a nearby restaurant's balcony, flooding the air.

Ocean Avenue is alive.

"Here." Nico holds one of those paper boats; the churros sit on a sheet of parchment paper. He quickly chucks a small container filled with chocolate dipping sauce in a nearby trash bin. They both love their churros as is.

"Uh." Nico chews slowly, barely making eye contact. "This isn't boring, right?"

An eyebrow slowly ascends Wes's forehead.

"I mean." Nico stammers. "This doesn't cement me in the top five unoriginal first dates, right? Because I can handle top ten. I'm even cool with a hard eight on the corniest dates metric. But not top five. I can't negotiate the emotional scarring that comes with that."

Ha. So, it's out there. This *is* a first date. An official, verbally committed first date between them. Hashtag relationship goals.

"Hmm." Wes chews, thinking.

Cinnamon-sugar dusts Nico's upper lip.

"Not lame at all," Wes says after swallowing. He passes Nico a napkin. "This is good."

It's better than that. Wes is finally on a date with Nico. Except for a grainy, sandy mouth, this is better than anything suggested by PopSugar.

They watch the city bloom into a nighttime circus: neon lights and noise and laughter for miles. Wes deliberately stands close to Nico; their elbows brush as they eat. He runs back to the food truck to buy them frozen lemonades.

When he returns, Nico has his phone in one hand. "I forgot to show you my newest Pinterest find."

Wes leans close, squinting against the screen's bright light. The image is black text against a plain white background. Wes inhales so quickly, his lungs ache. He reads over and over.

> *"I only want two things in this world. I want you. And I want us."*

"Do you like it?"

"Is this about me?" It takes every ounce of confidence and maybe a little bit of fear for Wes to ask the question. He's prepared if Nico just likes the quote. It's the kind of thing people get tattooed on their bodies. A love token of dark ink and years of heartbreak to follow when that person disappoints them.

"Possibly," Nico replies.

"Possibly?" There's that doubt Wes has been expecting.

Then the laugh lines around Nico's mouth deepen. "It's about you."

That's all it takes. It's the incentive Wes needs to go for it. He curls his hand around the nape of Nico's neck. He steps into Nico's space. Nico stands on his tiptoes to meet him halfway. Their lips find each other, clumsily at first, but then with the right amount of pressure. Nico's mouth parts. Wes tests his boldness with his tongue against Nico's teeth.

Their first kiss is sticky and sugary and un-freaking-forgettable.

THERE'S NOTHING DIFFERENT ABOUT WES'S bedroom.

His cap and gown are still on the desk chair. Posters layer his walls. His shelf of Funko Pop figurines is untouched. His dad's jersey is pinned next to a UCLA pennant. Spider-Man pajamas are kicked in a corner.

All the things he'll begin packing up next week.

Well, except for the shirtless Nico sitting on the edge of Wes's bed. Wes wishes he could pack him too. But, for now, he focuses on Nico's curious expression and artificial lights from outside streaming through his window and the way his heart jumps as if it's about to O.D. on anticipation.

They'd casually discussed continuing their date past frozen lemonades.

Wes suggested the loft. Then his bedroom. Nico grabbed Wes's hand. And their eyes said everything else: "Yes." "I want to." "We can take this slow; no pressure."

Now his bedroom door's locked. The interior lights are off. Wes didn't ask, but thankfully Nico was bold enough to tug out his wallet and pull out a shiny foil package. A condom. A preemptive measure if things escalated.

To be honest, Wes still isn't sure he wants things to escalate. But he's okay with Nico's preparedness. He's okay with the option.

Nico pats the spot next to him on the bed.

Wes struggles out of his own shirt, drops it, then eases down next to Nico.

"This is chill," Nico says. His hands are clenched in his lap, as if he's afraid to touch.

"It is," Wes agrees. He runs a hand over his curls. Grains of sand meet his fingers. *Ugh, gross.* He should've showered before this.

This. What is this? What are we going to do?

As if sensing Wes's indecision, Nico quickly says, "We don't have to do anything. At all. We can just talk." His eyes search around the room. "Here. I can put my shirt back—"

Wes cuts him off with a kiss. Well, an *attempt* at a kiss. His lips smack Nico's jaw. But he finds his way up, sealing Nico's words behind his teeth. He really likes kissing Nico.

He also appreciates that Nico knows Wes's stance on sex and isn't willing to pressure him into anything. He values Wes's beliefs. He's willing to sit in a darkened room, fully clothed, and talk. It's one of the six million things Wes loves about Nico: they can talk and talk, and nothing has to come of it. No epiphanies. No final destination. Nothing. They can be themselves.

"And if I want to?" Wes asks against Nico's mouth.

Nico slowly leans back, eyes scanning. "We could."

Wes doesn't tell Nico, but he has a bottle of lube. *Masturbation is very healthy, thank you, online doctors.* It's there, in his computer desk drawer. Wes is also criminally bad at establishing bulletproof hiding places.

"But, like." Nico sighs. "Sex is great…"

System malfunction.

In a very tactical decision, Wes has never once asked Nico how many partners he's had. He's been aware his brain is not capable of handling that kind of confidential information since that day at the skatepark. He should know Nico's history, especially if they're going to do anything. He needs to know if Nico's been tested. All the essentials. But Wes doesn't want the other details: Who? When? Was it any good? What does Wes have to live up to?

Yes, that's a thought. Comparison, on any level when it comes to people, is inevitable. It's so ingrained in human psychology that Wes isn't going to pretend he doesn't worry about it.

"… but it doesn't have to happen," Nico continues. "It shouldn't be the endgame."

Wes's mouth curls. "Are you about to say 'love' is the endgame?"

"It is!" Nico laughs. "But not necessarily romantic love. Just love in general. Being capable of extending the walls of your heart to make room for someone else in there. Being vulnerable."

Nico's head lowers. His hands are still knotted.

Carefully, Wes reaches out. He unties Nico's fingers. He slides his own between them. "Being vulnerable isn't easy."

"Fuck no. It's the worst."

Wes snorts.

"This." Nico nods at the condom between their hips. "It can happen. But it doesn't have to. I want you to be comfortable."

Wes is. When he's with Nico, even when they're fighting or not saying everything they should, he's comfortable.

He kisses Nico, eyes open for a second, waiting for Nico's reaction. But Nico's eyes are already closed, lashes fluttering. He's sighing hot breath against Wes's mouth. It's all very cinematic, but simple. As if they've been doing this forever.

Against Nico's swollen lips, Wes says it. The words just come out. "I love you."

He doesn't regret it. Except for the three hundred milliseconds when Nico doesn't say anything back. It's terrifying and embarrassing how, when some words are said, they live outside the mouth and heart. They're there, in the ether, waiting to be taken or ignored.

"I love you too, Wesley. I think for a very long time."

Wes doesn't say anything else. He negotiates their bodies until Nico's lying against the Green Lantern sheets and Wes is crawling on top of him. Pale silver light streaks through the window against Nico's cheeks. It shines on his scarred eyebrow, the mark Wes left on him. He wants to leave more. He wants to know the shape of Nico's collarbone under his fingertips. And his hands—Wes wants Nico's hands to know him.

He wants to remember Nico's body while he's away at UCLA.

He wants Nico to think of his kiss while in Palo Alto.

Indecision waves a red flag. Wes doesn't ignore it.

He keeps kissing Nico until one of their hands finds the condom in the sheets.

"WHY AM I NOT SURPRISED all you have in the fridge is a half-eaten slice of cheesecake, a gallon of milk that expires *tomorrow*, and cold Chinese food?"

Wes guffaws. His back is pressed against the wall his bed's tucked against as Nico sneaks back into the bedroom. They're both still shirtless, their chests sweaty, their skin flushed.

"And orange soda." He points at the items in Nico's arms.

"I'm not complaining."

Wes scoots over for Nico when he climbs onto the bed.

They crack open a carton of beef and broccoli. It smells rank, but Wes is *starved*. Making out burns a lot of calories. They eat with their hands, soy sauce on their fingers, re-microwaved rice on their lips.

"This is so bad, but so good," Nico says, stretching. His foot wiggles on the sheets, unearthing a shiny object.

The condom's still there, unopened. Nico doesn't mention it. Neither does Wes.

Thing is, Wes wasn't ready. His body wanted to—and is still a bit angry at him for ignoring that desire—but it wasn't time. Wes wasn't having sex because of a moment or because they said those three words. He knows that, by all definitions, Nico's "The One." They can share comic books. Nico loves—*loves*—Wes's geekiness. But he also didn't mind that Wes decided not to take it further. He was fine with kissing and trying to trace the shape of Wes's heart behind his ribs.

Wes is done with deadlines.

He doesn't need a five-year plan.

The other day, while talking to Calvin, they came to a compromise—Wes will attend UCLA in the fall. He'll dig deep, study, and give that first year a try. Maybe he'll like it. Maybe he'll want to transfer schools. Maybe he'll drop out. But Calvin wanted him to try, the same way Calvin's always tried. Wes could give his dad that. He could give himself a chance to succeed or fail or just figure out it's not for him. It's not the worst thing.

And Wes is done with this theory that all eighteen-year-olds are adults who know everything and aren't virgins and are incapable of having a voice. Wes has one. He's learning to use it.

Like now.

"I need to tell you something."

Nico sits up, attentive.

"And it's probably going to ruin the mood," Wes adds.

Nico's hair is pulled in every direction from Wes's fingers. He's squinting without his glasses or contacts. There's soy sauce on his bottom lip. His breath smells like orange soda. The old food isn't the only thing that's rank. They could both use a shower.

Consider the mood already ruined.

"After I say this, I don't want to discuss it," says Wes, frowning. "Not tonight, at least."

"Are you breaking up with me before we've even made it official?"

"*What?* No."

Then, because his brain's finally catching up with Nico's words, he says, "Wait. Do you want it to be official?"

Nico rolls his eyes, chugging more soda. "Your ineptitude is hella fascinating."

Fuck Stanford, they got a good one with Nico Alvarez.

"We're getting off track," Wes says. "This isn't about us. And there will be an us. To be discussed later."

Nico beams.

Wes clears his throat. "Mrs. Rossi is sick. She has a brain tumor." It's been a week, and this is the first time he's said it out loud. It aches. No, it tastes like vomit rushing up your throat, but you swallow it; the chunks wad in the saliva in your mouth. But Wes had to tell someone. And Nico's always been his Someone.

"Is it..." Nico's face tightens. "Is it cancer?"

Wes hesitated to ask Mrs. Rossi that morning. It took him hours and a lot of deep breathing in the bookstore bathroom before he got the words out.

Mrs. Rossi smiled, patted his hand, and said, "It'll be okay."

"I think so."

Nico blinks hard. Wes can see the wheels turning in his eyes. He's an idiot. He's leaning on Nico with this secret—the possibility of someone they both love dying—and completely forgetting that Nico's still living with his own mourning. He's so selfish.

But Nico inhales deeply, then says, "All right."

"All right?"

"Yes," Nico says, confident. "We're gonna... we're gonna get through this."

And that's it? They're going to get through this. It's the most adult thing Wes has ever heard Nico say. Maybe not all eighteen-year-olds are as screwed up as he is. Maybe some can handle more than people expect.

They sit quietly. Nico passes Wes the soda can; he chugs it until it dribbles down his chin, onto his chest. A shower is definitely a necessity now.

"Hey, Wesley." Nico's voice sounds far away. "About earlier."

"Yeah?"

"Do you want to try, uh." Nico's back to stammering. It's cute. "If it's okay with you, I'd like to try the long-distance thing. I mean, it's only six and a half hours..."

Which is eight hours in California traffic.

"But I want to."

Wes tilts his head back. He stares at his boring white ceiling. Nico wants this to last more than a moment. He wants it to last as long as Wes will allow it. Everything Wes loves is taken from him before its time. No one's ever offered him the chance to choose when or how something ends.

Blindly, his hand finds Nico's, sticky and warm. "There's no way I'm turning down that offer. No way." He squeezes Nico's hand twice.

"Hey. Skateboarding, orange soda or…" Wes's chest inflates with that kind of good feeling he associates with summer and comic books and the rules of Once Upon a Page. "… me?"

"You're asking me to go without orange soda?"

Heart dancing in his chest, Wes sighs. "Forget it."

Nico pulls on his hand. His orange-soda breath tickles Wes's cheek. The smile in his voice is Wes's favorite song.

"You."

Wes exhales happily. He considers turning his head to kiss Nico. Or just stare into his eyes. Or make a corny joke they'll both laugh at. But he doesn't need to.

This is enough. This is everything.

"It turns out life isn't a pile of bad days and then you fall in love with someone who fixes it all. Life is a series of embarrassing, funny, and sometimes brutal moments. Romance might be in there, too. But if you're lucky, you'll fall in love with your own amazingness and stumble upon a few kickass people to go on life's adventures with you."

—Savannah Kirk, *Laguna Love Blues*

EPILOGUE

WES'S BRAND-NEW TUX SHIRT IS ruined.

It only took five hours before he managed to get a Rorschach-style wine stain on it. Forget his boutonnière—that's a casualty of the dance floor and the DJ's obsession with replaying that wobble song. He survived an entire best man speech too. The stain came from Grace getting hammered and bumping into him on the way to the bathroom.

But at least the wedding's done.

Leeann Chen is officially a Hudson. Leo's married. And Wes needs a nap.

Also, Wes's phone is missing. Not missing. *Taken.* Heisted. It's currently owned by Cooper Shaw, who leads their pack into Little Tony's Big Slice, gossiping with Savannah Kirk on FaceTime.

"Is she really that bad?" Cooper asks, awed.

"The worst," Savannah announces. "Keep the bourbon away from that one."

Wes should never have introduced them.

Ella, in a green polka-dot dress, fedora, and large dark sunglasses, makes a beeline for their favorite booth in the back. She shuffles in, bookended by Zay and Wes. It took a lot of convincing, but Wes managed to talk Leeann into bumping a few guests off the reception list to make room for his friends. Ella even brought a gift.

The card read, *"To Leeann and Lucifer—may your reign in the Underworld be forever long."*

"What was that menu?" moans Ella, tugging off her sunglasses. "Did they want us to starve at the reception?"

"I thought the chicken was good," Zay says, passing out the plastic menus as if they're going to order anything other than the usual. His hair's cut short, a few waves at the top the only remains of his sick, curly Afro. Wes still hasn't adjusted to it. But it's also a reminder that more than Zay's hair has changed in a year.

"I can't believe you caught the bouquet," Ella says accusingly to Kyra.

Kyra has one arm resting lazily on Anna's bare shoulders, scanning the menu.

"That means you two are next," Zay teases.

Anna blushes from her hairline to her collarbones. But Kyra smirks, then says, "Don't jinx it," before pressing a loud kiss to Anna's cheek.

Wes is happy they're still a thing. Next to him, Nico finds Wes's hand under the table. Wes's glad they're still a thing too. A capitalized Thing.

"Can we hurry up and order? I can't be out too late," Zay says, repeatedly flipping his menu. "My moms have been on me about studying. I'm taking this summer course—"

Everyone groans. Zay graduated high school early. He started UCLA in the winter and is living his nerdish-musicology wet dreams by taking two summer classes. He's on a mission to finish college before he's twenty-two. Wes supports it.

In fact, he's behind all their decisions since Once Upon a Page closed.

Cooper's living his best life as a soon-to-be high school senior. He's up at least two hundred thousand social media followers thanks to a certain Savannah Kirk giving him a follow and commenting on all his Bookstagram posts. There's no blue checkmark next to his name yet, but Wes is betting on @coopsarrow being verified before the year's over.

Kyra quit Brews and Views. "Can't make a living when two competing coffeehouses are on the same block," she texted him a few months ago. "Who the hell does that? Fuck the Tea Leaf and Coffee Cup House." She has one more semester in the fall before graduation. In the meantime, she rakes in loads of cash as an online gamer. She's also moved in with Anna, who's a bank manager.

Huh. Wes didn't think she'd really pull it off.

"Yeah, whatever," Ella says to Zay. "Be a nerd. I have a date tonight, anyway."

Wes sputters. "A *date*-date?"

Ella rolls her eyes. "Here we go again."

Yup. Here we go again.

Since he's left UCLA, Wes no longer gets daily updates on Ella's social life over sandwiches at Fat Sal's. But before Wes can interrogate her, their waiter arrives with a tray of waters and a sour expression.

Constantine sighs. "Do you all need a mo' to figure out what you're having or what?"

"Artichoke or spinach?" Cooper asks the table.

"I'm thinking bacon," Zay says. "Bacon's life."

"Babe, veggie or Hawaiian?" Kyra says to Anna as they huddle over a menu.

"So." Constantine digs the heel of his hand into his eye socket the same way Wes's dad does when he's getting a stress headache. "Can we not give me hell tonight? I have plans afterward."

"Hey." Ella wriggles in her seat, back arched, her cheek resting against her knuckles. "Can you give us a sec? Five minutes, tops. I promise it'll be worth it."

And then, she winks. Constantine's a new shade of red. Wes's eyes widen, mouth falling open, but Constantine says, "Sure," and then spins around and walks off.

"No. Shit."

Ella pinches Wes's thigh hard under the table. He yelps, nearly knocking over all the waters.

"Ella Graham, are you kidding me?" he almost shouts.

"Shut. Up." Ella's eyes are soft; her lips are pulled into a sweet, self-conscious smile. It's peak Pining Wes Hudson. His brain can't digest it. But Wes decides not to grill her.

She deserves this moment with no judgment.

Wes turns to Nico, who wiggles his eyebrows knowingly. Nico never misses anything. Well, except that One Thing. Wes kisses him. They see each other every other weekend, but Wes has missed him. He looks incredible in an all-black tux with a rose-colored bow tie. His hair's slicked back with a single curl falling across his forehead, à la his prom look.

Wes also kisses Nico just because he can, as a boyfriend.

It's become Wes's favorite word. *Boyfriend*. He's made a list of ways to say it in other languages.

"How's the job?" Nico asks quietly.

"Ugh."

After an entire year and probably too much debt amassed, Wes is taking a gap year from UCLA. It wasn't that he failed. He just wasn't ready. Both his parents assured him that was okay. Leo did too.

Wes has moved back into the loft. He has a summer job working at his dad's Santa Monica restaurant. Waiter. Busboy. Assisting in the kitchen. Whatever Calvin needs. It's at least earning him gas money— Leo gave him his old car in exchange for promising to help plan Leeann's baby shower when the time comes—and an opportunity to think.

It's the universe's gift to Wes—a chance to figure himself out without any distractions.

Leaving Ella was hard, but they've adjusted.

"The worst thing you could do in this life is live it without ever knowing who you are," she said.

Wes thinks she stole that from her therapist.

"Has anyone been by the new shop since…" Zay trails off.

Around the table, everyone shares looks—sad, confused, and indifferent ones. This is one thing they don't talk about.

Wes shrugs, then says, "I've visited Lucas a few times."

Cooper nods. "We hang out there all the time after school, before their shift."

"I got an iced coffee the other day," Anna says. "Horrible."

"Told you," Kyra says smugly.

"Their book selections need work. They're showcasing the wrong stuff," Ella huffs.

Wes side-eyes her. He knows Lucas only has a small voice in what's featured in Mrs. Rossi's Book Corner, but they're trying. Secretly, he's certain Ella just wants a summer job bossing around young baristas and pissing off entitled customers. The usual.

But this is nice too. They're not tiptoeing around the fact that Once Upon a Page is gone. Their second home has been turned into a luxury apartment building with all the amenities and none of the heart that made the bookstore the soul of this community. But they're letting go.

"I heard there's a new indie bookshop opening up a few blocks away," Anna mentions.

Wes knows. He's already put in an online application. So he's *mostly* learned to let things go. But he loved life in a bookstore. He loves the things it gave him and the things he was able to give in return.

Zay raises his water. "To Mrs. Rossi."

It's quiet for a moment. They're all accepting that Once Upon a Page's not the only thing that's gone.

Wes stares resolutely at the Formica table. It's only been five months since the funeral, but it still aches like yesterday. Wes now owns two suits. He'll never wear either of them again. But he made it through the beautiful ceremony. He sat next to Mr. Rossi, holding his hand. He fought back tears, but only until Nico cornered him before the burial.

"It's not her. Her hair's not pink," he whimpered into Nico's shoulder. "They didn't even give her that."

She died in her sleep. She died living the last of her days reading, sitting in the sun, and being with her husband.

Wes clears his throat, then lifts his glass. "To Patty Rossi," he finally says. "She changed our lives."

Ella adds, softly, "She was a fighter."

They clink their glasses. Anna sniffles into a napkin. Nico drags his knuckles across his puffy, wet eyes. It's surreal. They're toasting Mrs. Rossi and the bookstore and all the things they can't take with them. Except the memories.

Wes will never leave those behind.

Constantine returns, brooding, but Wes now knows it's only for show. Constantine and Ella are posers. One day, he'll call them on their bullshit. "I put in an order for two pepperonis, a Hawaiian, and a veggie," he announces. "And a pitcher of Coke. Anything else?"

"The complimentary breadsticks," Ella reminds him.

Constantine stomps away, offering their table a one-fingered salute.

Wes yawns. It's almost eleven o'clock on a Saturday, and he's exhausted. Is this adulthood? Is this what he has to look forward to? In bed before midnight on a weekend? This is a tragedy.

He rests his head on Nico's shoulder. A dry kiss is pressed to his temple.

Across the table, Cooper hums something. It's familiar. It's also terrible.

"Coop." Wes's face wrinkles. "No. I'm embarrassed *for* you."

"What? Come on," Cooper tries to argue, but Wes is not having it.

"You have shamed your family," Wes accuses teasingly. "Semisonic? Gross."

"It's a classic," Cooper insists. The pizzeria's speakers hum to life as "Closing Time" fills in all the spaces between the empty tables and forgotten pitchers of beer and the heavy scent of baking bread.

Wes rolls his eyes, beaming. "Ohmygod, Canceled, dude."

They all laugh. And Wes breathes easy, adding one more item to his list of things he loves most about Santa Monica.

THE END.

ACKNOWLEDGMENTS

THIS BOOK WOULDN'T BE POSSIBLE without so many amazing people who encouraged me along the way.

My deepest gratitude to:

Annie Harper, my continuous cheerleader, the world's greatest editor, who had way too much faith in me tearing this book apart and stitching it back together again. When I didn't believe, you did.

C.B. Messer, all-star cover designer and my real-life Kyra. You're an inspiration. I love our talks and laughs and inability to take compliments.

Candysse Miller, idea wizard and coolest foodie. I love your fearlessness. I hope I did California some justice in this one. Tacos on me next time!

Nicki Harper, copyeditor supreme. I'm so grateful for your knowledge and for continuously pushing me to grow. I've had some hilarious Google searches thanks to you.

To all the incredible people who read, supported, and help make this book into what it is: My "lost in the city" friend, Jude Sierra. No more planes, trains, and automobiles for us! Lilah Suzanne, F.T. Lukens, Daniela "DB" Bailey, Tiffany Chapman.

To all the Interlude Press authors—I love the stories you've created and the lives you've changed.

Thao Le, agent with a vision and a mission. You make me excited to be a writer and a geek. I can't wait to see what happens next.

Becky Albertalli, my rock and French Toast buddy: I'm so thankful for your love and enthusiasm. Like, beyond grateful.

Nic Stone, the MVP of sneakers, deadlines, and realness: Thank you for your care, honesty, and overall dopeness.

Adib Khorram, my nerdy friend and confidant: I look forward to more tea, D&D, and smiles with you. Lots more.

C.B. Lee, my calm in the storm: You're such a shining star. Can't wait for you and your millions of ideas to take over the world.

To the countless friends I've made and who have held me up when I couldn't stand: Patrice Caldwell, Adam Silvera, Mark Oshiro, Roshani Chokshi, Dahlia Adler, Adam Sass, Kacen Callendar, Alex London, Angie Thomas, Eric Smith, Tiffany D. Jackson, Karen Strong, Natalie C. Parker, Simon James Green, Cale Dietrich, Camryn Garrett, Phil Stamper, Natasha Ngan, Tom Ryan, L.C. Rosen, Caleb Roehrig, Laura Stone, Natasha Ngan, Sabina Khan, Mason Deaver, Sandhya Menon, Brandy Colbert, Ashley Poston, Lamar Giles, Zoraida Córdova, Dhonielle Clayton, Kimberly Jones, Gilly Segal, Sierra Elmore, Katherine Locke, Justin A. Reynolds, David Arnold, Aiden Thomas, Kelly Loy Gilbert, Kiersten White, Sarah Enni, DJ DeSmyter, Saundra Mitchell, Laura Silverman, Kat Cho, Claribel A. Ortega, Ben Philippe, Katie Zhao, Ryan La Sala, Randy Ribay, Roselle Lim, Ray Stoeve, Rachel Strolle, Jennifer Dugan, Rachael Allen, Vania Stoyanova, and so, so many more.

To every independent bookstore that has welcomed me and to the ones I haven't visited yet: thank you for making a place for my books on your shelves. To the Atlanta indie bookstores—Little Shop of Stories, Charis Books & More, Brave and Kind Books, Read It Again, and many more—you're the heart and soul of our communities. Thank you for existing.

To the librarians, teachers, educators, bloggers, vloggers, bookstagrammers, podcasters, artists, agents, and publishing professionals who have uplifted me.

My family and friends, especially Mom, Sonya, Tamir, Tamica, Angela, Ahmad, Jason, and Tony—thanks for dealing with my constant disappearing acts. My nephews (Zeke, Daniel, Malachi) and niece (Jael)—you are my constant motivation.

To Santa Monica: You inspired me in ways I'll never forget. Stay beautiful.

To every reader who picked up one of my books, contacted me, shouted about them, made the coolest aesthetic posts, and made the most beautiful art: Let's continue this journey together. We decide what our future looks like.

ABOUT THE AUTHOR

JULIAN WINTERS IS A BESTSELLING and award-winning author of contemporary young adult fiction. His novels *Running with Lions* and *How to Be Remy Cameron* (Duet, 2018 and 2019 respectively) received accolades for their positive depictions of diverse, relatable characters. *Running with Lions* is the recipient of an IBPA Benjamin Franklin Gold Award. *How to Be Remy Cameron* was named a Junior Library Guild Gold Standard selection and received a starred review from School Library Journal.

A former management trainer, Julian currently lives outside of Atlanta, Georgia, where he can be found reading, being a self-proclaimed comic book geek, or watching the only two sports he can follow—volleyball and soccer. *The Summer of Everything* will be followed by his fourth novel, *Right Where I Left You*, from Viking Children's/Penguin in 2022.

CONNECT julianwinters.com
WITH julianw_writes
JULIAN wintersjulian
ONLINE julianwinters

duetbooks.com
@DuetBooks
duetbooks
store.interludepress.com

an imprint of inter**l**ude**press**

ALSO BY **JULIAN WINTERS**

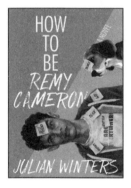

How to be Remy Cameron by Julian Winters
Junior Library Guild Gold Standard seal of approval

Remy Cameron is an out-and-proud guy who everyone admires for his cheerful confidence. The only person who isn't sure about Remy is Remy himself. Under pressure to write an A+ essay defining who he is and who he wants to be, Remy embarks on an emotional journey toward reconciling the outward labels people attach to him with the real Remy within.

ISBN (print) 978-1-945053-80-1 | (eBook) 978-1-945053-81-8

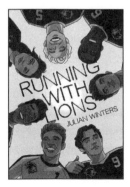

Running with Lions by Julian Winters
IBPA Benjamin Franklin Gold Award Winner

When his estranged childhood best friend Emir Shah joins his team, star goalie Sebastian Hughes must reconnect with the one guy who hates him. But to Sebastian's surprise, sweaty days on the pitch, wandering the town, and bonding on the weekends sparks more than just friendship between them.

ISBN (print) 978-1-945053-62-7 | (eBook) 978-1-945053-63-4